I0522660

The Black Bag of Dr. Wiltse

Murder on the Prairie

Published: November 24, 2021
ISBN: 978-0-9992635-5-6 (KDP/CreateSpace)
Library of Congress cataloging-in-Publication Data available upon request. Printed in the U.S.A

Book Covers: Lance Buckley Design

Read more about historical Fairbank, Iowa,
the town which inspired two historical books about Iowa at:
www.bettybrandtpassick.com.

The Black Bag of Dr. Wiltse

Murder on the Prairie

Historical Fiction

Book two in the Gangster Series

BETTY BRANDT PASSICK

Other books by this author:

Gangster in Our Midst, Bookkeeper, lieutenant and sometimes hitman for Al Capone (2017)—
Book one in the Gangster Series

Arlington Hills Presbyterian Church, 125 Years, 1888-2013 (2014)

We Are Eight, A Memoriam (2015)

ACKNOWLEDGEMENTS

Dedicated to Cousin Verla with my deepest love. Words can't express my gratitude for helping with this novel—plus three other books. What a blessing, that in the process…we've grown to be more like sisters.

A special thank you to my beta readers: Jo Bodeker, my go-to person for Wiltse family history; Dr. Cameron McConnell, who kept me on point writing about the practices of an 1850s physician; Frederick Scott, among Strawberry Point's oldest residents, was a knowledgeable resource of the town's history; and finally, Gary Ressler, Arnola Siggelkow, and Maurice and Wilma Welsh—resources for Fairbank, Iowa history. What a fun crew you were to work with on this project.

Cody Chamberlain, professional academic advisor, Metropolitan State University, St. Paul, Minnesota, helped with the Ho-Chunk language and customs.

Thank you to author Joan Young, who, after stating she had enjoyed reading Gangster in Our Midst (2017), offered to help with Book Two in the Gangster Series, The Black Bag of Dr. Wiltse. You are a skilled historical book coach—and friend.

I'm forever indebted to Connie Anderson, editor, Words & Deeds, Inc. Your honesty in suggesting significant changes were what made this book the best it can be. My highest praise to you for your role helping me have a book that I am very proud of.

My husband Clay has been my loyal encourager and supporter through four books and thirty years of marriage. I love you more than you can possibly know.

Finally, thank you to my readers. If you didn't read my books, I couldn't write them. So, thank you.

PROLOGUE

During the Colonial Era (1607-1776), many Dutch people immigrated to America seeking religious freedom. After the American Revolution (1775-1783), a significant emigration from the United States to Canada followed, including about 75,000 British Loyalists. For their service to Britain, they were given citizenship and land in the area that became known as Ontario. These Loyalists introduced English to the French and native-speaking people.

The Black Hawk Treaty of 1833 opened most of Iowa to white settlement. In 1834 Iowa became part of the Michigan Territory—which included what is today Michigan, Wisconsin, Iowa, Minnesota, and parts of the North and South Dakota. When Michigan withdrew to become a state in 1836, the remaining area was called the Wisconsin Territory. On February 6, 1838, Congress voted to establish the Iowa Territory. Iowa became a state on December 28, 1846.

After 1850, most European settlers came through ports in New York or Canada. The first European settlers to Iowa were French-Canadians who worked in the lead mines near present-day Dubuque. Between 1850-1860, the population of Iowa nearly tripled.

Before 1906, a man's wife and minor children were considered naturalized citizens when the man completed his application requirements.

CONTENTS

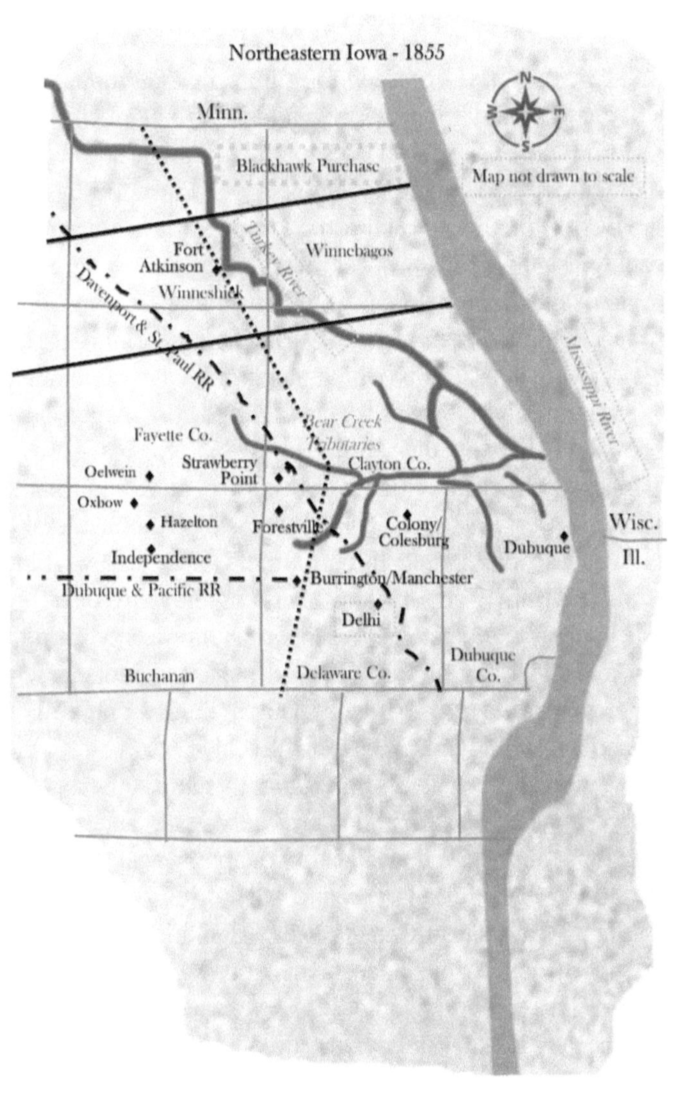

Northeastern Iowa - 1855
Minn.
Blackhawk Purchase
Map not drawn to scale
Turkey River
Fort Atkinson
Winnebagos
Winneshiek
Davenport & St. Paul RR
Mississippi River
Fayette Co.
Bear Creek Tributaries
Oelwein
Strawberry Point
Clayton Co.
Oxbow
Hazelton
Forestville
Colony/ Colesburg
Dubuque
Wisc.
Ill.
Independence
Dubuque & Pacific RR
Burrington/Manchester
Delhi
Buchanan
Delaware Co.
Dubuque Co.

CHAPTER ONE

Guérisseur, Healer - 1855

If I could have foreseen the future in *Amérique*, would I have changed anything? How could I have predicted the hideous murder at Stone's Grocery? I would ne'er forget the final moments my colleague Dr. Stout lay on the floor, gasping for air. How is it another avowing the Hippocratic Oath can kill? With each passing year, the list of murderous transgressions grew longer and more diverse—Indian massacres, mob hangings, prairie banditti; then a great war, sanctioned murder. In the end, 'twas my own mortality which taught me what none other could.

Admittedly, it was the Ontario newspaper article that beckoned me in the spring of 1855 to leave my beloved Canada—for Iowa, which had become a state and opened to new settlement. Being near *famille* was to my considerable liking; then the article named three murders in a nearby village where Cousin Uriah Wiltse resided. Perhaps only my dear wife Phebe knew of my interest in investigating murder. My durable oiled black canvas bag simply allowed me into emplacements where others may not go. Still, my Dutch family and fellow French Canadians called me *Guérisseur*—Healer.

Within the year we said *adieux* to family and friends, and to pretty stone chalets, rose flower gardens, and ancestral farms. My relations had started Wiltsetown, arriving at the time of the American Revolutionary War, when the British recompensed soldiers with land in Canada West. Benoni Wiltse, who'd served in the British Army, once owned my farm overlooking a vale. The Wiltse colony would look after our Ontario farm in our absence. If Iowa grasshoppers ate our crops or hailstorms forced us from the land, we could still return, but I dearly hoped our love for our *nouvelle* homeland would become as deep and wide as mine for my family. Phebe and our three *enfants*—Charles, age 5, Vidella, age 6, and Edwin, "Neddy," our youngest, age 4—plus, my parents, *Père* Philip, 55 years, and *Mère* Rachel, 54 years, as they wished to be called—and several stragglers, would join us on the voyage.

On the day of our departure, I insisted we stop at a fresh mound in Forest Home Cemetery, called out by undertaker Josiah in previous weeks. Clearly, the grave had been dug the previous fall, and the intruder spent the winter in Canada's frigid snow. Nearby, lay another soul who had left this world a decade earlier in horrible *douleur*, the result of a *fistule* on the rectum and *hernie*—I had signed the *homme's* death certificate. The vacant lot beside him awaited his wife Abigale. With her recent passing, the fresh grave was discovered, marked by a flat rock narrowly chiseled VIRGINIA C. My mind ached to encounter the *squatter*; how I itched to grab my shovel and identify the cause of the mysterious death.

From the rail of a side-wheeler tied up at the river's edge, each of us dressed in our finery, we watched barrel trunks filled to the rim with chattels—including one holding my diatonic *accordéon*, carefully painted in large letters *GENTLE, SINL VOUS PLAÎT*—brought aboard the 775 tons steamer built by the Ontario and St. Lawrence Steamboat Company's lines.

The twisting river required navigational changements, and by mid-afternoon our vessel had traversed the first of the Williamsburg Canals.

Days later, at the mouth of Lake Ontario, the schooner *Orcadian* awaited our transfer. The crew consisted of six persons including the captain. A heavy beam sea arose on our second evening, and we were frightfully tossed to and fro. More than once I went to the deck to empty my stomach. In the darkness it appeared the ship would surely capsize and sink, reminding me of my dream the night before leaving home. Had the dream been a presage—a warning? *Was I was embarking on a voyage of personal ambition, rather than of duty? Was I destiné for failure?* At one point, I thought I saw a roiling wave with two young boys waving—so real, I outstretched my hand before they disappeared before my eyes. The *visage*—face, of one resembled a childhood friend who had drowned in the Ottowa River twenty years earlier. By some fortune, the other lad swimming with him was saved.

Why wasn't the boy who remained the one taken?

Early the next morning I learned a woman had been washed overboard in the storm and perished.

The *Orcadian* moved onto Lake Huron, where we were delayed by several days to take on a heavy freight of merchandise. After a few days at sea, on one particularly calm morning around seven bells, Captain Stanard summoned all passengers to the deck for a burial at sea. The *âgé monsieur*—older man, had first complained of an infection upon boarding at Ontario. The captain requested I give an effective treatment, but applications of carbolic acid to his festering *blessure*—wound, did little to inverse his condition. He was in good health upon retiring the previous evening; at dawn, he was no more. His sudden death left me quite upset. Captain Stanard read a prayer for the dead before signaling to a member of the crew to raise one end of the slat, when the corpse dropped from beneath a *couverture* and splashed into the deep lake. A pealing of the ship's bell followed.

A second death was unknown to me. A man—nearly my age of 30 years—carried forth in his arms the body of a small boy whom I recognized, for he wore the same *vêtements*—clothing, as the day of his transfer onto Orcadian. He and Edwin had become fast friends. I watched the father tenderly place the corpse on the slat, and took one additional moment to glimpse his face, before covering him over. His mother nearby stoically clutched a Bible to her chest, drawing my eyes to what I perceived was a sizeable mass an inch above her left breast. Captain Stanard read the prayer once more. She did not breathe out so much as a sigh as her child slid from this world into the next. Once more the bell pealed.

The captain's final words, "Truly in the midst of life we are in death," hung in the air like the heavy grey clouds that now obscured the morning sun. A sense of *obscurité* shrouded my shoulders and enveloped me. My mind raced. Death touched many more voyagers. Even my courageous and intelligent Edwin fell ill—for two days keeping down only a little tea and biscuit and displaying a chill fever. I feared he, too, would die.

Within a short time, death swept through the overcrowded vessel like flames through straw. Those in good health at daybreak might be dead and buried by nightfall. Burials at sea became commonplace. Not until the freighter turned southerly onto Lake Michigan would my *esprits* begin to lift, when I knew our voyage neared its *fin*.

Mid-May 1854 we arrived at Chicago, Illinois. With considerable *difficulté* the ship navigated into port at Seal Bluff, as by then the entire crew had been stricken with *la dysenterie* from the *choléra*. Health officers boarded and a yellow flag swiftly arose on the mast. I was again enlisted to give aid with exams and distribution of equal parts of a tincture of opium, red pepper, rhubarb, peppermint, and camphor as treatment.

Choléra had been no stranger to Canada—it followed hordes of immigrants everywhere. Infant deaths in particular tore at my heart. From where did the disease originate? Teething babies? Miasmas from the ground at night? The wrath of an angry God? An electrical disturbance in the atmosphere?

The steady lineup of corpses for transport from the ship by plank to waiting carts on shore continued for weeks. Finally, liberated from quarantine, I found refuge for my family at a boarding house, and early the following morning I sought transport for our arduous voyage to Iowa.

I soon heard a merchant on a street call out: "*Bœufs*—oxen, raised and trained to pull together; plus, heavy, solid wagon to transport you to your destination, *où que ce soit*—wherever that may be." It was as if meant for my ears. So many adventurous people were bound for America's interior, the merchant also made available a hand-drawn map, for an extra dollar, with markings of rivers, streams, forests, and grandiose rocks—those used by Algonquin Indians, part of the same tribes who roamed the banks of the Saint-Laurent. The merchant added the wagonmaster was a veteran in Indian affairs.

In the end, I had no choice but to trust the merchant in all matters, whose final effort was to point me in the direction of the GENERAL STORE at the intersection of the Chicago River and Lake Michigan, to purchase supplies to last the six weeks' journey.

On the fifth day, just as the sun broke on the horizon, I carried Edwin, yet in a weakened condition, to a bed of straw on the floor of our narrow white canvas-domed wagon. I braced boards against stacked chests and dispositions to prevent shifting cargo of flour, sugar, vinegar, salt, pepper, potatoes, onions, and beans.

Within arm's reach were a sack of hardtack and urn of *cidre*—and my anti-cholera medicine, a homemade brew of laudanum and brandy. Phebe would remain at his side to tend to all his needs. Mère Rachel and Charles climbed to the bench seat beside me; Père Philip and Vidella would walk alongside the wagon on the first day.

Within the hour, the wagonmaster rode by on a painted stallion, bared rifle in one hand, and signaled to wagon drivers to find a place in the caravan. Once outside the noisy, dirty city limits, the hundred-plus units would follow a path snaking through dense forests, flowering thickets, and winding rivers—previously held Indian territory. From Canada I had heard stories of horrific scalpings of white men, and of women and children being taken captive, never to see loved ones again—stories reminding me of my Wiltse ancestors who were attacked and slain at Fort Orange by Mohawk Indians in the 1630s. Only two young boys in our family survived.

A *prémonitoire*—premonition, of foreboding death once more enjoined me, a fear that only abated whenever we crossed paths with the U.S. Militia. As it would turn out, I would never see Indians except from afar, though gunshots often rang out, though directed at a snake traversing through tall grasses or to scare off bears, coyotes, or wolves.

As for me, I listened for the booming grounds—the grassy openings where prairie chickens perform their mating rituals–the males creating loud booming sounds. Phebe made the best Canadian prairie *poulet*—chicken, stew with yam biscuits in all of Leeds and Greenville United Counties.

Our first most bitter experience of the trip occurred on the fifth day when a wheel from a sloughed down wagon in front of us hit a rock and broke into pieces. Hurled into the trunk of a tree was a yellow-haired *fille*—young girl, who had been seated alongside her father at the reins of the ox-team. Edwin—who had showed improvement with each passing day, retrieved my well-oiled black canvas bag, and I examined the female in an unconscious state. Rest was the best prescription, but within the hour a half dozen voyageurs stated their refusal to hold up until her upturn, and we watched as they boarded their wagons and left us behind.

We profited from our brief layover, however, to fish along a riverbed for bass. Phebe prepared *Chaudiere De Poisson*—with head, gill, and bones removed—potatoes, dried corn, tallow, onion, dried thyme, and basil in *un bouillon de lait de vache épaissi*, a thickened cow's milk broth.

Even though the young girl remained unconscious, with hundreds of miles to go, our caravan returned to the harrowing trail. Bedded on the wagon's floor, I knew she was tossed about mercilessly as we maneuvered through thick Illinois buckthorn.

With tremendous excitement, at last we reached the wide banks of the upper Mississippi River at Dubuque. Its water was beyond the banks from rapidly melting snow and spring rains. An enterprising pioneer, awaiting the arrival of caravans, offered to ferry us by flatboat for a dollar a unit—though a week or more would pass before it was safe to crossover.

Finally, ten days later, somewhere in the middle of the wide, muddy canal, we crossed over into Iowa and were met by the great forests along the state's eastern border. Wagons diverted in every direction, many to follow the broad military route which ran north from Dubuque to southern Minnesota and south to the Missouri border. Only a couple dozen units remained in our group.

By this time, provisions had greatly diminished, and skimming and stealing were rampant. I feared my children would become orphans on the second evening when a brawl escalated between two men just as I prepared to open my accordéon case to play traditional folk tunes before retiring to bed. Before I pulled the instrument from its case, I found myself in the middle of them—with knives drawn. Once separated, I hoped that would be the *fin*.

The next morning one of the men, traveling with a wife, a brood of children, two pigs, and a brindle cow, was found in the woods, his throat slit—and loaded shotgun nearby. The family's provisions, which had hung in a tree by fly rope, had been dropped and pillaged. The other man—and his wagon—were gone. The murder had not been at the hands of *Indians*.

We buried the man in a shallow grave marked by a pile of stones along the trail. Before the heat of the day could consume us, we plodded onward, with the dead husband's wife now at the reins of the oxen.

—

Eight weeks later in mid-June, we arrived in Moreland Colony, Iowa. Cousin Uriah had stated in a letter I would find his log cabin by following the Dakota path to a junction where a mature maple tree stood next to a post with a red-dyed skull at its top— painted by the *Indigènes* with the juice of red currents to warn the white man to leave their land. The grassy path would lead south to a fertile valley in Section 11.

Dusk was upon us by the time I caught sight of a plume of iridescent smoke rising from the tree line. The pathway, barely the width of our four-foot prairie schooner, took us through a dense forest, and we were soon plunged into near total darkness. The only sounds were the clanging of the tar-and-tallow bucket beneath the rear axle…the moaning mechanics of the wheels, axle assemblies, the reach, the hounds, and the bolsters of the undercarriage…and the oxen's heavy breathing.

I recalled Uri had immigrated from Canada in 1838 when he was sixteen. The first white man he met was Teeg, a trapper and Indian trader, who helped chink Uri's cabin on a hillside. In 1849 the American government had ordered the Sauk and Fox to resettle in Minnesota. On occasion, Winnebagoes, repudiated to have committed murders and depredations, still crisscrossed Uri's 160 acres. Uri had married within the year.

Just beyond a creek bed—likely, 'twas Bear Creek, according to Uri's letters—I spied the outline of a cabin on the hillside. Fog rising from the rippling creek bed merging with smoke wafting from the chimney presented a warm salutation. Hearing a bellowing cow from what appeared to be a stable forty yards beyond the cabin, my confidence grew we had reached Uri's homestead.

I halted the oxen outside the cabin and waited. A minute later the door opened a crack and a sliver of light pierced the blackness. The tip of a long gun appeared next, and a moment later, a half-wolf-half-dog, snarling and barking with a vengeance, bolted past the doorframe and onto the narrow porch.

Finally, the slender frame of a femme wearing vêtements of buckskin stepped into the *lumière* and ably raised the gun to her shoulder, pointing it in my direction.

"I'm Uri's cousin… Dr. Alex," I appealed from my perch… Rest of my family is in wagon… Uri said in his letters we would be welcome to stay with you 'til we got settled. There's more of us come all the way from Ontario, making their way to other Iowa relations tonight."

Cautiously she lowered the gun, grabbed hold of the wolf-dog's collar with her free hand, and the two slowly limped toward the wagon. She exhibited a slight *faiblesse* on her left side, perhaps from *apoplexie*, though she seemed too young for such an infirmity.

"Down! Ho-Chunk!" she said, as the wolf-dog struggled to break free. "*Cųk* smell wolves from hundred yards…saved my life more than *un*."

The waxing crescent of a strawberry moon, emerging just above the treetops, reflected upon her olive visage and brilliant black hair woven into a thick braid dangling nearly to her waist. She was narrow at the haunches, like my Phebe.

"Name, Louisa… Nice meet more Uri's clan," she said tentatively.

Père Philip leaped from the wagon's rear and dropped the toolbox onto the ground so Phebe, with Edwin in her arms, could step down onto it.

"I'm Phebe—and those are my other enfants," Phebe said, walking toward Louisa and pointing at Vidella and Charles who were seated next to me. Edwin here is not fully *récupéré* from our long voyage at sea. My husband's parents are with us, too."

Père Philip, standing at the rear of the wagon, tipped his ten-gallon hat, and Mère Rachel waved politely and tolerantly through the canvas drawstring opening behind the perch.

"*Haho*," Louisa said, as she and Phebe embraced with their eyes. "Not know when expect you—come in cabin for stew made of head of deer. Delicacy."

"*Merci*—first I'll bed my bœufs in the stable … Uri gone this evening?"

"At meetin'…where men from county gather regular since Mexico war. Talk of many immigrants come to

Colony…*wañgrá*—white man, fight over land. Railroad come here soon…" she paused and looked away, "and fight stray Winnebago who steal our fattened animals and *cykxéte*—horses. Uri be happy see you…home soon."

Her words reminded me Uri had answered the call to fight in the Mexican American War of 1846 with the *infâme Capitaine* John Parker's Company of Iowa Dragoon Volunteers, for which he received a pension of eight dollars a month. We Canadians knew winning that war meant America would add 500,000 square miles, stretching itself all the way to the Pacific Ocean. Americans perceived this land addition to be their *destinée manifeste*—manifest destiny.

"Phebe and young boy sleep lodge with Uri and me 'til well," she said, staring into Edwin's face. "Grandfather, Grandmother sleep lodge, too… Grandfather is sun and wife is moon, in Ho-Chunk tradition."

My family followed Louisa and the wolf-dog into the cabin.

Strangely, no one noticed or asked about the *other enfant* accompanying our troupe.

The cabin door closed, and the strawberry moon disappeared behind a cloud. Once more I was plunged into a blackness that enshrouded my senses like a thick blanket. A flick of the whip above the bœufs' heads, and the wagon crept up the hillside to a stable smelling of animals and last fall's hay and straw.

I stepped down from the bench perch and pulled open the bulky double doors. Inside, I searched for a lantern. A splinter of moonbeam reflected off a glass chimney on a shelf. I withdrew a match from a tin box beside it, struck the match on the shelf, raised the chimney, and held the flame to the wick.

Suddenly, the small stable lit up.

A shorthorn in a pen rose to her feet and began lowing, awakening her spring calf. A mule turned his head in my direction and *brayé*. Above, chickens fluttered from a perch, and what I perceived to be a feral cat scampered out of sight at my feet.

I released the oxen from the thick wooden yoke and metal arcs and directed them into a stall. Using a pitchfork thrust into a mound of hay nearby, I transferred forkfuls to the trough in their stall—then more hay into a vacant stall next to the cow to make a bed for Phebe and me and my children. From the wagon, I carried blankets, a small chest of vêtements and personal items, my accordéon, and black bag.

Preparing to extinguish the light, I raised the lantern to observe the stable filled with tools, hay, and animals.

Uri has done well for himself. I only hope to do as well in Amérique, I thought.

I reached for the latch, noticing a wide blotch the size of a man's palm. I sniffed for the indubitable metallic *odeur* of fresh blood. The streak ran along the frame to the floor; shards of discolored hay lay at my boots. Another flash of the lantern around the space revealed a long-handled wooden hatchet leaning against an exterior wall. Lifting it to the light, similar blotches emerged on the steel head, wooden shoulder, and belly of the hatchet.

This had been the tool of the crime. What violent thing had happened in this stable?

I extinguished the light, replaced the lantern on the shelf, and latched the doors behind me.

In the meager light of the moon, I marched blindly across rocks, thickets, and washouts—black bag in hand—to Uri's cabin.

Should I have brought along my accordéon? I wondered. Perhaps another evening.

—

The untethered warhorse outside the cabin informed me that Uri had returned. I stepped inside and awaited Ho-Chunk's attack. Instead, the wolf-dog was fixated on a deer antler between his jaws on the floor next to Louisa.

Uri instantly stood and, grabbing hold of a chairback then the tabletop in the center of the chambre to steady himself, hobbled toward me. His was a military injury from a horse startled by gunfire in the Mexican American War that fell on his knee. He had retained his curly blonde locks and boyish good looks—I was reminded of the Ontario schoolgirl who had been sorry to see him leave Canada so many years ago.

"Should-a come to the stable to greet you…Louisa said I'd encounter you on yer way back to the cabin…she said 'to save my steps.'"

Uri grabbed hold of my hands in the same manner as when we were *jeunes garçons*—young boys. For several seconds we stared into the visage of the other, realizing beyond all belief, we were together again at last.

Uri wore a home-spun pull-over shirt and cavalry fatigue trousers held up by suspenders. I couldn't help but notice his injured right hand. The *blessure* looked recent.

"My *bœufs* are settled, Uri… The family will rest well in the stable—perhaps a year or more, I expect… Couldn't help but notice, as I prepared to blow out the lantern in the stable…."

"Alex—or should I call you *Dr. Alex*?" Uri interrupted. "Pardon the *désordre*…had a visitor a day or two ago in the stable…."

Uri stopped abruptly, as though to catch himself.

"Well, it's a bit of a long story, and you've come a long distance… You must be fatigued from your voyage."

"I'm *Alex* to you, Uri…just like when we were garçons… Tell me your gory story then another time."

I sat on the table bench. Uri joined me.

Edwin took the prompt and leaped from the lap of Père Philip seated in Uri's rocking chaise, coming to rest at my knees.

"Stick out your tongue," I said, the same protocol I had followed several times a day since his illness began.

Pulling a handkerchief from my pocket, I grasped hold of his tongue and examined it for white spots or foul *odeur*.

"Remove your chemise, *s'inl vous plaît*."

Edwin withdrew the long grey tunic from his breeches and pulled it over his head, depositing it on the bench.

I reached for the stethoscope in my black bag that lay on top of dietary remedies, *bouteilles* of herbs, a small cake of tallow, and small pieces of *toile* to make a blister.

Edwin waited patiently as I placed the long wooden tubular instrument on his left chest wall where a stubborn congestion had lingered. I listened—one ear on the horn, the other on his chest, repositioning it multiple times along his chest, front to back. It took five minutes to register his body's temperature with the mercury thermometer. His blueish skin coloring had nigh disappeared. The last piece of my examination was *vérification* of his pulse.

"You have a strong heartbeat, and your lungs sound clearer, Edwin—I believe I shall soon pronounce you well."

Edwin smiled and reached for his tunic.

"Now, tell me again about your grand hope to grow up and become a *médecin*…and about how you and I will open a *bureau* and heal sick *personnes* everywhere one day."

"I wish to become doc-tor and *chir-ur-gien*, like you, Père," he said, looking into my eyes like a devoted puppy.

I hoisted the child onto my lap.

Phebe, who had been standing at the fireplace stirring the deer stew in a blackened *bouilloire*—kettle, now ladled several scoops into a clay bowl, and set it before me on the hatchet-hewn tabletop next to a half loaf of bread and a long knife. Finally, she slipped a metal spoon between the fingers of my right hand, bent over, and softly kissed me on my forehead.

And they call me guérisseur, I thought, as she cut a slice from the loaf and leaned it against the bowl.

"Run along, Neddy, let Père eat," Phebe said.

"Thought I might first take a look at Uri's hand…a splint would be a satisfactory aid."

Uri was about to repond when Louisa spoke from across the room, where she had been showing Mère Rachel the duvet she was weaving on her loom…*for a cradle*, I suspected.

"I do *mąką*—medicine stick." Louisa said.

Uri dropped his *blessée* hand to his side, stood, and made his way to the rag tapis on the dirt floor in front of the fire, seating himself in a way that allowed his damaged knee to remain extended.

"Tomorrow you may regard my hand, Alex. Tonight—eat, settle the family, and *repos*."

Replacing the thermometer and other items into my bag, I came across the Wiltse conch shell, a remnant of our ancestors engraved "1624," brought from Holland to America. I had placed it there for safekeeping during our voyage, as my bag was never out of my sight.

"See what I brought with me from Ontario, Uri."

His face brightened as I handed him the shell.

"We shall begin to blow it for the *dinner bell*, as did our *ancêtres*," he said, examining the shell as though a treasure he'd never expected to see again.

"What shall we do on the farm tomorrow…planting finished?" I inquired, as Uri returned the conch shell to me.

"Nearly…come Sunday, I'll you show you the land I've proved upon. But tonight, I should like to teach your enfants to play checkers."

Vidella, Charles, and Edwin joined Uri as he maneuvered a homemade checkerboard onto the tapis and positioned round pieces onto raised squares; Père Philip, too, slid forward in Uri's rocking chaise, looking on with keen interest.

I swallowed my first spoonful of hot stew and stared into the flickering fire. The lumière exposed the one-room chambre that served as parlor, sitting room, bedroom, and kitchen. Above, was a half-balcony with space for a straw tick in each corner—plenty of room for a growing family.

I caught sight once more of Louisa as she rose to her feet.

Perhaps she is pregnant, it occurred to me again. *An off-center placenta might explain the weakness in her gait.*

Staring at the buckskin thong around her waist, our eyes met from across the room.

"Is Indian treatment…sickness leave body and enter thong," she said, turning side to side for my benefit.

I acknowledged her interpretation and returned to eating, once more, caught up in examination of the cabin and its structure. The walls and gabled roof were built of 14-inches diameter logs corked with mud to protect Uri and Louisa from *des éléments*. If the mud was tight, the cabin would be impermeable, should there be rain—and from inside the stable, I thought I might have heard distant thunder in the western sky. Likely, it would be raining cow tails by the morn.

Outside, the coyotes commence to wail. How I looked forward to the sound of the whippoorwill calling in the night, though I'd have to wait for summer for that particular joy.

It was hard to recall a time I'd been so *satisfait*.

CHAPTER TWO

The Dirk Knife

Uriah Wiltse was among the first settlers to arrive in the region after the Black Hawk War of 1832, when settlement opened up along the eastern edge of Iowa. The Sauk Indians, unhappy with the loss of their land, killed dozens of pioneers, removing their fingers, toes, ears, and scalps—when *massacre* became a *nouveau* word in Uri's *vocabulaire*. 'Twas a fancy word for murder perpetrated by a group against defenseless victims.

Delaware County was organized by 1837. Uri played an important role in the development of all *civiques* matters, while developing his farm into one of the most enviable properties.

A few years later, David Moreland and his colony chartered a steamboat at Uniontown, Pennsylvania, and steamed down the Ohio River and up the Mississippi to the northeastern part of Iowa. He named the place where he landed the Colony—later renamed Colesburg. In 1841, he was appointed by the Iowa legislature to build the territorial road by way of the Colony from Dubuque to Camp Atkinson. Though a strong fear of Indians persisted, he then set about establishing the *première* inter-state stage line between Wheeling, Washington, and Baltimore. The first school and religious service also happened at the Colony. David Moreland's contributions to Delaware County became myriad.

Joel Bailey arrived thereafter, along with the Leonard Wiltse Sr. family—with sons Wellington and Amasa, Leonard Jr.— and a handful of others. In 1846, he became the first postmaster, then school fund commissioner, county treasurer, and county judge. Joel Bailey's name became *une légende*.

Now, the Alexander Wiltse family was listed on the county records. I hoped to leave my own legacy of grand proportion.

While Phebe and our children settled in at Uri's homestead, my most urgent wish was to find a community in need of good doctor…no need to trample on another's territory if it could be helped. Uri encouraged me to journey to Delhi, the county seat of Delaware County, twenty miles southeast, to file my name at the courthouse as a *certifié médecin*—a certified physician.

My overnight stay en route to Delhi was with Cousin Wellington Wiltse and his wife Aurilla. Most Wiltses were of average height and slight construction, but I found Wellington had grown into a big man with a splendid physique…thick arms, and legs, well adapted for the difficulties of pioneering. His farming abilities became renowned. In 1842, he sold his premier forty acres for $1,000 to a man who wished to live close to a school. He acquired another 160 acres to farm, and in 1851, he could have sold his property again for considerable profit when lead ore was discovered at Colesburg—and the area changed into a second California of 1842. Miners flocked into the area from all directions—and steamboats, which had rarely called at the place before—were loaded with miners, merchants, mechanics, speculators, and pickpockets, all in search of the almighty dollar. What yield of mineral came from the mine was unknown, but the village continued to prosper.

Currently, Wellington and Aurilla were hosts to one of the families from our Ontario voyage. It was an enjoyable *réunion* seeing these hommes again.

He and I arose early in the morning to travel via the mill road to Delhi. By mid-afternoon we had reached the place where the prairie inclined southward to the magnifique Silver Lake surrounded by a bur oak grove. I left my ox-team to graze on the grassy knoll outside the two-story brick courthouse, and we marched up the steps to the door—where inside, a huge room with a six-foot-high bench and tile engraved JUDGE F. DOOLITTLE awaited us. According to Uri, this was the place one was brought who murdered and left a corpse next to a log along Elk Creek—the first murder in the region. In a single year, Judge Doolittle had garnered a reputation for stopping settlers from taking the law into their own hands and meting out justice to lawbreakers.

Another sign pointed us to the CLERK'S OFFICE on the second floor. The steep wooden stairs delivered us to a long corridor; at the halfway point, we came upon an open counter.

"This the place to register as *praticien régulier de la médecine?*" I said, directing my remarks to two white men conversing at the rear of the room behind the counter.

A lean, bespectacled middle-aged man walked toward me, stopping briefly to pull sheets of paper from layered, divided wood bins stacked along one wall.

"Good afternoon, sir, thou art new to the county?"

Before I could speak, my eyes became preoccupied with the digits of his left hand, which seemed contrived to misbehave badly as he tried grasping a lead pencil from a box just beyond my reach. Awkwardly, finally he haphazardly dropped the pencil and paper before me.

"I am H. A. Carter, commissioner for Delaware County at thy service."

"Dr. Alexander Wiltse's my name…from Ontario, Canada…staying with kin in Colesburg—'til- I can get my practice established."

"Welcome to Delaware County, Dr. Wiltse. Thou shall want to fill out this form in triplicate and return it with a $1. 00 registration fee… Is Wellington Wiltse at your side your relations?"

I reviewed the form requesting my legal name, country of origin, physician I studied under, the university I had attended, and more.

"*Oui,*" I responded. "This herculean homme is my Cousin Wellington whom you probably know, as he helped settle Moreland Colony. Tell me, *s'il vous plait,* how many médecins and chirurgiens currently reside in the county seat."

"Plenty…and Dr. Albert Boomer informs me of a newly organized Delaware County *Société Médicale*–medical society to establish basic requirements for regular practitioners… though likely not every physician shall like the loss of independence and freedom a membership imposes. He can answer any questions. I'll draw you a map to the Boomer farm."

I waited for him to finish drawing, then folded the map along with the form, and placed them in a pocket.

"Where might I purchase products and dry *marchandises* for my femme?"

"Andrew Stone runs a grocery store at the end of the street… Walk out the front door—take a left."

—

Wellington and I found the bald Mr. Stone perched on a stool in the center of the long narrow structure—entrenched like an overgrown vegetable amid sacks of coffee, flour, meal, and potatoes, and dried venison and wild turkeys suspended on long crochets from the ceiling. At first sight, he might easily be confused with an immense yellow onion, his beard appearing like grey-black roots curling 'round the chin.

Upon closer examination, he was an elderly *Anglais* man with all the makings of a modern businessman: white chemise with narrow black garter over his sleeves, black bowtie, and dark pantalon—all covered by a white apron tied neatly at the neck and waist.

Not until the bell above the door had nearly ceased its clanging did he raise his eyes from the board balancing atop a pickle barrel, and then for only a moment.

"Love jigsaw puzzles. Careful! don't upset the puzzle as thou join near… Don't e'en sneeze," he pleaded.

Almost in unison Wellington and I took a half dozen steps forward to peer at the puzzle. Two hundred or so wooden pieces lay distributed across a four-feet square board…a few pieces attached in clusters—one, which appeared to be the beginning of young rabbits in a burrow; another, blue sky with white fluffy, clouds; and another, a nursery rhyme, or perhaps Scripture written in cursive.

"Never saw anythin' like it," Wellington said. "How do you know what goes where?"

"That's the trick, isn't it? The puzzles were created for children, though I find 'em quite entertaining. Preacher Clark, who passes hither from time to time, hath granted it to me on loan. I have another of the White Cliffs of Dover…that'll be harder to fix."

I pulled the clock from the pocket of my *gilet*—vest.

"Wouldn't want to interrupt your puzzle fixation, but perhaps you would be so gentile as to fill the elements on this list—and cut us some cheese, along with a few handfuls of craquelins…and a drink for our voyage home."

"It shall be mine pleasure, sirs," Mr. Stone said, grasping the list from my hand—then, steading the board with both hands, he prepared to stand. Convinced the pieces remained secure, he slipped behind a wooden counter where he ripped a sheet of brown paper from a lateral roll, pulled a cheese round from beneath a glass globe, placed it on the paper, and prepared to cut slices with a butcher knife.

The bell above the door sounded once more. Glancing in that direction, I felt my right knee brush against the board.

Mr. Stone, noticing my sudden movement, looked up in horror.

I studied the puzzle and signaled all was well.

The patron quickly advanced down the center aisle toward Mr. Stone.

"My order content?" he demanded in a husky voice, standing nigh parallel to Wellington and me.

I looked up to see a white-haired man with a beard of the same color and density which ended midway of his breastbone.

The man's a professional, I thought…dressed in gilet over single cut piping and corded chemise, his pantalons upheld by suspenders, and black boots that bear the worn signs of traversing rough vegetation and rocky routes; his head covering, an old black chapeau weathered by sun, rain, sleet, and snow. Bottom fact, he looked a lot like me.

"Yes, Dr. Sharp—got it content for thou hither."

Mr. Stone put aside the butcher knife and replaced the cheese round beneath the glass globe before reaching for a brown paper-wrapped package tied with string on one end of the counter.

The man waited restlessly, shifting from one foot to the other.

"Mine wife awaits these supplies…and I must tend to a young wench with fever…" he added, then pulled a notebook from a rear pocket and flipped through the pages.

Mr. Stone negotiated his way past the counter to the area of the puzzle board, where he extended the package to Dr. Sharp, conveniently leaving his hand open in the hand-off.

"Put on mine account...pay up end of month," he barked, before grabbing the package and placing it under one arm.

In Dr. Sharp's haste, a long-bladed knife dropped to the floor from the unhinged leather case attached at his waist. He bent down to retrieve it. Standing, a look of embarrassment emerged on his face.

"Wouldn't crave to lose this...belonged to mine father in the navy," he said, as his fingers coursed along the ornate handle.

Normally, I remembered some infirmity about the individuals I met—but at this moment I began to equate the name *Dr. Sharp* as the man with a *sharp knife*.

Then, without *au revoir* to me, or the gargantuan Wellington, or Mr. Stone—Dr. Sharp departed through the door, discharging the bell once more.

"The man's aye in a hurry...apologize I didn't introduce thou," Mr. Stone said. "Quite a bit of professional jealousy 'twixt him and Dr. Stout. I try to fill their orders such that they aren't in the market towards the like day."

"I am perplexed that I, too, have failed to introduce myself 'til this very moment... Dr. Alex Wiltse—of Colesburg. I've come to Delhi to register at the courthouse as a praticien régulier de la médecine. My femme Phebe and I are thinking of settling in the county. The homme at my side is my Cousin Wellington."

"Pleasure to meet thee," Mr. Stone said, once more passing by the board with great care as he returned to the counter. "I am aware of Mr. Wellington Wiltse—your reputation as a pioneer in these parts precedes you."

Mr. Stone completed my order and poured two small tins of milk.

"'Tis from our cow from this morning, milked by mine wife, Priscilla. That'll be a twenty-seven cents."

"I nearly forgot...add a box of toothpowder...and Gunther candies for mes enfants."

Mr. Stone raised an eyebrow as he reached into the jar of candy.

"The candy is for your *children*, eh?"

He pulled the toothpowder box from a shelf, and with much precaution, handed it across the puzzle board, along with the cheese, craquelins, and candies, into Wellington's massive open hands.

"Thirty-three cents, sir."

"Is it possible to start an account, or perhaps—will you take drugs in commerce?"

Mr. Stone nodded. "Bring by your inventory next time thou art in town."

"Delhi a worthy place to hang a shingle?"

"Grows day by day… We do lack good doctors hither as much as any other. One word of warning, though: I adjure thee to keep clear of that Dr. Sharp."

"*Baas boven baas*, eh!… There's always someone who can do it better," Wellington said, heaving open the door and sending the bell clanging wildly once more.

—

The sun had fallen below the horizon on the fourth day of my *voyage* by the time I brought the ox-team outside Uri's stable. Preparing to unhitch the oxen, I heard a grating noise from beyond the north stable wall. I walked with lantern in hand toward the strange sound. In a single moment, all was made clear to me why Uri had not delivered on his promise to take my family for a view of his property on Sunday—or any day since.

Uri was building a *bateau*—a boat.

"What's this, Uri?"

"I hope to have the bateau done to launch on the Turkey River before summer's end."

I encircled the twenty-foot wood carcass, noticing the weird materials on a half-bench nearby.

"Did you acquire any of these articles from my black bag? And are you sure this thing will float?"

"Remains to be seen, doesn't it?" Uri said, his joy undaunted by my skepticism.

I picked up a crude sketch laying on the hull. Best I could

make out, the contraption appeared to be built of a strip plank frame using steel wire covered with sand and cement plaster.

"This your conception, Uri?"

"'Tis a rough design…rest of the details are in my *tête*," he said, pointing to his brain.

"I have to admit 'tis inventive—but won't it sink as soon as it touches *la rivière*?"

"The post leaning against the stable wall is for the mast… It's like this, Alex, I've always wanted to sail. The Turkey River gets wide and treacherous after heavy rains… I've always wondered what it would be like to navigate in turbulent winds and seas like our ancestors"

I watched Uri continue to apply sand and cement plaster to the framework. Louisa had wound strips of cloth around his injured hand for support, along with what appeared to be ginger root for the swelling. He grimaced in pain with each swath.

"My offer remains good to put *une attelle*—a splint, on your hand… ."

"Pain is *temporelle*…hardly feel anything," he said.

—

Ho-Chunk paid no attention as I stepped through the doorframe of the cabin. The only light was the glow of embers on the fireplace floor. I placed the package from Stone's Grocery, map, and medical form on the table. From the balcony, I could hear Phebe and Louisa installing the enfants into bed. Walking to the ladder, three sets of eyes suddenly peered down at me.

"I-I-Indians… S-s-saw n-n-naked Indians t-t-today," Charles said, now standing at the top of the ladder.

"*Avez-vous eu peur*?"—were you scared, I asked as I climbed to the balcony, allowing him the opportunity to respond with a one-word answer.

"Oui, Père, I-I-I w-w-was a-a-afraid."

"They stole all our food," Vidella added.

"Well, not quite everything," Phebe said, "but the savages took the wild blueberry tarte we had baked earlier."

Louisa added: "Rifle by door…not reach."

"Where was Ho-Chunk?"

"Uri took *cuk* to check crops."

Phebe suddenly broke into laughter, her cheeks instantly turning snapdragon pink.

"We were too afraid to do anything…they hardly wore any vêtements—yes, they were almost *naked*."

Louisa looked away, informing me there might be more to the story.

I wondered whether the visit by these Indians had anything to do with the violent crime that had taken place in Uri's stable.

"I saw a garçon, Père…through win-dow…with limp. You should repair his leg," Edwin said.

"It's late to look for him tonight, but I'll watch for him tomorrow."

I kissed my children on the forehead before returning to the ladder.

"*Slaapwel*," I whispered.

And sleep well my little one, too, I thought, looking heavenward.

—

I could count on a few hands the nights that Phebe and I had been alone since Edwin's birth. In this evening, she looked more beautiful than ever…her long auburn hair, unwound from the bun, swirling across my arms as we whispered secrets in the lantern's flickering lumière in the stable.

I told her of the physical change from the Wellington I'd known in his youth—albeit his joyous temperament even now warmed the hearts of all he met. And how quickly I had come to love his Aurilla—a woman with the face of an angel. The Ontario family staying in their home sent Phebe their salutations.

She listened with great interest of my visit to the Delhi courthouse and of the formation of the Delaware County Société Médicale. Dues were $1.00 per year, which we could well afford, though we would need to keep an eye on *een appeltje voor de dorst*—our nest egg put away for harder times. Several doctors made up the society, including Dr. Boomer, whom Wellington and I found at his farm south of Delhi. Dr. Boomer proposed helping me prepare for my examination by the Board of Censors. "The man is of Scottish descent, and a bit hard to comprehend—though a fellow *Methodist*," I pointed out.

Phebe's gray-green eyes grew large as I told of the visit to Stone's Grocery—and of my discovery of the "picture puzzle." Each piece butted up against others, which, when in the end, revealed a beautiful landscape. Phebe insisted I inquire about borrowing the puzzle for our children's amusement.

Her visage changed to worry as I spoke of my introduction to Dr. Sharp.

"What's the source of his anger?"

"*Professional jealousy*, according to Mr. Stone."

"But surely Delhi can support many médical professionals."

"Perhaps mental illness is at play here… A physician would know how to mask symptoms," I explained. "My initial consideration was *dementia*…his impatience, embarrassment at dropping a simple thing like a knife…and he rummaged through a notepad as though unable to recall his next client."

"Keep attentive, Alex. An unwell homme—in particular, a physician, can result of perilous injury to himself and to others."

Phebe spoke excitedly of the recent visit to Uri's homestead by a midwife to examine Louisa. Listening to the telltale heartbeats of the fetus with a stethoscope—which had registered 130—the midwife determined Louisa's first child would be a girl. Her baby was due after the new year.

Teacher Miss Amalia Phillips had also stopped by for a visit, after learning Vidella and Charles would attend Colesburg's new one-story brick school building in the fall. She seemed an accomplished teacher in her knowledge of mathematics and lectures on the sciences. "She teaches *American English*, of course—not the Queen's English, god forbid," Phebe noted.

Miss Amalia remarked of the addition of the divisive topic of "slavery" to her fall schedule, stating: "Our nation is hovering on a bloody and divisive battle over slavery, though Abraham Lincoln, who is running as a candidate for the office of United States President on the Republican ticket, says he has no intention of interfering with slavery in the southern states. Our children need to understand that our very *democracy* is at stake."

Phebe had responded: As long as the message is not that slavery is the natural condition of any portion of humanity—nor did I wish our children to be taught the Fugitive Slave Law should be observed and enforced.

She provided me with news about Uri, too: Louisa informed her Uri had begun construction of a transfer boat as a *financial enterprise*. He would use it to transport immigrants arriving monthly, numbering in the hundreds, to communities along the Turkey River.

"Oh, yes," Phebe added, "and two farmers stopped by, upon hearing Uri's cousin practiced médicine… They hoped you might treat their sick animals."

During my four days away from Phebe, upon my return I had envisioned, playing her favorite accordéon serenade. Now, I withdrew the instrument from the case and commenced to play an old Dutch *mélodie*, "G du Bree en J. Blok."

In and out went the bellows on the squeezebox, ten buttons and keys alternately depressed; pallets opened to allow air to flow across brass reeds. Out came the melodious bass sound from deep within its body. Nouvelles lyrics overflowed from my heart, ones echoing the true signification of life.

> *Cher Phebe, my beloved. Come lie beside me in my*
> *bed,*
> *And take me to heaven, for in your arms, I long to*
> *inhabit,*
> *Too long have I been without you,*
> *And as oft as has been said, since whence first we wed,*
> *My Phebe, ma bien-aimée, my l'amour, I am yours*
> *forever.*

The longer I played and sang, the more inviting became Phebe's smile.

—

Cucumber time—the long growing season of summer—was upon us. Finally, our family, plus Uri and Louisa, boarded our wagon for a tour of Uri's property. He pointed out his acreages in Section 11…fields of green corn stalks and wheat, the heads already turning a golden hue. Broomcorn was his *novelle* cash crop, next to the usual field of potatoes. A stretch of land along the timberland by the Turkey River provided ample wood and plentiful wildlife: droves of deer from a dozen to forty at any given time, bears and turkeys. Large packs of gray wolves roamed the prairies. Wolf scalps were worth $1.50 each.

Uri noted that the explosion of immigrants had created an excellent home market for all kinds of produce, and the hardy pioneers who had paved the way for all this prosperity were beginning to reap a reward for their years of toil and privation. Money was plentiful, labor in active demand at good prices, towns were growing, farms were improving— even beggars were getting rich. Three-quarters of the land in Delaware County was now inhabited.

He spoke well of the partnership with his father, Leonard, and brothers—Wellington, Leonard Jr., and Amasa, whose farms were within a few miles of his.

I provided an update on building my medical practice. Monthly meetings of the Delaware County *Société Médicale* were held at a room at the Delhi courthouse. We were an energetic lot, and the first order of business was drafting the Constitution and By-laws. Dr. Albert Boomer was one of Delhi's most prosperous physicians, a good citizen, and a prominent churchman. With his tutorage, I was confident in passing the examination by the Board of Censors.

Dr. Stout, another founding member—and Dr. Acers—had kindly invited our family to visit the Stout homestead for the annual prairie chicken hunt. We looked forward to attending.

—

By the time summer turned to autumn, malady befell Uri's farm. After Phebe and Louisa delivered lunch to Uri and me as we pulled weeds in the fields, Louisa suddenly tumbled to the ground, writhing in pain throughout the abdomen. Soon, an escape of blood appeared on an interior calf. Phebe removed her apron to cover Louisa. My examination deemed her pulse a hundred and ten, irregular and fluttering. It appeared she was in early labor. The day prior, she had shot and gutted a mule deer buck with a skinning knife—quite an accomplishment considering her condition. Now, Louisa lay on the ground, perhaps near death, and that of her unborn enfant.

Uri climbed his warhorse to ride to the home of the midwife. Phebe and I helped Louisa into the two-wheeled cart to return her to the cabin—the same cart used weeks earlier to transport piglets from a neighbor's farm to Uri's kitchen, their place of temporary lodging.

Hours passed before Uri reappeared with the midwife, who immediately set about giving Louisa "muterkorn three"—but her stomach would not take it. Not until evening did her expulsive pains begin to cease. The midwife told Uri she would remain at Louisa's side day and night for as long as Louisa remained in a weakened and precarious condition. She expected the child could be born at any time.

Uri set about relocating the piglets to the timber to allow room for a cot in the kitchen.

The next morning Phebe took charge of all household chores. Preparing the morning meal, her foremost suggestion to Louisa was: "Wouldn't a grand wood-burning cookstove be an improvement?" After more days passed, Phebe encouraged Louisa to envision adding an outdoor kitchen. The arduous work of hauling water from the creek to wash the dirt from vêtements promoted discussion by Phebe about the construction of a windmill to deliver water directly to the cabin—and in short order, Phebe produced her sketch of a windmill structure emerging through the stable roof.

Furthermore, Phebe assigned Père Philip and Mère Rachel the responsibility of growing and harvesting the corn and beans in the gardens. Vidella, Charles, and Edwin would perform daily chores…removal of manure with a push shovel from pens in the stable, and gathering eggs—nevertheless, allowing them lavish time for play on the hillside picking *horse flowers*—dandelions, fishing and wading and tossing stones in Bear Creek. In the evenings, Phebe would continue teaching our enfants the alphabet and numbers, though the only books she'd brought from Ontario were a *Lefevre* Bible, an almanac, and a few ragged schoolbooks, also written in French.

In the days and weeks that followed, we waited to see what was to become of Louisa and her baby.

—

The Sabbath was a day of rest when we boarded our wagon to attend the Methodist Episcopal service at a cabin in the Delhi woods. The midwife kept Louisa bedridden so we left them behind. We Methodists were a group of a dozen or so families, who, seated side by side on the ground beneath shady bur oak trees, relished the opportunity to joyously sing hymns and listen attentively as Rev. S. C. Churchill—the most recent pastor sent from the Burrington Circuit—taught the simple Gospel of doing good.

Sunday afternoons were spent along the shores of the Turkey River, where our children searched for agates, pieces of slate, and pebbles of quartz foreign to this region. Boulders scattered over the surface were the silent monuments of the glacial period. The river's depth increased to as much as four hundred feet in places.

It was on these shores Uri gave the children instructions on how to fly a kite. His first invention was a twelve-foot kite, which he hoped to use for the transportation of small chests carried by immigrants, across the Turkey River. Word had spread among the immigrants that these lands, rich with fertile soil, an abundance of animal life, splendid forests, and beautiful streams, were all to be had but for the asking.

We watched Uri's inaugural kite launch, hoisting our Edwin into the chest, as a measure of how much weight it could lift. With considerable wonderment, we watched the kite lift...and lift...and lift, then drift toward the water's edge until floating float high above the channel.

Edwin's movement waving to his family caused the chest to tip, and soon we watched as he toppled into the water.

I hoped there should never come another day when I would hear Phebe's scream of *hystérique*, as with much urgency we fished our Edwin from the Turkey River.

—

Week by week my pioneering life as an Iowa physician grew. I carried calomel, jalop, castor oil, anti-inflammation creams, and herbal pills to treat everything from toothaches to stomach aches, fevers—and sick livestock. I went on foot, through paths so overhung with dense undergrowth and obstructed with logs and roots that a team and wagon seemingly could not pass, through muddy and flooded tidelands wearing tall gumboots to keep my feet and pantalon legs dry.

One evening, I admitted to Phebe my disappointment that not one murder had crossed my pathway since our arrival in America. Nonetheless, I was reminded with every voyage to Delhi of the death of an Anglais man in the town square a decade earlier, where thousands of people had assembled to watch him hang by the neck until dead—though no one could any longer recall his crime.

In more recent months, horse thievery—a single horse valued at fifty dollars—and counterfeiting had become endemic in the county, and increasingly there was talk of "hanging-bees."

Once the hangings began, how many would follow?

Of this, I was certain...whether the staunchest Methodist, the town's most venerated citizen, or a vagabond—if one could *watch* a hanging, he or she was culpable in murder.

CHAPTER THREE

The Hunt

A mere four years earlier, Dr. Joshua Stout had emigrated from Herkimer County, New York, along with Dr. John Acers, his brother-in-law. Both Germans were of considerable character and ability and had developed successful medical practices. But prosperity has both its recompenses and deprivations—neither was aware how soon murder would befall one of them.

The Iowa law on hunting prairie chickens would expire for the season at dawn on September 30th. A few weeks prior, Dr. Stout invited families, neighbors, elected aristocracy, and others from the Burrington and Delhi citizenry to join in the annual prairie chicken hunt. Spouses would prepare the evening meal for the huntsmen.

Overnight lodgment, midway in our two days' journey to the Stout farm, occurred at Honey Creek, where I gave treatment to more of my fellow Ontario voyagers. I found many suffered from lingering fatigue and maladies, bad teeth, swollen ankles, broken bones, and arthritis.

There, I also learned of the multitudes of new immigrants arriving daily from the Ohio Valley, complaining of nausea, vomiting, chills, thirst, diarrhea, and violent spasms. The fear of the deadly cholera epidemic resurfaced in my mind's eye—the scene where hundreds of corpses were carried from our ship at the port in Chicago. I had access now to the newest journals through the Delaware County *Société Médicale* that linked cleanliness with morbidity, and I urged these people to boil the water they drank and wash their hands to prevent the spread of disease—knowing few, if any, would believe me.

Our journey resumed on the third day, with my black bag dismally low on supplies. I would need to submit a request for replenishment from Manufacturing Chemists and Druggists upon my return to Uri's homestead.

—

Dr. Stout had described the route to his 320 acres as bordered by split rail fence and wheat fields. I knew with certainty we had arrived when a two-story stable came into view. He said it held the tools he'd used in felling timber and grubbing, burning brush, and breaking the stump land. Large stones brought to the surface during the glacier era were those used to erect his stone house. Within the first year, he was in the initial stages of a cultivated farm with roaming chickens, rooting pigs, and a smokehouse.

Forty yards beyond, a huge multi-room habitation was arising from the prairie.

Phebe gasped at the magnificence of the structure. I, too, was quite charmed by Dr. Stout…the house only added to his charm.

No sooner had I halted my ox-team than a woman stepped through the front door of the stone house, and gracefully strolled toward us in greeting.

"On behalf of Mr. and Mrs. Stout, Ich bid thee willkommen. I am the wife of Dr. Acers, Melinda Acers…sister to Mrs. Stout."

She paused in her struggle to speak in English—"Sie offer hospitality für thy problem im das stable…but alas, das lodge shall nicht be finished für months—Samuel Knee is das devoted contractor."

Then, speaking directly to Phebe, she added: "Mrs. Stout hath implored me to kindly offer, should thou require, a mehr comfortable place of slumber…space has been made available in the stone haus—though hurlyburly of food preparation für hunters can affect thy rest somewhat."

Phebe was caught off guard by the gesture.

"Merci… but I shall choose to remain with my family in the stable."

"Get settled und come für refreshments towards das lawn then," Mrs. Acers said.

I tipped my hat to the woman and directed the oxen toward the stable amid the convergence of arriving carriages and wagons.

"Why should I require special lodgment, do you imagine?" Phebe inquired once out of Mrs. Acers' earshot.

"You must admit, *ma chère*, you've not been feeling well… I may have made mention of your illness to Dr. Stout and Dr. Acers."

Our children, seeing a game of tug of war in progress, jumped from the wagon's rear and ran off.

'Twas the sound of an *oom-pah-pah* German band playing a polka that caused me to hurry Phebe's descent from the wagon. I, too, looked forward to joining in the festivities.

—

The next morning the hunt commenced at daylight. Dr. Stout directed me to hunt with my Delhi colleagues—Drs. Acers, Boomer, Smith, Doran, Taylor, and Wright. We lined up along the western side of a hillside overlooking an open treeless expanse of dewy yellow Indiangrass; ammunitions and game sack at our sides, brass trim from our rifles glinting as the sunlight broke on the eastern horizon.

Dr. Stout's hired hand sent bird dogs through the grasses to flush out the birds, when the sharp cracks of firing flintlock rifles first pierced the air.

Another signal from the hired hand and the dogs rushed the field to retrieve the fallen fowl.

Dr. Boomer, hunting to my left, was quick off the mark and soon brought down two fowl with his 50-caliber flintlock. According to the Scot, 'twas not unusual for him to sack twenty-five birds in a single day. A fervent disciplinarian, Dr. Boomer did not choose to mix business affairs with pleasure, nor speak of the tutorage he was providing me; nor make mention of the position of county agent for the sale of liquors, for which I believed he sought, though his aspirations went well beyond county agent. He kept all personal things confidential.

"Th' most desperate o' tactics is th' ambush wey," Dr. Boomer explained. "Prairie chickens are creatures o' habit and 'kin be scouted in upland species. Ye kin watch them in their routines as they fly over th' exact identical fence post each night in a roosting field on their way to a feeding pasture, then from th' feeding pasture back to the exact identical roost field... Don't have muckle o 'a chance to survive, if ye'r any kind o' hunter."

We both knew I had yet to drop a single bird with my Parker shotgun.

"I am outta practice—little time to hunt these days," I said, as a way of explaining for my poor performance.

I observed Dr. Stout hunting a short distance away, using a new model Smith and Wesson. Hunting seemed effortless with a fully self-contained cartridge and stunning precision, seemingly giving him a distinctive edge over the others. Within the hour he rotated next to me, standing to my right.

"I admire your *fusil*, Dr. Stout."

"This weapon hast begun new era in hunting rifles," he said, once more raising the Smith and Wesson to fire at a fresh lot of birds lifting thirty feet above the grasslands. Straightaway, two fowl fluttered and dropped near the trees.

"I have idee for you, Wiltse," he added, as we observed the dogs locate his birds.

I felt an immediate rise in my heart rhythm and my lungs fully inflate... *Did he wish for me to join his practice? Burrington would be an excellent choice to hang my shingle and construct my nouvelle life in America. Surely, within a few years, I should possess a farm such as Dr. Stout's, and be the envy of every physician in the region.*

"Surely, however, may I be of aid?" I said with enthusiasm.

"Dr. Acers says ich come up with hair-brained ideas from time to time...but what do sie think of sending up a live ox in a balloon as part of some future Burrington festivity—perhaps the next Independence Day celebration...with the town bürgermeister trotting up Franklin to speaker's stand, talking 'til all are bored, crackers going off— beer and whiskey running das full channel of the Maquoketa River. Nein expense spared...make it day to be remembered. Charge: perhaps twenty-five cents for adults, kinder under ten feet—hälfte price."

The look in his eyes informed me his idea was sincere, and he believed it the equivalent to the glorious invention of, say—a plow, to reduce by half the hours of labor it takes to cut through a foot of prairie sod.

"*Amerika ist* greatest land of all—think can be done?"

"I assure you, my oxen should not care to premier such a balloon-rising event," hoping to hide my skepticism of his idea without offense.

Just then, I heard the whiz of a lead ball fly by in close proximity to my head. Out of the corner of one eye, I saw Dr. Stout reach for his jaw and fall to the ground.

I dropped my gun and bent over him to determine the significance of his injury. Fresh blood flowed from his lips.

"Appears it's only a graze… Where the hell did that come from?" I said.

I stood again to canvass the landscape, trying to identify the source of the projectile. My eyes focused on the tree line to my right.

Dr. Stout slowly sat up, retrieved a handkerchief from a pocket, and wiped the blood from his mouth.

Dr. Acers, alerted of his brother-in-law's injury, arrived at his side in a panicky state.

"What happened, Joshua?"

"I've been shot by some *dummkopf*."

"Likely, *ein* accidental discharge…a rifle misfiring, a flash-hole."

"I tell you…no one was firing to mein*e* right."

Dr. Acers helped Joshua to his feet, and together they limped off toward the wagons, which, but an hour earlier, had delivered the hunters to Dr. Stout's prairie.

"I should come with you...," I offered.

"I'm alright, Alex… John will tend to meine injury. You enjoy das hunt."

—

Dr. Stout called for a three-hour intermission for lunch. Phebe and I and our enfants ate seated in the long grasses under the shade of leafy oak trees in full view of the imposing new framed lodge. I wondered if the house was modeled after Abiathar Richardson's home near Mudville, of which Miss Amalia had spoken. Richardson had worked in shipbuilding in his native Maine, and he alone had fashioned every joint and beam, and split the shingles out of native oak and walnut from his timber.

I should be intrigué to look into the eyes of such a bold homme who painted his habitation— romantique rouge, I thought, musing about the very idea of a red house.

The German band clad in colorful costumes moved throughout the families, playing lively waltzes on guitar, harmonica, violin, bass tuba, and accordéon. It was an enviable exposition. I would have enjoyed playing with them very much.

Vidella, Charles, and Edwin told of passing the morning amused with the game of grace, and chase and capture—earning prizes of apples and nuts. Phebe had found herself light-headed, such that she was unable to aid in dressing the birds for the evening meal, though she did manage to teach the others a quick one-step method of dismembering the meaty breast from entrails and feathers: Inverting the deceased fowl on the ground, she placed a foot upon each wing, then grasping the bird's feet with her hands, she pulled until the breast and wings separated from the feathered carcass.

She had been complimented numerous times, for hers was quite a system to behold. Already, Phebe had found favor among her new acquaintances.

Dr. and Mrs. Stout emerged from the old stone house—he, with notable swelling about the mouth, but without bandage so as not to curry sympathy, I imagined. They greeted guests, one by one. He made light of his misfortune, or so I imagined by his gesturing. The identification of the man and woman at their side, for whom he was making presentations, was a mystery to me.

My family and I stood as they approached.

"Dr. Alex and Mrs. Wiltse, ich should like to introduce you to Dr. A. B. and Mrs. Ward and their young son Griffy. Sie are new to Oxbow in Buchanan County. Ich thought it a friendly gesture to present them to Delaware County physicians at the annual prairie chicken hunt."

"*Bonjour*! I admit to learning of your arrival. We are recent immigré from Ontario...these three are our children," I said.

Mrs. Ward, dressed fashionably in a fine silk dress, black

velvet neck ribbon with brooch tied with a knot around her slender neck, quickly dropped to one knee in the grass, until Griffy, about three months in age in her arms, was at eye level to my children.

"I should like you to meet our son Griffy… Dr. Ward and I and Griffy reside in Oxbow. We shall be most pleased to receive you for a visit at your earliest opportunity."

Looking kindly into Edwin's eyes, she added, "Perhaps you and Griffy shall grow up to become friends."

Dr. Ward's booming voice spoke over Mrs. Ward's last words.

"Dangerous business being a doctor," he said, gesturing with one hand at Dr. Stout's face.

"I started carrying a revolver after almost a capture by some rough characters who wished to run my buggy off the road… They ran away when I pulled a revolver from my black bag. Didn't take long in this profession before I realized Indians, bandits, and chicken thieves are all patients—und enemies. Same for you, Wiltse, I suspect."

"I should graciously accept your aid in the selection of appropriate hand revolver at your convenience, Dr. Ward."

"And acquire a buggy and horse—so people will begin to recognize you as you cut across the prairie and backwoods…might help thine ass from being killed."

I looked at my children, who paid no mind to Dr. Ward's discouragements, but were preoccupied with the childish comportment of poking one another.

The young physician continued: "I studied under Dr. Parson out-a Blanchard, Ohio for three years; then practiced in Rock Port, before attending the medical department at the University of Michigan at Ann Arbor. Ended up in the flourishing hamlet of Oxbow, which bids fair to be a large place. What about you, Wiltse?"

Phebe's face informed me of her boredom with the subject at hand.

"I fear, Dr. Ward, we are boring our women with talk of la médecine. Perhaps we shall have the occasion to speak more thoroughly another day. We gratefully accept your hospitality and shall enjoy a voyage to Oxbow one day very soon."

"I shall come, too, Père?" Edwin said.

"Yes, my son." I said, surprised at his attentiveness to the conversation. I lifted him to my chest.

"Already Edwin is tutored to become a splendid physician… Our other *enfants* shall also do well, perhaps marrying and becoming honorable *des agriculteurs*—farmers."

Mrs. Stout spoke, addressing Phebe: "I believe you and Mrs. Ward met in the kitchen earlier."

"Maria and I have become fast friends and have much in common," Phebe said, with a strange twinkle in her eye. The meaning was beyond my immediate comprehension—more so when Phebe reached for Mrs. Ward's hand and drew her near, as though the two were *inséparables*.

The three women huddled to digress into their ideas further.

"Und we discussed das growing threat of *counterfeiters*," continued Mrs. Stout. "Most claim to be—d*octors*, assumed doubtless to gain the confidence of the public more readily, as is there any class of men so honest as regular-bred physicians?

"Though we spoke nothing of the great rebellion, soon to be upon us. *Dies ist immer noch ein glücklich Zeit im America*—this is still a happy time in the America," Mrs. Stout added.

Phebe interjected: "*Prairie banditti* are of more urgent concern. At this instant, my Alex is preoccupied with the fact that all horses in Delaware County are in danger of being rounded up for illegal transfer and sale into Wisconsin's interior. I believe he's correct in his thinking. Most people blame the Indians, but white men are being rounded up for the crime left and right."

—

The remainder of the day, the only additional hunting incidents amounted to exploding powder in gun barrels from improper muzzle charges that produced blackened faces, hands, and *vêtements*. Hunters had been instructed to fire *en volée*—on the fly; instead, they fired off rounds like on an army battlefield—as though instructed to kill every prairie chicken by noon.

Around mid-afternoon, Dr. Sharp arrived on the hillside,

breathless and without fanfare or introduction by Dr. Stout, and promptly inserted himself in the lineup between Dr. James Wright and me. Dr. Wright had his sights set on being Iowa's next Secretary of State, according to rumors.

"We meet again, Dr. Sharp… Agreeable you could join us," I said.

Dr. Sharp made no gesture that he'd heard my greeting, nor could I tell whether the Anglais recognized me from our initial encounter weeks earlier at Andrew Stone's Grocery. Even now, the angle of his black hat seemed positioned to shield his face from mine. Was he embarrassed over his comportment that day, or did he simply prefer to avoid making eye contact, even as a common courtesy?

"Mine invitation 'twas overlooked, I should imagine… Overheard Mr. Stone speak at the market this morning of today's exalted hunt. I am outstanding member of community, too…which Dr. Stout seems reticent to concede."

Dr. Sharp prepared to fill his muzzle-loading fusil, steadying himself on the uneven ground, one foot above the other on the hillside, each anchored in a tall black boot from which a willowy panted leg arose to a jacketed torso. Perched at the summit of his drooping shoulders sat an immense head of thick white hair sticking out beneath a weathered black hat. And attached at the waist was his leather case holding the dirk knife, which I had yet to see him without.

His footing secure, he pulled the gun powder sack from his shoulder harness, lifted it just above the octagonal barrel, and poured in the coarse black powder.

'Twas the first time I noticed his dense white brows, suspended like a narrow shelf cloud over his eye sockets that nearly overtook his poignant, piercing eyes from which he dispensed sharp daggers with precision. Profound furrows lined the soft tissue around his eyes and high forehead. His thick, white beard largely hid his prominent Anglais-structured weathered cheeks through which a gigantic reddish nose emerged—all of it, masking the conduit of anger driving his true intentions.

"I'm certain indeed there's been a miscommunication, Dr. Sharp," I continued. "I bid thee *bienvenue*! You arrived in time for a good hunt; the final two hours of twilight should be the best of the day's journey."

Dr. Wright—also a Scot, ceased his firing to reload and briefly looked in Dr. Sharp's direction.

"It shall be *mah* great pleasure to hunt beside *ye* this day."

Again, Dr. Sharp made no gesture he'd heard the comment.

Dr. Sharp killed his share of fowl in a short duration. I observed his cheeks glow with excitement. His eyes grow soft and kind and heaviness lift from his face.

As late afternoon dampness crept over the valley, which effectively weakened the black powder, the day's hunt was cut short. Total prairie chicken killed by all *chasseurs*—hunters: four hundred eight-seven.

Dr. Sharp stated he could not attend the twilight meal, demanding, Dr. Stout's hired hand produce his killed birds before his departure, without so much as a farewell to the host.

Once more I found my family seated near the German band, this time in a dewy sea of horse flowers, where we enjoyed the bountiful harvest of the fowl, beans, pastries, watermelon, and sweet cider.

My Dutch ancestors would have described such happiness: *Alsof er een engeltje over je tong piest*—as if an angel is peeing on your tongue.

—

I awoke the next morning to the sound of heavy rain against the stable's windowpanes. Phebe declared her desire to return to Uri's homestead; her lightheadedness and stomach issues were persuasive. However, I sensed she, too, was weakened by the lack of a premier letter from her parents, Père Henry and Mère Hannah Wiltse, who had resided in Floyd County for some time. Indeed, by the time we bade farewell to the Stouts, Phebe made a request to stop and inquire of a letter at Bailey's Ford, where the stagecoach runs to connect Dubuque to Independence.

I shouted words of gratitude to the Stouts: "Thank you for the fine day of hunting—and most profoundly, for the German band…nice touch! particularly the *l'accordéonon*, for which I have personal knowledge... Perhaps I shall play for you sometime."

The rain quickly transformed the county road to Colesburg into a muddy, treacherous mire. At the approach to the Plumb Creek bridge, even now in an embryonic state without side rails, the wagon slid off the roadway. But for the robust oxen's efforts, the unit and all of us with it, would have slid into a deep ravine.

Closer examination revealed the rear axle had lodged on a boulder. I searched in the trees for a sturdy branch to excise the box and observed a suspect band of horses in a roped area beneath me at the creek's edge. In the center, stood a gray stallion with spotted loin…I recalled Dr. Stout had announced the theft of a horse fitting that description.

Within the hour, I managed to free the wagon then felt obliged to return to Dr. Stout to inform him of the location of his stallion.

Dr. Stout instantly prepared to set off for the bridge to claim his prized horse, though Dr. Acers implored him to wait, as he remained unwell from the mishap the previous day. And wasn't it more prudent to summon the sheriff to join him than to meet the thieves alone in the woods? Dr. Acers asked.

Dr. Stout refused to wait and followed us on horseback through the muck to the bridge. There, he wasted no time sliding down the embankment to identify his bay—shouting up to us from the creek bed that he recognized other horses reported missing by neighbors. Retrieving his animal, he urged us to continue on our way home.

Once safely beyond the bridge, I looked back at Dr. Stout on horseback leading his mare by rope, and noticed he did not return home the way he had come, making me wonder: *Where is he off to? Surely, he has guests to get back to.*

—

The next day we arrived at the home of Postmaster Joel Bailey. Phebe explained she sought a letter from her Père Henry and Mère Hannah. He searched in his Dead Letter bin, and found a letter addressed to Mr. and Mrs. Alexander Wiltse, which he'd been holding for several weeks, not knowing where we had settled in the area.

With enthusiasm, Phebe tore open the envelope, but her look turned to consternation. She handed me the letter. I learned my *schoonmoeder*—Phebe's mother, was ill with consumption and longed for Phebe to come to her side.

Phebe's teary eyes informed me the hundred-miles *voyage* would be too much to endure at this moment, which greatly saddened her.

—

Upon our return to Uri's cabin, we found a grim-faced midwife attending to Louisa. Ho-Chunk lay on the floor beneath the cot, also in a melancholy manner, without so much as lifting her head. Mère Rachel and Père Philip stoically looked on from across the room.

Louisa immediately reached for Phebe's hand.

"Baby gone," Louisa said, struggling to breathe through her agony.

Phebe let out a wail that I understood all too well.

She placed her hands against Louisa's wet cheeks, and the two tortured souls joined forces with the universe.

Louisa continued: "Name him *Šųkjąk*. English name: *Wolf Runs Alone*…wish bury next to creek where Uri sits."

She began fingering the string of beads as though attempting to lift them from her neck.

"Phebe, you have beads…are from mother."

Phebe refused the gesture.

"I shall help care for you… You can have another *bébé* another year."

The midwife beckoned me to follow her out of Louisa's earshot. Père Philip followed. She wished to inform me of Louisa's condition.

Within recent days, Louisa had begun displaying affectations of the nervous system, at times developing into a hysterical nature, depressing forebodings of impending evil; feeling some great calamity was about to befall herself or some of her family. At other times, Louisa seemed incredulous of her own condition, even inventing the most ingenious arguments to convince herself and others that all her peculiar symptoms were attributable to any cause but pregnancy. The midwife explained Louisa's was a peculiar kind of insanity to develop, and she may have to consider some sort of restraint be put upon her.

I left the cabin in search of Uri. Père Philip grabbed his ten-gallon hat and followed.

"Tell me what perplexes you so my garçon," Père Philip asked.

"'Muterkorn three' is not *modern* médecine. Nonetheless, Louisa continues in the care of the midwife…as is Louisa and Uri's wish."

We found Uri at the place along Bear Creek where he went for a rest many evenings.

Noticing our approach, Uri stood and greeted us with his usual exuberant handshake.

"We have come from Louisa's bedside, Uri…is there anything Phebe and I can do for Louisa or you?"

"You can pray, Alex," he mumbled, "I fear all we can do…is pray."

Uri stumbled back to his seat, facing away from us.

In the solemness of the babbling creek, I placed my hand upon Uri's shoulder.

He began to ramble.

"I have ended my work on the bateau and await launch day.

"The pigs are flourishing in the timber and have created a large mud hole to find relief from hot days… I shall show you the shed I built to shield them from their first Iowa winter."

With every word, he gestured with his damaged hand. Finally, catching sight of it, he flashed it before my eyes as though to invite my inspection.

"'Tis now well enough," he said.

"Where is Louisa's family? Who can we notify of her dire malady?" I inquired.

"Louisa's father, a white man, was stationed at a military post…said to be of some refinement and education. He died before she was born. She grew up on the Half-Breed Tract for the Sac and Fox in the southern part of the state between the Des

Moines and Mississippi Rivers."

He continued: "Another white man, who had taken a squaw wife asked that Louisa, then a young girl, be released to serve her. She taught Louisa to read and write Anglais—and to hold onto her Indian ways. Every day since, Louisa has wondered, whenever she crossed paths with another *Hochunkra*, whether her blood flowed in his veins… This was her life as a half-breed. There is no one to notify of her impending death in her family."

I now felt the pressure of my father's hand on my shoulder. I was aware, as I stood at Uri's side, once more Père Philip stood at mine. Since a young boy, I had been keenly aware that he understood my joys and sorrows—a blessing of being the eldest child of eight, I imagined. Surely, Père had sensed Uri and Louisa's loss would remind me of the deep sorrow Phebe and I had shared a year earlier—the loss of our bébé.

I felt a familiar brush against my forehead and instinctively raised my hand, in search of perhaps a leaf or twig deposited by the wind, or insect of the night. I found nothing—again. The sensation had become almost routine: at the Forest Home Cemetery as I stood over the grave marked by a rock chiseled "VIRGINIA C"; at the port of Chicago, treating cholera victims; and many, many evenings as I lay awake thinking of the day's perplexities on a bed of straw in Uri's stable. Perhaps it was God reminding me of his love and care. Or perhaps, only a wang-doodle of my imagination.

My Canadian médecin mentor, whom I trained with for several years, had told me that medicine either works well or not with patients who believe a holy entity will come to their aid and heal them of indigestion, infected toenail, and every other malady that comes their way, just because they asked. But faith routinely gets in the way of their seeking timely medical remedies, and they often end up dead—much sooner than they ought to be.

I glanced at Uri, who now stared blankly at the last remnant of the setting sun.

A part of him had died; another part of him was on the brink of death.

I resolved this was not an appropriate time to question him about the violent thing that had occurred in his stable.

—

In territory like Delaware County, where the average rainfall is forty inches, if there were not sufficient slope and an adequate number of stream valleys to afford timely escape for the surplus water, the whole surface of the land would become one continuous marsh, breeding pestilence for the destruction of humans, plants, and animals, rather than furnishing arable fields for their support. I knew of only one man who thought day and night of harnessing that rain—for the purpose of floating a cement boat.

With the approach of fall, Uri began studying every ominous cloud arising from the sky that seemed to promise rain. For weeks clouds appeared and grew, tantalizing him with their broad propositions, containing the liquid foundations he was thirsting for, but week after week they passed over, giving nary a drop to his parched dream.

Finally, a drenching rain began to fall that crept across much of the eastern half of the county and continued for days. And so, came the time for Uri, in his thirtieth year, to move his large round-bilged bateau through the rain and mud from the north side of the stable to the Turkey River—or more precisely, he employed the use of my oxen to drag his boat. The cement hull created such a trench in the earth that a canal was cut all the way to the riverbed, one which quickly filled with run-off water and gave buoyancy to the beast.

Then, in the spirited affair, he walked to the cabin to retrieve his Louisa from her bed and carry her in his arms to the same two-wheeled cart he'd used to haul pigs only months earlier. There, he gently placed her on a fresh bed of straw, sheltered beneath a tarp attached to poles at the four corners, and covered her over with blankets. Finally, he delivered her to the *canapé* beneath the cottonwood trees at the river's edge.

Phebe, our children, the midwife, and I awaited her arrival, all quite caught up in the swell of his noble strain.

Watching her amateur sailor climb aboard the twenty-foot truss framed vessel, Louisa applauded with seemingly limitless energy, as the storm raged just beyond the tree line.

Uri then raised a small vessel of apple vinegar above the bow and smashed it against the hull, declaring during a fissure of thunder, "I crown thee 'Sweet, Louisa.'"

Once more, Louisa's glee echoed throughout the canyon.

With every passing minute, the rain grew more violent. The wind gusts seemed forty miles per hour or more. Uri watched from the deck, keeping attentive to the rise of water along the hull. When small whitecapped waves gave lift to the keel, Uri started raising the rigging on the stayed mast. Ever so slowly, the little boat bowed to the wind and floated from her mooring.

Finally, Uri opened the mainsail and the cloth unfurled, exposing large rouge hand-painted *HO!* at its top, a word meaning *rendre grâce*—render grace—in Siouan.

Tears flowed from Louisa's glowing cheeks. 'Twas the same for Phebe. The midwife, too. Our children seemed bedazzled by it all.

Then Uri, at the helm of his bateau, disappeared in the heavy haze of rain, carried on the water, moved only by the wind, making his way down the Turkey River.

Louisa screamed and applauded in delight, waving until she knew Uri could hear her no more. Then she stared after him a bit longer, and longer still.

A sense of shame washed over me.

I had anticipated Uri's vessel would sink.

But Uri had built his boat of concrete.

I was reminded: In life, you have to make room for *rêves brises*—for broken dreams.

CHAPTER FOUR

A Group Called Murder

In the fall of 1855, my oxen followed the Indian slough—
only wide enough for a 1.2 meters-wide wagon to pass—that
would take us to the hamlet of Oxbow, fifty miles west of
Colesburg. Phebe and Edwin accompanied me on the
voyage; Vidella and Charles now attended Miss Amalia's school.
Unbeknownst to me, murder of another kind would find us at this
place.

Midway, we passed signage pointing north to a village called
STRAWBERRY POINT. I made mental note I should like to
investigate this civilization more fully another day—'twas a
name that charmed my senses.

Outside Oxbow, we came upon an Indian encampment. *La
fumée* curled from the tops of wigwams, filling the morning air
with the smell of boiled samp and roast venison. We remained a
few moments to watch as braves dressed in buckskin moved
between huts, tended to their horses in preparation for the fall
hunt, or so I imagined. If they were Winnebago, they came from
Minnesota, where the tribe had moved a decade earlier after the
U.S. Government bought their land in Iowa and Wisconsin for
habitation of the white man.

It was the premier moment when I saw the colossal wheel set
in motion, whose accelerated revolutions were to keep time with
the pulsations of a new state's ambitious heart and hurry forward
the multitudinous throng that were to white men Iowa's vast
domains, developer resources, and buildup of her villages and
cities—landmarks of her liberation from the darkness of *la
barbarie*, extreme cruelty.

An Indian wearing a distinctive headdress, whom I imagined
was Chief, emerged through a cloth opening in a wigwam. As a
physician in Ontario, I had learned to speak Canadian French,
Dutch, broken-English, and bits of the language of the Siouan.

Now I found myself longing to sit at the Chief's campfire to inquire about the mighty changes wrought by the arrival of the white man, and what it meant to be forced from the land of his forefathers.

"Get up" I finally called to my oxen. I looked forward to visiting the place Dr. Ward had described as a "most industrious place." Perhaps this would be an appealing location to establish my practice.

Oxbow greeted us with two small farms before the road opened wide into a principal street lined by log cabins, a livery, bureau of *de poste*, a place of lodging, a two-story mercantile under construction, a blacksmith, and harness maker.

Dr. Ward said I would find his office above the grist mill on the west end of the village along the Wapsipinicon River.

My eyes soon fell upon a fine filly tied to a hitchrack, hitched to a covered four-seater black buggy next to the mill—and posted just beyond was a small sign: "Dr. J. A. WARD & DRUGS."

I abandoned Phebe and Edwin in the wagon to climb the narrow wooden staircase along the exterior of the three-story structure. Halfway up, the tall, spindly frame of the black-bearded Dr. Ward stepped through a doorway and onto the short landing at the top.

"Wilste…here thou art!"

A quick glance at the perch of my wagon informed him Phebe and Edwin had joined me on my voyage.

"We shall deliver thy sweet wife and child to mine cabin, then myself should'st like thou to accompany me on mine sick calls… Some interesting cases, me thinks thou shall hit together," he said, as I retraced my steps down the stairs, with Dr. Ward fast on my heels.

In an instant, he had climbed into his buggy and his black beauty trotted south.

My ox-team followed from a vantage point that allowed me to observe the six-inches rouge plume at the top of the headpiece bounce with the high-spirited horse's every step.

At a crossroads, he turned east onto Prosperity Street, where a sole log cabin appeared atop a hillock in the woods.

Nearing the dwelling, a sizeable colorful garden of orange and red *légumes* and yellowing vines became visible in a clearing to the right. It appeared Mrs. Ward was a good gardener, like my Phebe.

Dr. Ward bounded from his buggy and waited for us to follow him up the footpath outlined in wood planks. The austere home could have belonged to any pioneer but for the sign by the front door: DR. & MRS. WARD.

Inside, we surprised Mrs. Ward, who was bathing Griffy in a washtub before the blazing hearth. The nine-month-old boy seemed delighted at the sight of our Edwin, now age 4.

"You shall resolve to keep the night," Mrs. Ward said. "We shall board thou at a nice accommodation for the weary traveler. And I hast made plans for Phebe to meet the ladies of the town at the noon hour—our children shall be minded by Grandmother Fairbank. You'll see we are a social bunch, closely linked to one another."

Dr. Ward signaled his readiness to depart, when I felt Edwin's hand tugging on the edges of my coat.

"I shall come, too, Père?"

As our eyes met, I was reminded he had the same gray-green eyes as his mother.

"We will be gone all day, and you will surely miss your Mère," I said, before following Dr. Ward through the door.

I dropped my ox-unit at the Balwin Hotel livery a block away and boarded Dr. Ward's buggy.

"First thing—" Dr. Ward said, "a forbear at McCuniff's to view his hardy selection of pocket pistols."

A crack of the whip and his Missouri Fox Trotter headed back to the main street of the village.

Outside a general store, three burly men unloaded freshly milled oak beams and planks from a long, narrow wagon, its sides emblazoned with EVERETT & BACON in cursive lettering.

Dr. Ward leaped from the buggy, and I followed.

A sizable shiny, bluish violet *corbeau*—crow—swooped down from top a lantern pole and landed in an oak tree nearby, nearly knocking me off my feet.

"Did you know corbeaus live in a group called a murder?" I

said. "They're known for grouping together to attack, a behavior known as *mobbing*—much like people."

"Ya comin', Wiltse?"

"Did you see that big crow?"

"Lots of birds i' these parts."

Dr. Ward continued, pointing to the EVERETT & BACON signage.

"If thou aye find yourself in crave of a loan to build thy cabin, you might try Mr. Everett…in addition to his sawmill, he is part owner of a gristmill in Black Hawk County and owns quite an extensive amount of property in the village."

One of the men unloading lumber, noticing our arrival, ceased his labor and walked toward Dr. Ward, as though awaiting introduction.

Dr. Ward took the signal.

"Mr. McCuniff meet Dr. Alexander Wiltse—originally from Ontario, Canada. He'd like to see thy display of pistols, if thou hast the time."

Mr. McCuniff motioned for us to follow him inside the skeletal building, passing by piles of dry good boxes and wooden barrels. At a rear wall, he stopped and knelt on the floor to open a long, wooden chest. From it he lifted a half dozen rifles and handheld firearms and spread them at my feet.

"Fur what use doth thou seek to purchase a gun? Dr. Wiltse?" he said, handing me a pistol for examination.

"Dr. Ward recommends I carry a pistol as I travel about Delaware County—though I doubt I shall ever fire a pistol at homme nor beast, except perhaps to protect myself from, say—a mad dog."

"The Allen and Thurber model 1850 pepperbox gun is my best seller…multiple-barrel repeating firearm hath three barrels— four inches lang, eight inches total—which revolves around a central axis; bears 6 shots of .32. Just purpose the gun n' shoot from the hip. Identical handgun ah sold to Dr. Ward… or, ah kin discover thou a derringer, too."

"Dr. Ward commends the pistol for staving off Indians and local bandits seeking to remove him from his treasures."

Mr. McCuniff added: "The Ojibway encampment thou passed

on thy way into the village is friendly—most are not, 'tis true. Even so, thou are more likely to shoot yourself with a pistol…and 'tis a dangerous companion fur wee *jimmies*—children."

"I believe I shall be satisfied with this model, though I require credit—half today, the rest, in say, six months?"

I pulled money from my lambskin vest as Mr. McCuniff wrote the sale in his register. He handed me the pistol, cleaning accessories, and box of munitions.

Dr. Ward and I returned to his buggy. I slid the pistol and supplies into my black bag on the floorboard at my feet.

"You'll find McCuniff an accomplished carpenter, Wiltse…built Everett's cabin—and mine own," he added with a certain twinkle in his eye I did not grasp at first. Then I realized he might be hoping Phebe and I would settle in Oxbow.

"I shall surely find a carpenter in Delaware County, too, I suspect," I said.

The crow returned to the lantern pole and squawked angrily as Dr. Ward's black beauty took us south again, this time through a dense forest to a colony called Kier.

"Seen any surgeries, Wiltse? Today we'll be stopping to see a young boy with bowel pain complaint localized towards the right side of the umbilical area…presents with constipation preceded by mild diarrhea, nausea, and vomiting. If he's not improved, I resolve to slice him ope as a monkey and doff his appendix. Likely, I'd find nearly a pint of puss inside… Not afraid of blood and puss, are ye, Wiltse?

"I have acquired books on surgery—I shall be fine, fine."

"Read the writing of Claudius Aymand? He successfully operated on an 11-year-old boy with a right scrotal hernia and a fistula. Identified the appendix perforated by a pin within the intestine; ligated the appendix, then doffed it. The boy's pain originated from peritonitis muscularis, a perforated appendix. Not caught in time—if the extremities become cold—the patient is certain to die. By then, gangrene hath set in.

"This is modern pathology—not to be confused with *barber surgery*, who'll bleed thou 'til half dead…until thou are in fact dead.

"He used diethyl ether for pain—only used opium poppy and

other herbal remedies for setting a bone, that kind of thing."

I stared at Dr. Ward, such that I must have looked as though I thought him a madman.

—

Dr. Ward's first sick visit was to a Mrs. Thomas whose complaint was cramps and spasms in the stomach. Mrs. and Mr. Thomas resided alone at their farm, he said. Mr. Thomas had recently come into money from Wisconsin and fixed up the place most nice.

Mr. Thomas coolly welcomed Dr. Ward and me inside the cabin, initially directing us to stand on the good-quality braided rug by the door.

"Good day, Mr. Thomas," Dr. Ward said. "Dr. Wiltse is accompanying me on mine sick calls today. He's hoping to set up his practice in the area... I'm showing him around Buchanan County."

"Mrs. Thomas is in the bedroom. She's expecting thee...you may ask when thy companion may join thee."

Dr. Ward halted in place as a meek voice from across the room addressed us.

"May I get you a cup of coffee or tea?"

The person speaking was a handsome young woman standing in front of a modern kitchen stove, though I interpreted from the body language she wished to be invisible.

"Dr. Ward—you remember the widow Mrs. Fay, helping out while Mrs. Thomas is under the weather," Mr. Thomas said. "Dr. Wiltse, meet Mrs. Fay."

"Nice to see you again, Mrs. Fay," Dr. Ward said. "I'll just tend to my patient," and he departed with his black bag in hand. My eyes followed him to a room down a short hallway, noticing the wallpaper lined with vertical rows of wheat printed in varnish green wallpaper that smelled of fresh paste.

I extended my hand to Mrs. Fay, and, taking hers into mine own, felt drawn to her eyes. I observed a *démonstration d'innocence—a* demonstration of innocence, but in what reference, I could not ascertain.

"I require nothing, at this moment. Merci," I said, glancing again in the direction from where Dr. Ward had disappeared. I returned to wait on the rug.

Mrs. Fay poured two coffees from the silver pot on the stove into two delicate porcelain cups and placed them on saucers on a covered breakfast table—a table that also held the sugar bowl, creamer, and small glass of stir spoons

"I am unfamiliar with Mrs. Thomas' commons, or myself should stir up some sweetbread or muffins," Mrs. Fay added.

Mrs. Fay and Mr. Thomas sat on chairs across from each other at the table and sipped coffee in silence.

Several minutes passed before Dr. Ward, with stethoscope in hand, stepped into the hallway to motion for me to join him.

Mr. Thomas followed.

I found Mrs. Thomas lying in bed in the ornately decorated room.

"Mrs. Thomas, this is Dr. Wiltse, of whom I just spoke."

I nodded my acknowledgment though remained a distance from her bedside, should there be contagion.

Dr. Ward continued to speak: "Your pulse is elevated—perhaps from the spasms, and thou hast a slight temperature, also understandable. Hath your diet changed recently? Have you taken any cures? Signs of black bile? How long have you been bedridden?"

"It's hard to tell exactly," she stated. "Perhaps a month or longer since the muscle cramping and fatigue began, more severe spasms with every passing week. I'm not one granted to trying new cures, for which I hast few ailments, as I am a young woman, busy with garden and the farm from morning 'til night—until recently, when I find myself now unable to rise from my bed."

"I shall confer with Dr. Wiltse, Mrs. Thomas... For now, I leave thee with this bottle of curare for biliousness—indigestion, which should'st grant noticeable alleviation of thy symptoms. Drink plenty of liquids...and wash your hands. I've read in a recent medical journal that a prickly Hungarian physician hath determined thou may unknowingly be incorporating some plant poison or virus from the animals by touching thy hands to thy mouth or eyes. And keep a journal of all that thou consume. I shall return in a week for reevaluation."

Mr. Thomas followed us from the room.

Dr. Ward prepared an invoice, as I took my leave to return to his carriage, quickly followed by Dr. Ward.

"What regard thee, Dr. Wiltse?" he said, returning his black bag to the rear floorboard before climbing aboard. "I shall be grateful for your intuition."

"How long has Mrs. Thompson been your patient? Have her symptoms become worse as she described?"

"'Twas mine second visit—and her symptoms hast substantially inclined… Possibly, it's arsenic poisoning."

"She is in peril then, I believe…*grave peril*."

Dr. Ward paused. A look of preoccupation appeared on his face.

"You should know, Wiltse—Mr. Thomson hath told me ne'r to return again."

—

The second sick call was to the home of Miss Matie Sherwood, who, in the company of a Mr. Towman, had been accosted upon leaving Oxbow township one evening several weeks earlier, while the young couple made their way to the town of Independence, a community twenty miles south.

Miss Sherwood had been roughed up by vandals, who, awaiting their passage along the Catholic Cemetery, stopped their buggy, and shot Mr. Towman twice in the head during a scuffle—another physician was treating him. Mr. Towman had also been relieved of his wallet. She remained anxious over the incident. Dr. Ward replenished her bottle of morphine with instructions to continue to add several droplets to her evening tea before bed, and throughout the day, as necessary. He handed Miss Sherwood's father an invoice for $3.50.

Next, Dr. Ward and I attended to two persons involved in a quarrel on the day prior over property rights. The elderly woman had suffered a pitchfork puncture to a leg; the man, of about the same age, a bullet from a Derringer to his *derrière*. It was easy enough to treat both the same day as they lived on adjoining farms.

It was late afternoon before we arrived at the farm where the boy of ten years complained of bowel pain. I should have thought Dr. Ward would have called on him earlier in the day, while fresh in mind and body, but he pushed forward, seemingly healthy as a fish.

Fear of what was to come plagued me as we deboarded his carriage a few feet from the front of the cabin. If Dr. Ward found the boy unchanged, was his intention removal of the appendix—*to slice him ope as a monkey and doff his appendix*—today? Would he demand I give aid with application of ether, for which I was professionally ill-prepared. Significant blood loss would result from cutting into the abdomen, another problem for which I was without experience. If the patient survived surgery, what would be Dr. Ward's remedy be for infection? At that moment I was unsure if he might be *avoir son voyage*—at the end of his tether.

Near the front door, we came upon two white chickens pecking in the dirt, greeting us with a happy cackling song, each with leg tied to a stake. Likely, they were payment for Dr. Ward's visit.

The mature man and woman who opened the door and invited us into the one-room cabin showed faces strained from worry.

Dr. Ward addressed the couple: "I wish to introduce you to Dr. Wiltse from Delaware County, accompanying me on sick calls today… How is Alijah?"

The mother looked across the room at the child in a bed partially encircled by a six-foot-long curtain tacked at several points along two walls.

"His fever rages throughout the night, clothing is soaked, and he cries out non-stop in horrible pain…can't bear to see him suffer so," she said.

We walked to his bedside. Dr. Ward pushed aside the water basin on the nightstand, dropped his black bag, and opened it to withdraw a few instruments.

"How you are feeling today?"

The boy pointed to his abdomen. Fresh tears flowed from his

soft blue eyes.

Dr. Ward ran his fingers lightly along the right side of his abdomen. The boy cried out in agony and curled up in a ball.

The mother, unnerved by the screams, stepped to the nightstand and dipped a cloth in the water basin, wrung out the excess water, and caressingly draped it across the boy's forehead.

"There, there…the doctor shall take away thy pain," she said.

Suddenly I became aware of five additional children seated at the edge of another bed along an opposite wall watching in stoic silence. I estimated they ranged in ages from about two to twelve years.

I took a few steps in their direction to address them.

"My children are in school… No school for you today?"

"Father said we should'st keep home, and one or twain days more," said what appeared to be the eldest child.

Without words to comfort, I could only nod.

Dr. Ward checked the child's vitals before speaking to the mother.

"I shall leave thee with this bottle of medicine to ease the pain. Feed him broth as oft as he shall accept it. Keep him dry and warm…that's the meetest we can grant him at this hour."

He closed his bag and prepared to depart.

The father thanked Dr. Ward for coming. "The chickens outside are for thee, please take 'em with our praise."

"No invoice today…your account is paid in full."

Dr. Ward beckoned me to follow him to the door. I looked once more in sympathy at the children seated on the other bed.

Our senses numbed by the boy's senseless imminent death, we staggered back onto the porch, past the chickens, and into Dr. Ward's buggy without a single word spoken. Even his horse seemingly required no instruction, as the mare took off in a trot without knowing the direction Dr. Ward wished to go.

Several minutes passed before Dr. Ward inquired whether I should care to accompany him the next day on sick calls to families in quarantine with cholera. His treatment would be the same remedies available to me. Most men, women, and children with cholera died quickly, but painfully.

"I should like to remain but will be dependent upon Phebe,

who is fatigued easily these days. Our journey today has been medically informative; I have learned a great deal."

A long pause followed.

"One question remains: How long before we shall have the knowledge we need to save lives? I didn't choose to become a physician to watch people die. And it appears, more often than not, people die quicker with medicine, than without," I said.

—

We returned to Dr. Ward's residence around seven that evening—famished, for we had barely stopped to eat more than butterham on bread and drink water from a canteen the day long.

"Your place of lodging hath a hot meal awaiting thee and a sturdy roof over thine heads for thy good night's rest," Mrs. Ward said. "I hope thou shall find the Baldwin Hotel sufficient at $1.00 per day."

Phebe's exhausted face soon informed me that the day's activities had strained her. She spoke softly during our short walk—Phebe, Edwin, and me—to the hostelry. She described her new friend, Mrs. Ward, as a fine and pleasurable woman. Among the young companions who Edwin met at the home of Grandmother Fairbank were two girls: Miss Lucy Dean, age 3, and her elder sister, Hattie, age 5, who resided in the village with an aunt. Their mother, according to the aunt, is an innkeeper in Vermont state.

"How strange that these little girls should grow up without their mother," Phebe said in agony.

Then she added a statement about Oxbow I didn't expect: "*C'est une belle communauté*—Yes, you heard me correctly, I believe I could reside here. Think on that, *ma chère*...think on that."

Outside the two-story hotel at the corner of Prosperity and Second streets, a man—who carried a small, red-collared monkey on his shoulder—and I presumed was Mr. Baldwin, held open the door for us. A corbeau again swooped down, coming to rest on the roofline, its raucous *caw-caw* rising to a deafening pitch. Frightened, the monkey jumped to the man's opposite shoulder.

"I believe that corbeau has remembered my face from this morning…and now follows me," I said to Phebe, lifting Edwin from the stoop into my arms, shielding his head with one hand while urging Phebe inside.

"Ich apologize—the crows are an annoyance," the German said. "Sie seek to antagonize their predators—perhaps an eagle perched next to river to das west. They shall soon roost in das tree für das night."

"I trust you have fed and watered my oxen," I said. "And we seek a spread of food to our room then shall be off to bed—*pas de perturbations*—no disturbances."

"All have been tended to, I assure you," the man with the monkey on his shoulder said.

CHAPTER FIVE

———

Night Dreams

Before sunrise the next morning, we boarded the wagon to begin our return trip to Uri's homestead. Phebe, seated on the perch beside me with Edwin on her lap, had swaddled the two of them like a cocoon in a wool horse blanket to shield them from the brisk headwind. It would have been better had I prepared for an unnerving encounter with Indians.

By the time we neared the Ojibway encampment, Phebe announced: "I fear an upcoming winter of unusual gravity…and am fatigued living in a stable. I have decided, either construct me a *maison*—a house—or I shall insist upon returning to Ontario in the spring."

Her reasoning was just, I knew. It was time to put down deep roots here, though on this morning my attention was preoccupied with a dream from the last night:

> *One of my bœufs, stood but a few feet before me in a green meadow, snorting, voluminous amounts of vapeur coming from its nostrils, his front hoofs pawing at the bloodied terrain where the lifeless corpse of a young male homme laid at its feet. A black corbeau circled overhead for remnants of the kill.*

I had not had such a hideous dream since departing Canada, and it left me anxious.

It did not help that a corbeau had followed us from Oxbow, perching from time to time on a curled horn of my oxen, apparently intent on accompanying us on our return journey. I flicked my whip at the black devil from time to time, only to have it return, *caw-cawing* in protest.

Phebe abruptly demanded I stop long enough for her and

Edwin to climb into the wagon's rear to rest on straw ticks, where she wished to remain 'til reaching Uri's homestead.

I readily complied with the request, though the boredom of the trail left time to obsess about the dream—perhaps, a remnant of my fear of Phebe losing another baby. I could not bear another loss of such magnitude—neither could she.

A premonition of the good Dr. Stout, too, flashed before my mind's eye... *Had his "near miss" at the prairie chicken hunt been an décharge accidentelle? Or was his life in real danger?*

And, I thought about Mr. Thomas trying to poison his wife. *What more could Dr. Ward do to give her aid?*

Like a lightning bolt from hell another old fear beset me, one I most dreaded to embrace: *Am I a faux médecin? I have no competencies beyond my study with a Canadian physician. Was my ego responsible for delivering my family to America? Would our lofty endeavor end in failure?*

How I wished I could remove feelings of insufficiency from my mind.

My thoughts returned to the road before me just as the corbeau *cawed* in alarm and lifted into the sky. My ox-team also reacted strangely. A moment later, Indians on horseback appeared like phantoms through the forest to my right—three in number, as far as I could tell. I reached for my pistol in the black bag at my feet, remembering it was without munition in its chambers. One of the Indians, without speaking, beckoned me to follow him back into the dense pines. I turned around to check on Phebe and Edwin. They were fast asleep. The two other braves spurred my oxen from the road onto the grassy pathway.

I recalled hearing Uri tell of a white man named Atkins, who, years earlier, had been murdered by Winnebagoes after selling them whiskey. They became offended when he tried to get them out of his cabin. After killing Atkins, the Indians went after his son and daughter. The son escaped, and the daughter was ravished by the demons and left for dead. Eventually, the two children showed up at a neighboring homestead. The Indians were later caught and arrested at Fort Atkinson and taken to Dubuque, where they were confined to the old log jail.

Did these Indians seek to purchase whiskey from me? Were

they brutal Winnebago, or friendly Ojibway, or warring Dakota from Minnesota? Or Sauks and Foxes who traversed the state.

Recent rains left the forest floor a soggy bog. My two thousand pounds oxen bore down with every rotation of the wagon wheels. The mechanics groaned and creaked. Tree branches tore at the domed white canvas. Not once did the leader turn around, nor did Phebe or Edwin awaken though the wood box churned like a small boat on a tumultuous sea.

At a small clearing, a brave exhorted me from my perch and directed me to sit on a bark sheet on the forest floor next to a campfire encircled by a dozen Indians from the clan.

Merde! I thought. I recalled Uri's admonition: "If Indians dance, it means murders and scalpings will follow."

None were dancing, yet.

A brave offered me what appeared to be roast venison and a drink that tasted like herbal tea.

For the purpose of getting me unfit? I wondered.

The Chief arrived at the camp, with scalping knife hanging in a sheath at his breast atop his buckskin, and sat next to me.

A pipe—a delicately carved, hollowed-out light piece of wood—was brought to him. Smoke flowed from one end. He took in an inordinate amount of air, holding *de fumé* in his lungs for a long time, before passing it to me.

All eyes fell upon me—I wondered whether they might look upon me strangely because of my full, long, light-brown beard. Canadian Indians viewed facial hair as savage, barbaric, and feminine.

The Chief passed me the pipe and I lifted it to my lips, inhaled, and filled my lungs with smoke. Not having smoked since leaving Ontario, I coughed considerably.

I saw laughter on their faces. Suddenly, I perceived the Chief's gesture with the pipe might have been a demonstration of his virility.

He began speaking in an unfamiliar dialect. Another brave came and knelt before him to interpret. *Perhaps he had learned Anglais at the reservation*, I thought.

As the interpreter spoke, other braves began carrying animal pelts from the backs of pack horses and piling them on the ground before me.

As much as I was able to comprehend, with the coming of winter, the chief sought commerce: a trade of furs for pigs.

The pipe returned to me once more. Taking another drag, the thought came to me: *Had the growing numbers of European and Canadian immigrants created a decline of game animals, such that these people were starving?*

I explained in my best French-Canadian-Dutch and broken-Anglais that I was a doctor—I did not own a farm; the only animals in my possession were my oxen. My wagon was home for myself and my family. Even so, I thought: *Perhaps I can aid in the Chief's demand.... I know farmers who raise pigs.*

The translator repeated my declaration, though I could not ascertain how well.

The pipe was returned to the Chief who again offered it to me. This time I took in less smoke to minimize my coughing.

His final act was to hand me a buckskin sack of wild rice. I gift of similar value from me to him was surely required. I walked to the wagon, where Phebe and Edwin now peered at me beyond the drawstring canvas opening. Her hand was clasped over Edwin's mouth. I beckoned her to remain hidden, fearing she would be taken captive by the Indians and never heard from again—as had been the case of the brazen Mrs. Holt a few years prior.

At the floor of the wagon's perch, I rummaged through my black bag in search of a small bottle of rum. I had noticed the chief favored one side of his mouth when he chewed the venison—perhaps a sign of poor teeth.

Upon my return, I handed him the bottle.

"You may find this good medicine for your teeth," I said, pointing to the Chief's cheek.

He accepted my gift and offered me the pipe once more. This time, I refused.

Two braves loaded the pelts into the rear of my wagon before mounting horses to accompany me back to the intersection where we had met. I whispered to Phebe and Edwin to remain hidden.

Reaching the slough, I brought the oxen to a stop, and with the Indians looking on, I loaded my pistol and rifle and placed them next to me on the seat.

The braves kept watch 'til we were out of sight, perhaps fearing I would return and ambush the clan for more pelts—a pervasive trick of the white man.

After several minutes had passed, I turned around to see if the braves remained. The second time I looked, they were gone.

I remembered the corbeau and scanned the sky. It, too, had vanished.

"Get up! you beasts. Take us home!"

By the time we neared the place where we would camp for the night, I had already begun to question whether I would ever see the Indians again.

But the memory of the horrific dream from the previous night returned, which seemed an omen.

—

The next morning, as we came upon the path that forked north to Strawberry Point, I tapped the near ox on the head and the off ox on the rump to follow the sign—and within the hour, I smelled the pong of fermented mash. I knew a large brewery sat nestled along a hillside stream just outside of town.

A mile beyond the brewery the route widened—enough for four wagons to pass—where I saw with my own eyes the substantial industriousness of the village underway. Men unloaded lumber from a wagon marked STEARNS BROS. for a building of considerable consequence, and new signage was being raised over what had been the STEARNS store. Opposite, a schoolhouse was going up. A sign, "Now Open for Business," hung in the window of MR. PEARS'S DAGUERREAN PARLOR above the store of "Messrs. Tremain & Blake."

Diligently I searched for any indication a physician occupied space in the village—I found none.

Could it be true we had 'fallen with our nose in butter'?

Strawberry Point was one more colossal place to start a medical practice. It appeared what Uri had said was true: "There were no more than a handful of paupers in the whole state of Iowa."

Nearing Uri's homestead, I detected a panther had suited its gait to ours; it stopped when I rested the oxen, then continued to dog the wagon mile after mile. The oxen, too, sensed a threat and turned their heads side to side in attempts to see behind them. I knew the cat could easily tear the flesh of my team to ribbons. Once more, I maneuvered my pistol and rifle within easy reach. I had never heard of a man who had fought with a panther—and survived.

—

Uri met us on his porch with a remorseful story. Only an hour earlier he'd returned home, after giving aid to other homesteaders tracking a span of horses believed taken into the timber in Dubuque County. "The proprietor offered a five-dollar reward for the return of any horse," Uri explained. Some citizens had jumped to the conclusion the horses had been stolen by a man named Peters. They went to his home, called him out and seized him, carried him to a nearby grove, tied a cord around his neck, threw the other end over a limb, and strung him up—twice, to make him confess. Peters' wife appeared, and the cowardly lynchers fled leaving their victim hanging. Two of them finally returned, cut him down, and helped Mrs. Peters return him to his home to be nurtured back to good health.

"I should-a held back," Uri said. "'Twas impulsive to run off and leave Louisa... I am married now...and have *j'ai des responsabilités*."

"*How is* Louisa?" Phebe inquired.

"No change... She refused to leave the cabin, not eating, prefers to remain in bed most days. Is it possible to lose a bébé— then your femme?"

Hearing Phebe's voice, Vidella and Charles, Père Philip, and Mère Rachel appeared through the hand-chiseled doorway which framed their sad faces.

I reached for Charles and Vidella and pulled them close, as one does with those things more precious than nuggets of gold.

"I-I-I-I w-w-w-ish to b-b-become *m-m*-médecin like you, Père," Charles said.

I thought it a shame the garçon has a stutter; médecin would be an impossibility.

"*Je t'aime tellement*—I love you so much," I said, kissing each of them on the forehead.

Phebe handed Vidella the Chief's gift of wild rice as they retreated inside the cabin.

Uri jumped to the perch to accompany me to the stable.

"I wish to inform you, Uri, we shall leave your residence in coming months," I said. "Phebe sorely desires her own home, and we shall soon need space for another enfant. I shall purchase land and begin building this autumn, hopefully."

"'Tis time for you move into our cabin for the winter…with nine of us under one roof, we shall be cozy. Hopefully, you shall not depart until after…"

"Hold tight, Uri. Phebe and I shall not abandon you in your hour of need."

Reaching the stable's double doors, we stopped. The animals seemed nervous. I was certain the panther had followed us to Uri's homestead.

"In your absence, I have made a list of sick calls from neighbors asking for your aid," Uri said, leaping from the perch to lift the heavy yoke from the shoulders of the oxen.

His bad knee put him off balance, and I rushed to give him aid.

"Homme—or animaux?" I asked, as together we hung the yoke on hooks on the stable wall.

He handed me the list.

"Animals—three, the usual: diseased horse; cow with sore teats; porcs in need de castration. People—two, well maybe only one. Ye may not wish to treat the homme who goes by the name Wilson—he's a desperate character and member of a gang of prairie banditti," Uri said.

"I've taken the Hippocratic Oath to *ne pas faire de mal*—to treat everyone in need to the utmost of my power and judgment. I am a *Guérisseu*—a healer.

Uri picked up the curry comb and began moving it in gentle circular movements along the back of one of the oxen, while I picked up the pitchfork to carry hay to a trough.

"I assisted Dr. Ward with sick calls yesterday…we made one sick call to a boy in need of an appendix removal… At the end of the intestine is the appendix, Uri—I'll draw a picture of the intestine and show you sometime. No doctor can remedy the ailment. The boy will die soon.

"Only spent one day with Dr. Ward… He's a promising physician and surgeon—graduated from a university in Michigan. He tried everything but offer to construct us a house if we settled in Oxbow. I admit I'm interested a joint practice would be of mutual advantage."

"We need good doctors in Colesburg, too—like *you*," Uri said.

"Phebe prefers to be closer to her parents… We passed through Strawberry Point on our way home—a lot of construction, but no sign of a doctor's shingle anywhere in the town."

"Do what you need to do, Alex."

Uri set the brush aside and reached for a horse saddle spanning a sawhorse and lifted it onto the back of the ox he'd been grooming.

"You know you can ride an ox like a horse, Alex. Only need to get a proper saddle…would help you facilitate making calls to hommes who require a jolt over rough road back in the thickets. You're probably aware though, without the cover of a wagon, you'll have less protection from Indians—and oxen don't gallop."

"We will certainly get that piglet washed! I can promise you that," I said.

For a few moments, Uri was doubled over in laughter. Again, I caught a glimpse of the boy I had known from our childhood so many years ago. I also grasped how little I laughed any longer, and for several minutes I laughed heartily alongside Uri.

"I'll comb the other ox in the matin'," Uri finally said, returning the saddle to the sawhorse. "I'm ready to call it a night… You comin'?"

I caught sight again of the streak along the door frame. *Had a murder occurred here—of an Indian? Was Uri confident authorities wouldn't investigate if a red man had been killed? Was that why he chose to put me off when I had asked about the blood in the stable? The hatchet still leaned against the exterior wall, without any attempt to wipe the blotches from it.*

"I'll join you and the family in a few minutes," I said.

Alone in the stable, I sensed the crisp, damp evening breeze wafting through the double doors. It smelled of hydrogen sulphide from wafting across foggy Bear Creek, then encircling the stable to mix with the *au parfum* of animal manure, hay, and chickens. This was the aroma that had lulled Phebe and me to sleep many evenings since our arrival at Uri's homestead.

Tonight, I appreciated that the breeze also carried the light, airy song of the whip-poor-will; as well as the course, gravely sound of a single *cawing* crow.

In between bird sounds, I found myself listening for the silence of a wily black cat.

Before departing the stable, I confirmed the double doors were latched and tied off, so tightly they would not fly open even if a two hundred pounds predator clawed and threw its body against it in desperate pursuit of fresh meat.

CHAPTER SIX

A Sincere Offer

Within the week, I journeyed to Delhi to attend a *société médicale* meeting. Along the way, I planned to make a sick call on Mr. Wilson, currently residing at Mr. Sullivan's backwoods log cabin at Coffin's Grove. Mr. Wilson had a far-reaching reputation for being a horse thief—and a murderer.

I found the aging Scot bedridden with complaint of external fatigue, night sweats, coughing up blood—symptoms of consumption. His vitals were remarkably normal, considering he had progressed to where within six months he would be dead. Nothing more could be done beyond rest and good nutrition and moving to a dryer climate. Consumption was a dreadful way to die; lungs filled with white phlegm and left its victims gasping for air.

I surprised myself, remaining at his bedside far beyond the hour of my diagnosis—lured by his stories of him selling liquor to the Indians, even after it became a federal infraction in the early 1830s. He noted, about that time the Indians had been particularly troublesome. At his trial, a witness testified seeing Wilson furnish Indians with *something*, but could not identify it as the *something* coming from the same bottle out of which Wilson had drunk. Wilson was ultimately acquitted. Folks in the county were angry he got off…said he should have been severely punished for the crime of selling liquor to Indians.

Wilson also spoke with great detail of the murder of the Garden family near neighboring Fayette in the 1840s, which made me curious about his implication. Presumably, Indians had committed the murders, he said.

I thought it curious never once did he brag of his days as a horse thief—not once.

It was late afternoon before I departed his bedside. With the fast approach of sunset, I found a cove to abide for the night. En route, I had hit a rough patch and believed damage had been done to the wagon's reach, hounds, or bolsters. I kept tools in the jockey box but would wait for Uri's aid upon my return to his homestead—in Canada we called the likes of Uri, a *bricoleur*—a handy man.

At the crack of dawn, I arose and bathed in the stream, all the while sensing I was being watched from beyond the trees, which had not fully leafed-out. Then, for a split second I thought I saw a painted stallion vanish between the towering gray-brown trunks on the other side of the water. *Was I being tracked by Indians? For what purpose? Uri's stable...that could be the reason. I needed to know if Uri had committed murder.*

I fixed coffee over an open fire and ate beans and venison. Before departing, I made final adjustments to my pants, shirt, vest, and black tie, when I recalled a phrase Wilson had spoken on the day prior: "A pretty face suits the dish-cloot"—never fuss over what to wear when going to a hanging." His words lifted my humor, which I should hope to never forget came from a horse thief and a murderer, whom many believed was deserving of a hangin'.

I found my Delhi colleagues—Drs. Acers, Boomer, Smith, Doran, Stout, Taylor, and Wright, and a few new stragglers—assembled in the room behind Judge Doolittle's bench at the courthouse. Dr. Boomer—whom, by now, I had come to refer to as my dear Scottish friend—immediately expressed enthusiasm to learn of my visit to Dr. Ward in Oxbow.

"I am willing to share my experience, as you wish... 'twas quite a privilege to consult on sick calls with such a médecin savant—yes, a very smart doctor."

Dr. Boomer ended our conversation to confer with Dr. Acers who was about to gavel the meeting to order.

Dr. Acers began: "Under-Secretary Boomer, who shall be taking our minutes again today, hath indicated all active members are present and accounted for.

"Our agenda is to break into two or three groups to draft portions of the Constitution and By-laws. We shall meet till four o'clock when each committee member shall provide a progress update. Our goal is to finalize the official document by March of next year.

"Before we begin the work of the committees, we shall discuss the new application for membership by Dr. C. C. Sharp. He, of course, must first take the examination establishing basic requirements for regular practitioners."

A tide of grumbling rose in the room. After a minute passed, Dr. Acers gaveled the meeting to order again.

"There shall be time enough to hark to pros and cons from each of thou towards the subject of Dr. Sharp at four o'clock. First, I'm privy that Dr. Alexander Wiltse—who recently assisted Dr. A. B. Ward from Buchanan County with sick calls—offers an evaluation. I grant thee now, Dr. Wiltse."

With some hesitation, I proceeded to stand beside the table where Dr. Acers and the board were seated. I hoped my words would augment my professionalism within the eyes of this community of physicians. Lacking in clarity or sincerity in presentation could poorly reflect my readiness for allowance into the society.

"As you are aware, I am a recent *immigré* from Ontario, and as English is not my native language, I shall do my best for my *première* discourse before this prestigious group. Already, I am acutely aware the state of Iowa is blessed with quality physicians—those in this room, among them. In my estimation, few shall become more highly appreciated than Dr. A. B. Ward, a recent resident of Oxbow. He studied under the celebrated Dr. Parson in Blanchard, Ohio for three years, before attending the medical department at the university in Ann Arbor, Michigan.

"I, myself, became acquainted with Dr. Ward at Dr. Stout's annual prairie chicken hunt this past September, at which time my beloved Phebe, family, and I were invited to travel to Oxbow by Dr. and Mrs. Ward—an invitation we accepted with gratitude.

"For a single day, I consulted with Dr. Ward on sick calls to address a variety of maladies: A woman, whom Dr. Ward believes is undergoing strychnine poisoning by her *conjoint*—husband, though she has made no complaint to authorities, thus far. Then, we called on a man and a woman—neighbors, whom, after a quarrel over property rights, had severely injured the other; the woman received a pitchfork blessure to her leg, and the man a bullet from a Derringer in his *derrière*. Finally, we called on a young boy in his final days of a burst appendix—for which, sadly there can be found no *remède* in the entire state of Iowa. While Dr. Ward has considerable knowledge of such treatment and surgery and would be willing to apply himself to the task when appropriate tools and medicines become available. At this time, however, he could do no more than minimally reduce the boy's discomfort in his final hours.

"In closing, I wish to add that Dr. Ward, in his short time in Oxbow, already garners an excellent reputation. I found him exceptionally intelligent, enthusiastic, and imbued with considerable curiosity of modern pathology, anatomy, and the human *l'esprit*—characteristics one rarely sees in a single man. I wholeheartedly encourage extending an invitation to Dr. Ward for a practicum of a general nature in the future, from which we should all benefit. This now concludes my remarks."

"Thank you, Dr. Wiltse, for the interesting report. We shall take thy suggestion under consideration," Dr. Acers said. "When art thou planning to take the examination as regular practitioner ere the Board of Censors—when thy $1. 00 fee shall also be required?"

"Our esteemed colleague Dr. Albert Boomer is preparing me for the exam. Hopefully, I shall be ready the first half of the new year."

Dr. Acers continued: "At this time, allow us to break into committees. We shall meet back in this room at four o'clock. And may I suggest one change in process…that we divulge into the issue of the membership of Dr. C. C. Sharp at a later date, as can be fit into our monthly schedule."

—

At the meeting's conclusion, I found myself in need of a visit to Stone's Grocery. The bell above the door set off its usual wild *sonnerie* upon my entrance. I found Mrs. Stone who appeared to balance midway on a vertical ladder that slid along a horizontal rail fixed to a wall of shelving. Startled by the bell, she jerked her body in such a way that I considered, for a brief moment, the necessity to rapidly move along the long, narrow center aisle in an attempt to aid in breaking her fall.

As it turned out, with prodigious authority, she grasped hold of the ladder's side rails with both hands, re-centered her two-inch heeled blue velvet ankle-high boots on the narrow rung, checked her long skirt for any remnant of an exposed petticoat—and only then, having steadied herself, did she utter any word of salutation.

"If you're looking for Mr. Stone, he's making deliveries," she said quite calmly.

My eyes canvassed the zone for the puzzle board, which during my previous visit, lay balanced atop the pickle barrel.

I located the barrel and approached the board.

"New puzzle...I see."

Mrs. Stone let out a gasp. "It'll be the perpetual wink—death—of both of us if thou topple that board."

"I'm aware...'tis not my first visit to the market, Mrs. Stone."

"What may I get for thee, Dr. Wiltse?"

"You remember my name?"

"It's mine job to recall the faces of patrons... Composed a decision about settling in Delhi?"

"I'm in Delhi to attend a medical society meeting...no certainty where for certain I shall hang my shingle. I believe I heard Mr. Stone say your name is—Priscilla."

The bell sounded once more. Mrs. Stone remained poised on the ladder until seeing the man's face—then, I noticed she began to check for loose hairs about her face that might have worked themselves free of her bun, which she promptly whisked back into place. 'Twas the first time I became aware Mrs. Stone appeared to be years younger than Mr. Stone.

"Dr. Boomer, been watching for thee; I hast all content for thy missus," Mrs. Stone said, cautiously descending the ladder, then making her way to the counter where two boxes of foodstuffs sat next to a jar of pickled eggs. There, she awaited his approach, fingering at the length of velvet that encircled her narrow neck while she waited.

He proceeded to make his way down the center aisle. Out of caution, while sliding onto the tall stool I grabbed hold of the puzzle board.

"Albert—I could have saved you a stop if you had mentioned at the meeting your need for supplies," I said.

"Ah hoped to leave early to shop fur a few articles; my wife hopes to have them in time fur our dinner this evening—she's preparin' *yer* favorite dish."

"I have brought along my accordéon and shall plan to entertain your family long into the evening."

I fished out the clock in the pocket of my *gilet* and stared at the dial.

"I shall tarry at the market an hour to give her ample occasion for preparation."

"What's th' picture?" Dr. Boomer asked, gazing at the board.

"Appears to be an angel outside a crypt, a Christian theme, I believe—not many pieces aligned at this time."

"Which reminds me, Madame Stone," I said, turning on the stool to speak directly to her. "My Phebe asks that I inquire about borrowing a puzzle for my children… They have not seen such a thing in their young lives."

Mrs. Stone appeared absorbed with verification of the items listed on Dr. Boomer's invoice, leaving me uncertain she'd heard my request.

"Can't see a reason for declining thy crave, Mr. Wiltse, providing the puzzle is returned by the next time Preacher Clark passes through—mid-month," she said eventually. "I shall compose note of it at the register."

"I have a grocery list to be fulfilled, as well," I added. "I should care to pick it up tomorrow, on my return home, plus, medicines for sale at the market, upon agreement with Mr. Stone. Among them, "Munnels Great American Preparation" may be recommended for cholera, stomach, and bowel ailments. I'll leave a case with you before my departure."

Mrs. Stone nodded in agreement.

Dr. Boomer made his way to the counter. His eyes now appeared fixated on the dried venison hanging mid-air from ceiling hooks.

"I kin furnish thou with fresh wild turkeys, geese, prairie chickens—only a day auld—whin ah could get them ta yea…ah hunt most evenings."

"We should'st be most grateful, I'm certain… I'll inform Mr. Stone—who's in charge of all procurements."

Dr. Boomer pulled his wallet from a pocket, withdrew money, and paid the invoice.

"Thank thee, Dr. Boomer. It's *aye* a pleasure doing business with thou," Mrs. Stone said.

Dr. Boomer lifted a box into each arm, turned, and walked toward the front door.

Just then the bell sounded, and a white ball of thick hair appeared on a large head in the door frame.

"Good day, Dr. Sharp," Dr. Boomer said as the two passed in the aisle near the stool where I was seated.

Dr. Sharp halted at my stool, without giving so much as a glance in my direction.

"We meet again, Dr. Sharp," I said. "My dear Scottish friend Dr. Boomer, whom you just passed in the aisle, and I have come from a meeting of the société médicale meeting… It's my understanding you have submitted application for membership. Dr. Boomer is tutoring me to prepare for my exam before the Board of Censors—perhaps he could be persuaded to allow you to join our little group. We shall meet again on the morrow… It would be my privilege to study alongside such a learned physician, having had the opportunity to hunt beside you, from which I learned a good deal about the successful shooting of the prairie chicken."

I waited for a response from Dr. Boomer, who had frozen in place just inside the door, presumably upon hearing mention of his name.

"Albert, what say ye? Do you wish to assist Dr. Sharp with preparation for his exam, too?" I said.

Dr. Boomer turned his head around far enough to look in Dr. Sharp's direction.

"Yes, yes—*wid* be fine, o' course. We shall heartedly welcome ye. Begin at ten o'clock. *Ye* need th' direction to *mah* farm?"

Hearing no reply after several seconds had passed, Dr. Boomer attempted to lift the door latch for his departure. Finding himself encumbered by the boxes he held in his arms, I stood to give aid just as the bell sounded and the door burst open.

"Let me help with das door," came the gentle, kind voice of a German man whom I knew well.

It was the unmistakable voice of Dr. Stout. The sound of his voice provoked a reminder that I needed to talk to him about his willingness to trade pigs for pelts with the Indians. I was certain he and Dr. Acers had more pigs than they had market to sell them. Perhaps, delivering the pigs directly to the clan at Fort Atkinson was the answer. With multiple ox-teams they could easily deliver hundreds of pigs in time for Christmas.

To my great surprise, the sound of Dr. Stout's voice elicited a violent response from Dr. Sharp, such that he abruptly turned—which severely adjusted my position on the stool, causing the board to be dislodged from its mooring—wherein hundreds of puzzle pieces were ejected into the room in all directions.

Next, I heard Mrs. Stone let out a frantic moan as she fled through the market's rear door.

Dr. Sharp then unhinged the leather case hanging at his waist and withdrew his dirk knife. I glimpsed his eyes beneath the dense white brows that appeared mean-spirited. His focus remained trained on Dr. Stout, who was making his way toward the store's interior, seemingly unaware of Dr. Sharp's presence.

Finally, Dr. Sharp lifted the long knife blade above his head and advanced toward Dr. Stout, shouting, "I shall dispatch thee!"

Dr. Stout bolted toward an outer aisle, and a moment later, I felt his hands bracing against my back.

Out the corner of one eye, I saw Dr. Boomer drop his boxes and begin moving in Dr. Sharp's direction down the center aisle. Reaching him, he made attempts to control the hand with the knife that repeatedly cut through the air.

Blood droplets spurting into the room was the first to inform me the knife blade had connected with Dr. Boomer.

Dr. Sharp took a step backwards as the red droplets landed on his face and clothing.

Dr. Boomer—with one arm now incapacitated—saw a

moment of opportunity, and yet managed to wrangle the knife free from Dr. Sharp's hand.

Dr. Sharp, then defenseless, fled out the front door and was gone.

I eased Dr. Boomer to the floor as Dr. Stout went in search of a belt or cloth to use as a tourniquet to stop the flow of blood to the wound. Seconds later he arrived with a cotton towel, tore it into strips, and tied it tightly above the wound on Dr. Boomer's left arm.

At that moment, we three physicians of Delaware County, huddled in the small space above a pool of blood on the wooden floor—a stain not easily lifted from view, or a market's *histoire*—looked at the other in quiet consternation.

Dr. Boomer lifted the bloodied dirk knife, cupped in his hand.

"Whit shall we do wi' this?"

"Joshua, assist me with getting Dr. Boomer to your office for sutures," I said. "Albert, your wife Charlotte will have to do without the items on your list for our dinner."

I assisted Dr. Boomer to his feet, noticing the many puzzle pieces strewn at our feet were now sprinkled with fresh blood.

That calamity would also be dreadful to explain to Mr. Stone.

CHAPTER SEVEN

Three Deaths - Two Murders

Christmas 1855 was of little merriment, for by then Louisa's life hung suspended by a thread. On the first Sunday in February 1856, she passed. A severe fever one day—and by the next, she had breathed her last. Phebe bathed Louisa, dressed her in buckskin vêtements, and placed a bandana and feather 'round the crown of her head. Uri lifted her into a coffin he had built in the shape of a bateau. Hers would be the first death; two murders within the month would follow.

A surprising number of pioneers began arriving at Uri's homestead for Louisa's funeral, likely due to the notoriety in Delaware County of Uri's eldest brothers, Wellington and Leonard Jr. My oxen and I rescued three travelers arriving by sleigh and carriage from winter mishaps along their route. Those requiring overnight lodging found sanctuary and warmth in co-habituating with the animals in Uri's stable. The windmill, too, proved to be a godsend, delivering ample water to the stable and cabin.

The Rev. Daniel Smith, a traveling Methodist minister, had offered to officiate over Louisa's funeral. But Methodist—not the creed of the Ho-Chunk—Uri chose Wellington to give Louisa's eulogy.

Wellington began: "Louisa Wiltse was born about 1834, the daughter of a white man stationed at a military post and a Ho-Chunk squaw, a member of the clan Thunder. She never knew her father, as he died before she was born. She grew up on the Half-Breed Tract, until, as a young girl, she found favor in the eyes of another white woman, Mrs. Fuller, who had also married a military man. She was re-named Louisa, though taught to honor her Ho-Chunk traditions. Over her brief lifetime, she grew to love the lofty mountains and the land skirting the shores of the great rivers of her ancestors.

"Uri took notice of the beautiful Louisa during a county-wide gathering in the winter of 1853, and they married a few months later. In the second year, they lost their first baby, which Louisa named Šųkjąk—Wolf Runs Alone. Sadly, she never regained the strength she had known as a young, ardent, and resolute squaw.

"We shall miss the bright smile of this Ho-Chunk woman, and the light she cast upon all who knew her. Ours is not to question why the Great Earthmaker in His *infinie* wisdom hath seen fit to release your ship, Louisa, in the spring of your years to begin the wild adventures in the hereafter.

"*À Dieu d'être la gloire*—To God be the glory."

Uri's seven brothers lifted Louisa in her coffin and carried her from the cabin to the rear of the ox-team pulled cart. In the knee-deep snow, mourners followed behind him to the edge of Bear Creek, where Louisa was placed next to the tomb of bébé Šųkjąk—in "the place where Uri sits," as Louisa had requested.

Uri led the Ho-Chunk tradition of covering her coffin with stones and boulders he'd carried from the glacial shoreline along the Turkey River.

In the distance, I thought I heard the eerie echo of chanting and drums throughout the valley and hillside, as though a sorrowful wailing of Ho-Chunk ancestors had begun.

—

In early 1856, I learned that horse thief Wilson had decided to leave Mr. Sullivan's cabin and to express his gratitude for the kind care he had received, he stole Mrs. Sullivan's stockings and various other articles and removed himself to settle near Buffalo, Iowa, where he was shot and killed by a party of settlers from whom he had stolen some horses. He was buried where he fell.

—

Approval of the Constitution and By-laws of the Delaware County Société Médicale happened in March 1856. Beyond that, occupying much of our discussion was the recent knife attack at

Stone's Grocery. Unanswered questions hung in the air: *Why had Dr. Sharp sought to harm the good Dr. Stout? Was Dr. Sharp at discord with other doctors in Delhi? Who might be attacked next?*

The knife that had been in Dr. Stout's possession, awaiting the arrival of Sheriff Parker, had come up missing a day later. The culprit broke the lock of Dr. Stout's office door, rummaged through desk drawers, and found where the weapon had been kept. Dr. Sharp remained at large

Another of my dreams brought home the vulnerability I felt at the hand of Dr. Sharp—or any other who should choose to objectify me as the cause of their distress:

> *I lay along a stream, having been thrown by one of my bœufs, after attempting to ride it like a horse. An unknown assailant appeared, lifted me from the ground, and threw me into the river. Then the assailant tried to force my head below the water line, again, and again.*

At the meeting's conclusion, Dr. Boomer, Dr. Stout, and I departed for Stone's Grocery for supplies. I followed behind Dr. Stout in his carriage and observed he interfered so badly in giving commands that his little spotted bay horse seemed to have either its right or left hind leg in the air all the time. I recalled the last time I had seen that horse—hidden in a roped area beneath a bridge near Dr. Stout's homestead. I never heard if the thieves were ever found and brought to justice.

At the market I promptly returned the puzzle to Mrs. Stone and inquired about the loan of another. A young boy about twelve years in age appeared at her side. Being a school day, it was unlikely for him to be helping at the market.

"This is my son, Chester," Mrs. Stone said. "He craved to miss his place of learning today to help fulfill orders at the market… He wishes to take over the business at a time that's appropriate."

"'Tis nice to follow in a father's stead," I said, laying my hand on the boy's shoulder.

While waiting for Mrs. Stone to fix our orders, we three

physicians—along with Mr. Stone—took seats around the puzzle board. Mrs. Stone had added three chairs to the region as a "gathering place," though the chairs now made it difficult to pass by along the center aisle.

Mr. Stone asked that Mrs. Stone deliver coffee and fresh tartes for all.

I fixed my attention on the puzzle pieces, noticing they had been wiped clean of blood spatterings, although a faint odor of vinegar lingered in the air.

Dr. Boomer arose and cleared his throat as though about to deliver a political address.

"I believe, Alexander, you're fully prepared for your examination before the Board of Censors. And you can be proud o' your efforts to diligently apply yourself in your study with Dr. Ward of Oxbow," he said.

The other physicians echoed their congratulations, for which I was certain I blushed.

"Merci, for your excellent tutoring, Albert—I shall be forever in your debt."

Mrs. Stone and Chester arrived with a tray of plates, cups, and tarts. With one hand, she pushed the puzzle pieces aside to make room for the tray.

The ease at which she moved them aside I found amazing.

"Next, Wiltse," Dr. Boomer continued, "I suggest you investigate obtaining o' a diploma o' medicine to help you favorably compete with other physicians. I will get the names o' schools in Chicago where ye might wish to apply."

Handing Dr. Stout a plated tarte, and retrieving one for myself, my eyes caught the discoloration in the floorboards at my feet.

Dr. Stout noticed my glance and looked at the floor.

In a hushed tone, he asked: "Is it because I am German that Dr. Sharp seeks to harm me?"

The same question had relentlessly encircled my feeble brain, though I had come up void of any sensible explanation.

"Impossible to say, Joshua," I said matter-of-factly, forking the first bite of tarte into my mouth.

"The apple tarte is *délicieuse*, Madame Stone—merci!" I

called out to her and the boy heading toward to the counter.

Dr. Stout added: "Perhaps there are those who prefer my family and Dr. Acers' family had settled by Elkader in the German communal colony. The state of Iowa has two thousand Germans—half the farmers in Iowa speak German."

"'Tis possible, but you have every right to live as you wish," Mr. Stone reminded.

"Are we nicht more industrious than every other pioneer in das state? Have we Germans not built homes, barns, neatly kept und highly cultivated fields—attesting das industry, thrift, und progress from the German immigrant?" Dr. Stout continued.

"What ye say is a credit to yer culture," Dr. Boomer said. "Unfortunately, jealousies arise, over which ye hae na control."

The bell above the door sounded, and in unison, we jerked our heads to see who had entered the space. The bell sounded twice more in rapid succession. The space was now quite full.

Dr. Stout removed his chair and set it aside to allow passage of new patrons along the center aisle, before taking Mr. Stone's abandoned tall stool after he departed to wait on customers.

The three of us attempted to continue our discussion until noticing the eyes staring down upon us. Word had spread in the community of the knife attack weeks earlier.

Dr. Stout fidgeted as he sipped the last dregs of coffee and finished his tarte.

Again, the bell sounded.

My heart sank at the sight of the tall, willowy frame of Dr. Sharp. His winter cloak lay open, exposing the long dirk knife hanging at his waist.

I observed Mrs. Stone quietly send Chester...to find the deputy sheriff, I presumed.

When Dr. Sharp caught sight of Dr. Stout seated on the tall stool, he instantly reached for his dagger and charged him like a raging bull.

"I never take thy threats to try me harm lightly, Stout... I shall not keep silent... The woman thou dwell with is of ill repute— you hide behind the saintly goodness of a physician's discretion, while you carry on with another, not thy wife."

Dr. Stout rose to his feet and stepped backward as Dr. Sharp advanced.

"You know not of what you speak—I made no threats to you." Said Dr. Stout.

They met in the center aisle, where a fierce battle began.

Dr. Boomer and I alternated in our attempts to confine Dr. Sharp and protect Dr. Stout.

'Twas like controlling a match between a sheepdog and a basset hound, though Dr. Sharp clearly had the advantage, even without the knife. The towering Englishman sought to corner the little German, who was nimbler on his feet and ducked between pillars and bins in the attempt to keep his life. If there was a blow with a fist in their close exchanges or a cut from a knife or injury from flying debris, 'twas unseeable to my eyes. Neither appeared bloodied or bruised, only exhausted the longer the battle persisted.

"This time I'm aff to murder ye!" said Dr. Sharp, eventually backing Dr. Stout into the crowd.

With each slash of the blade, patrons swayed back and forth like waves of an ocean, hoping to avoid being fileted open like the belly of a fish. Barrels turned onto their sides. Glass jars teetered, fell, and broke open. When the tip of the blade caught a sack of ground wheat, a brownish powder filled the market like an Iowa snowfall.

The skirmish ended when Dr. Stout let out a noxious moan and fell to the floor in a heap.

Dr. Sharp retreated when realizing what he had done, and two broad-shouldered patrons jumped him from behind, and knocked the knife from his bloodied hand onto the floor.

I picked up the knife and moved a distance away.

Dr. Boomer rushed to Dr. Stout's side, and gently rolled Dr. Stout onto his back to determine his injuries. Fresh blood emerged chest-high through his shirt. Gasping for air, a trickle of blood appeared at one corner of Dr. Stout's mouth.

"Help me hurl the jimmy 'n' carry him to a day cot in the rear," Dr. Boomer said, addressing those standing nearby; he sent another to his carriage to secure his bag.

"Allow me passage," Mr. Stone said, en route with a stack of towels.

Patrons wrestled Dr. Sharp to the floor near the potato bin as Dr. Sharp continued to writhe to break free. I hurried to give aid. His body smelled sour, like Mr. Bomgartner's after a day of hard work in the fields. The leather knife case, attached midway to his body, lay undone and empty. With the knife, I cut the buttons off his suspenders, and using the leather straps, tied his hands behind his back. I noticed he had now wet himself, adding to the *eau de toilette* of the space.

Sheriff Parker arrived within the hour. I handed the dirk knife over to him—*the symbol of a Highland man's honor*. Sheriff Parker took Dr. Sharp to the jail in the basement of the courthouse. Dr. Acers informed Sheriff Parker he would file the complaint later.

I joined Dr. Boomer in the rear of the market where we vigorously sought to stop the flow of blood and to address Dr. Stout's difficulty breathing from what appeared to be two stab wounds to the chest.

Within the hour, Dr. Acers transported his brother-in-law to Dr. Stout's newly completed multi-room house to care for him day and night, until which time his life would expire.

Dr. Stout died six days later.

On the 19th of March, Sheriff Parker arrested Dr. Sharp and took him to the Dubuque County jail to await judicial process.

—

On the day of Dr. Stout's funeral, a steady line of people filed past his casket in the parlor of his home. The vast majority were Germans and physicians. Upon demand of Dr. Acers, a group of German men kept guard of the Stout's property to turn away anyone suspected of being a journalist, as every news outlet in the region had carried a story similar to: "Murder flashed its red hand in Delhi." They longed to publish an interview with Mrs. Stout. She kept her young face shrouded in a thick black veil and cared for her young son William.

The following day the casket was removed from the home for interment at Dr. Acers' family burial site in Oakland Cemetery at Burrington.

At the prescribed hour, a German band—for which I was an honorary participant—preceded the horse-drawn hearse to the cemetery. The contingent attracted more attention than usually bestowed upon a funeral procession, as the corpse of the murdered Dr. Joshua Stout was interred with all the normal rites of the German Lutheran Evangelical Church.

—

I moved forward with the establishment of my medical practice at The Point—much to the delight of my Phebe. Twenty families now established claims along Old Mission Road, built by the army as a military wagon road when the government began moving Winnebagoes from Wisconsin to the safety of Fort Atkinson. Moreover, three new businesses just opened their doors: M. O. Barnes, a merchant; J. B. Miller, lawyer; and E. P. Rawson, the proprietor of a hotel. It was my good fortune to meet Mr. R. Elvidge, who sold insurance under the name Consolidated Patrons and Farmers Mutual Insurance Company of Buchanan County Iowa. We promptly formalized plans to hang a WILTSE & ELVIDGE shingle outside Bailey's store where we rented space.

Next, Phebe and I selected 160 acres in Section 26 in Clayton County. Dr. Boomer suggested I apply to borrow five hundred dollars from the School Fund to purchase the property at the rate of six percent interest.

Phebe and I caused quite a stir when we filed for Title to the property at the courthouse, for she wrote her maiden name "Wiltse."

"There must be some misunderstanding," said the clerk. "You have written your married name."

"My husband and I shared the same surname when we married," she explained. "'Tis no different than one Hanson marrying another Hansen, or a Smith marrying another Smithe. 'Tis how it's done in Wiltsetown, Ontario, Canada."

Phebe and I chose Samuel Knee of Colesburg, and his competent assistant Charles Bomgartner, to erect our cabin—though it would be a meager dwelling initially, framed with logs from my trees cut to dimension at The Point's sawmill.

In the fall, just as Uri began removal of crops from the fields, a slump in prices began. Then, the price of wheat fell twenty cents within a single week. The first snowfall also came early, covering the earth like rabbit skins. For the remainder of the winter, his crops remained buried under heavy snow.

CHAPTER EIGHT

One-half Grain of Poison

In early April 1857, I found myself longing for the company of my comrade Dr. Ward, hoping he had something *under the knee*—a few lifting words to render sensible the premature death of my friend Dr. Stout. His death taught me that murder is not nothing. After it occurs, one cannot comprehend why it happened. I had also become afraid of what I had let die inside of me while I still lived.

The sun was rising over the pines as my bœufs delivered me to the eastern edge of Oxbow. The sound of their hooves trampling on the frozen slough, covered over by icy leaves and a layer of yesterday's glittering snow, echoed a hollowness to the earth. The creak and moan of the wagon's mechanics reminded me of the hard struggle of life.

Edwin, nearing his sixth birthday, insisted on coming with me, and I welcomed his company. He yearned to visit his new friends, Griffy and Miss Lucy, and carried with him the borrowed puzzle from Mrs. Stone, along with a wild young rabbit collared by a short length of twine that he and his siblings had captured at the cemetery on the day of Dr. Stout's funeral.

Before departing Uri's homestead, I had tucked Edwin and the rabbit on a fresh bed of straw in the wagon and covered them over with a woolen blanket and pelts from the pigs for pelts exchange between Uri, Dr. Acers, Joel Bailey, and four other farmers from the Delhi area. Using three ox-teams, loaded with corn and supplies, in December they drove the hogs along Old Mission Road to Fort Atkinson. The weather was glacial and the snow deep, but after eight days, camping every night, they reached the fort and were joyfully welcomed by the Indians— who had begun to fear they might be forced to live without meat during the winter. It was not an easy or comfortable task to then kill and dress twenty-five hogs a day on the frigid prairie.

Pelts also draped my shoulders and legs as I sat exposed to the brisk spring wind on the wagon's perch. On occasion, I heard Edwin speaking to the rabbit in soft murmurings.

We found Dr. Ward at his cabin in an encumbered state. The injury, he said, happened during a runaway of his fine high-spirited filly, which resulted in his toss from his buggy—and a protruding double fracture of the bones in his left ankle. A surgeon from nearby Oelwein had set the bone. A great degree of contraction and shortening of the muscles had occurred; he also survived a case of tetanus. He would be able to walk, albeit, with a limp the remainder of his days.

"I can use thy assistance on sick calls and keeping the drug market," Wiltse," he said, pointing to the set of wooden crutches leaning against the wall by the door.

"I shall do what I can within my time allotted in Oxbow, for since we last spoke, I opened my *pratique* at The Point."

He seemed to take my news in stride, better than I anticipated.

"You shall doth well, of that I'm certain," Dr. Ward said. "Might we depart now? There is much to accomplish during thy stay."

"You want thy rest—A. B.," Mrs. Ward interjected. "Thou shall not depart until after the noon meal… Catch up Dr. Wiltse on thy appointments for now."

"Père has brought me a puzzle for my muse-ment," Edwin said, lifting the box for Mrs. Ward's examination.

Mrs. Ward knelt to see what Edwin had in his hand. She took the box and carried it toward the stone fireplace, her long, thick, custom skirt swishing with every step. She set the box on the floorboards in front of the fire, and removed Griffy from the cradle, and propped him with a blanket in a sitting position on a rug.

Opening the puzzle box, she lifted the pieces, examining them one by one. I watched her face turn to wonderment.

It was only then her eyes caught sight of the young hare Edwin had carried in under his coat.

She stared at the rabbit endearingly as Edwin lifted the furry grey bundle onto his lap.

Griffy reached for the animal, and startled, the rabbit darted from Edwin's lap. Edwin grabbed hold of the length of twine that loosely encircled its neck to prevent escape.

"Tis a wild creature and great care should be given, Edwin," I said, from my chair at the table across from Dr. Ward.

"While Edwin is entertained with his delightful puzzle, I shall prepare the table…carry on, A. B.," Mrs. Ward said.

Dr. Ward updated me on the status of the young boy with the burst appendix—who had died, as expected. Such avoidable deaths would continue, he explained, until which time a hospital and surgery unit could be established.

Mrs. Thomas had also died, and Mr. Thomas was eventually arrested for poisoning his wife.

"He likely would hast gotten by with murder if he had only acted, e'en for a short time, as a bereft widower," Dr. Ward noted. "On the very day of the funeral it was reported that Mr. Thomas had taken the widow Mrs. Fay out for a tour in his buggy. The neighbors became aroused and sent for County Coroner Dr. H. H. Hunt, who filed an allegation that Mrs. Thomas had possibly been poisoned. The Thomas' home was searched, and a bottle of strychnine found—which isn't unusual, as the poison is found on most farms to kill rodents who eat the harvested crops. The coroner then had her corpse exhumed, a postmortem made, the stomach taken out, placed in a stoup with a jar, and sent to a chemist for analyses. The coroner's jury spent some time in examination, and finally established that Mrs. Thomas had been killed by poison.

"The physician who made the postmortem examination testified there were no indications she had died from disease. Strychnine produces convulsions and witnesses present when she died said she had experienced numerous convulsions—which was confirmed by the condition of the body when exhumed, and by her general appearance: arching of the neck and back; also, a well-defined rigidity in the arms and legs, and masseter muscles, in particular. The jaw was twisted by muscular contraction, giving the victim's mouth what appeared to be a sardonic grin at the time of death.

"The chemist, Professor Hinrichs of Iowa State University,

who analyzed her stomach, testified to finding strychnine that would indicate she had taken about a one-half grain of the poison a day—enough to produce the convulsions, and her ultimate decline in health leading finally to death.

"A witness testified to the facts as to the intimacy 'twixt Mr. Thomas and the widow Fay; that he gave her money frequently and had built her home and improved her farm. Also, he ordered merchants at Independence to sell her goods that she might crave, and he would pay for 'em, and the fact that he didst pay for large amounts of goods that she purchased.

"I was called to testify, too," Dr. Ward added. "As you know, I made sick calls to Mrs. Thomas, when Mr. Thomas told me she had these spasms and had been subject to 'em for some time… She would die in a spasm someday, and that 'twere no use to doctor her, as naught could cure her, and told me, her physician, that 'I need not come again.

"Mr. Thomas has remained confined to the county jail, and being a corky and feeble man, is allowed large liberty by the jailors and has had a fairly comfortable time."

I asked Dr. Ward if it had ever occurred to him to report the presumed poisoning to officials after Mr. Thomas asked him not to return to care for Mrs. Thomas?

As the poisoning had been only hearsay, he responded, there was not precedent for action by the law.

Dr. Ward continued: "My concern this day is for you, Wiltse. I've learned of the savage murder of Dr. Stout in Delhi. Maria and I appreciated his kind invitation to meet my fellow physicians at the prairie chicken hunt on the Stout farm this past fall. His death has been a great tragedy for Delaware County… Tell me what brought this about."

At that moment I felt the flood gates open as I began to speak of Dr. Stout's murder, which, heretofore, had left me sitting with *a mouth full of teeth.*

"'Tis the very reason I have come…seeking your solace and words of comfort," I said. "The source of the enmity between the two physicians was apparently professional jealousy. Dr. Stout was a founder of the Delaware County Société Médicale—where I have made application. I had met Dr. Sharp—Dr. Stout's attacker—on a few occasions. He appeared to be an angry man, though I knew not with certainty the cause of his passion. Dr. Sharp's trial is scheduled for May, when I expect to learn all matters of the case."

"This must be a very difficult time for you and thy comrades… Shall thou be called to testify, Wiltse?"

"Yes, I surely will, in that I was present at Stone's Grocery on the day of the attack against Dr. Stout, which six days later led to his death. Since, I have been haunted by a stream of disturbing dreams:

> *Someone of great personal wealth offered me a beautiful maison, with every amenity—beyond my wildest dreams. Even the animals I desired most suddenly appeared, as though my mind had been read. 'Twas everything, and more, any homme could desire. But what was required of me for these gifts in return? My heart sank. The cost was more than I wished to pay.*

"My dream has to do with the loss of Dr. Stout, don't you see? What good are riches… Whatever would my Phebe and my enfants do if I should die? I fear the whole country is coming apart just as our lives are beginning in our new homeland."

"A physician's work is dangerous from many perspectives, but Dr. Stout's death is a baffling waste. The ethos of the physician is to save a life for as long as possible—this has been an ancient way of knowing and being since the beginning of time. It was even the way of the *Indians*," he said.

I heard myself sigh. Dr. Ward had reminded me there were no clever words to subdue such tragedy. The healing would take the required time, as it always must.

"How is thy Phebe? I wish I might assist her as midwife at the time of the delivery," Mrs. Ward said.

"Her time is nearing… She is exhausted with the great care of Uri's homestead required since the death of his wife, Louisa."

"I should like to discuss with Phebe, too, the coming of the great rebellion, which I foresee, over the issue of slavery. The

Union will not abide the loss of such valued property as Fort Sumter."

"I'm certain she welcomes your visit."

Griffy suddenly let out a wail, and Mrs. Ward walked to his side, grabbed the rabbit, and carried it to the floor by the woodbin, where she promptly tied the twine to a log.

"I believe Cloudy hath bitten Griffy's finger," she said, quickly delivering the child to Dr. Ward.

Edwin left his puzzle and crawled onto my lap.

"There, there, Griffy—Papa shall see to whatever is wrong and fix it."

The soothing tone of Dr. Ward's voice hypnotized Griffy, and he soon ceased his crying.

While Dr. Ward examined Griffy's fingers, Mrs. Ward, who had assisted him countless times on sick calls, straightaway delivered the black bag to his side, marched to the teakettle suspended above the fire, lifted it, and poured steaming hot water into a bowl and carried it to the tabletop. This was followed by delivery of a bar of soap smelling of lye, a small towel puffed by a fresh breath of winter wind, and a silver teaspoon.

"If this were a bite from a dog, fox, or wolf—well, that would be quite another matter; but a nip from an insignificant little rodent like a rabbit…a good cleaning is all that's required," Dr. Ward said.

He finished cleaning the puncture wound and reached into the bag for a corked bottle of laudanum, poured a tincture of the syrup into the silver spoon, and fed it to Griffy.

"Something else to keep in mind about medicine, Wiltse; it goes beyond the corporal."

Mrs. Ward retrieved Griffy with his tiny finger wrapped in gauze and placed him in the cradle by the fire.

"Use the water to wash thy hands—lunch shall be on the table in a minute," she said, as she set about retrieving two pots hanging above the red coals in the fireplace.

"What were we speaking of before Griffy's mishap?" Dr. Ward said, reaching for the bar soap.

"The harsh winter we've had, I believe… I should add 'tis already estimated one-third of Judge Doolittle's grove in

Delaware County of 100,000 grafted apple trees and several hundred thousand younger trees have died."

"Most unfortunate, indeed… I shall check with thy orchardist to see about the start of a grove in Oxbow," Mrs. Ward said.

Dr. Ward continued: "Do thou estimate the Iowa winters are too vigorous to be most attractive to Negroes, Wiltse?"

Surprised he held an opinion on the plight of colored people, I was momentarily rendered speechless.

He continued: "There are about half a dozen people of that race now living in Independence who are honest, frugal, and industrious people, enjoying in a good degree the confidence and respect of their neighbors. The sore coldness of our Iowa winters is the only reason I would agree so few of 'em are here, or I expect more should'st flee to 'scape slavery in the South."

"I imagine you may be correct…but if one can find a way to survive being treated like un animal, a piece of property, and working in the summer heat of cotton fields, then think they can find a way to prosper in the rigueur of an Iowa winter," I responded.

"Right, Wiltse—very correct thou are in thy statement."

Mrs. Ward contributed her thoughts while clearing the table.

"From what I've read, the question of wither or not slavery had been allowed in the new western states shadows every conversation in the county. Our Governor Grimes is against slavery, though Iowa, part of the Louisiana Purchase, had been considered a slave territory. How uncanny that our blasted, inhospitable wilderness—only fit for roving Indian bands—has quickly become the attraction of the nation."

Finally, she spread a fresh cloth and deposited plates and utensils—a pot of cornbread and another which appeared to be mutton stew.

She glanced at Cloudy, who now quietly sniffed the air at the end of the rope. Carrying a saucer of water to the animal, her whisper was loud enough to be heard. "If that were mine rabbit, I know what our meal had been."

Edwin climbed into the high chair. I looked across the room at Griffy, now fast asleep. Mrs. Ward covered him with a blanket before joining us at the table. She reached for my hand, and her husband's, as Dr. Ward bowed his head and said grace.

—

Contrary to Dr. Ward's original request, he refused my aid as we departed the cabin after lunch. Instead, the tall, spindly, black-bearded *homme*, ten years my junior, energetically hobbled out the door on crutches like a teenager, and down the hillside to the rear of my wagon parked along Prosperity. Neither did he respond to my offer of a hand to steady his walk across the frozen, rutted dirt road that was created by the narrow wheels of his fine buggy. I withdrew my toolbox from the rear of the wagon box and placed it on the ground to assist his climb onto the bed of straw. Again, he pushed aside my hand.

Dropping his black bag next to him, I chided: "'Tis a good thing I have not traded my wagon for a fancy buggy, for your thick cast fits far more comfortably into the rear of my wagon."

I heard him call out to me as I climbed to the bench perch: "Wiltse—we shall not depart without thy Allen & Thurber pistol, shall we?"

"Do not worry, *mon ami*, I am prepared for whatever occurs."

I waved at Edwin standing at the cabin door. After Griffy awoke from a nap, Mrs. Ward would deliver the three of them to the home of Grandmother Fairbank. I looked forward to her report later, particularly should Miss Lucy Dean and her sister stop by for a visit.

A block away I heard the familiar *cawing* of crows. *Murderous things!* I thought, as I raised my eyes to the rooftop of the Baldwin Hotel where the black-feathered leader had perched with a dozen others. The large one I had named "Devil"—he who had dared curl his talons on the horns of my oxen and stared his steely eyes into mine.

"Leave me alone!" I shouted, "Be gone with you."

"Have you changed thy mind, Wiltse?" Dr. Ward asked from the wagon's rear. "Do ye no longer wish to do client visits with me?"

"A black devil of a crow is intent on accompanying us on our journey," I said, "and I'll have none of it."

Reaching into my black bag at my feet, I pulled out my Allen & Thurber, stood, and pointed the pistol high above the heads of my oxen.

With the click of the hammer, the oxen jerked the wagon, knocking me from my feet, and I dropped onto the perch with a thud.

"What are you shooting at?" Dr. Ward asked.

"Your crows have antagonized me—one too many times."

The shot had cleanly missed the crows who lifted to the safety of an oak tree.

Lucky for you, I thought. *Lucky for you.*

Dr. Ward planned for a sick call at the farm of Alexander Stevenson, who had arrived in Oxbow from Indiana five years earlier. Nearly all his family members were indisposed from vomiting with drought of water accompanying it, as if the stomach were parched up and cramps were fixed in the tendons of the joints—all symptoms of cholera. He'd urge rehydration and the intake of zinc. Finally, he would help Mr. Stevenson deal with the manifestation of flies born in the excrements of his hogs—flies, which he had come to believe largely contributed to the spread of the disease. Dr. Ward estimated about seven percent of his clients currently suffered from cholera.

So flies are the culprits behind cholera...*not the wrath of an angry God, after all.*

—

Mrs. Ward informed me Grandmother Fairbank had again warmly welcomed Griffy and my Edwin into her home in the afternoon. The rabbit remained tied to the woodbin at Ward's cabin, lest it be tempted to bite another in error, Mrs. Ward explained.

Her home was perhaps the first log cabin in the township, built in 1855 of logs hewn square with the adze—an axlike tool—and broadaxe; the spaces between logs were filled with wattle—wooden strips, and daubing, a combination of wet soil, clay, sand, animal dung, and straw. She made the voyage from New York with her Grandson C. W. Bacon, and F. J. Everett. Two years earlier the two men had platted the north part of the township, and a year later, they built the steam sawmill along the eastern bank of the Wapsie River. The cabin now served duly as post office.

Mrs. Sarah Ann Leffingwell and her daughter, Mabel—along with nieces Lucy and sister Hattie—stopped by the Fairbank's cabin three times weekly—on the days the stagecoach dropped off mail at Kier, which was then transported to Oxbow by horseback. The two Dean girls eagerly awaited letters from their mother in Vermont with word of their return home.

Edwin produced the puzzle box and spread the pieces on Grandmother Fairbank's tabletop, much to the girls' delight. He was careful not to let on the puzzle would produce a picture of The White Cliffs of Dover, so as not to spoil their fun... Something a boy going on six years would know to do, Mrs. Ward bragged, surprisingly.

The strangest occurrence happened next, she added. Miss Lucy was dressed daintily in a simple frock reaching midway to her ankles, with long legs bound in heavy black stockings, and shoes of the ordinary kind one might expect of a child abandoned by her mother...but a lass of extraordinary beauty, whose dark curly hair so very nicely framed her cherub face... No sooner had Edwin finished turning over the puzzle pieces exposing the fractured picture when Lucy reached for Edwin's neck and the two embraced.

"I love you, Edwin Wiltse," Lucy said. "Some day I'm going to marry you."

"I love you, too," Edwin responded in kind.

"What doth thee think of that?" Mrs. Ward inquired of me. "It was almost foreboding."

"We shall see, Mrs. Ward, "won't we?"

CHAPTER NINE

The Trial of Dr. C. C. Sharp

In May 1856, awaiting the premier run of the Chicago and Burlington Rail-Road Line, the trial of Dr. C. C. Sharp commenced at the District Court of Dubuque. Murder causes agony and suffering that ripples throughout families and entire communities, but none so much as *premeditated murder*. Difficult to explain then the gripping allure to attend the trial of a murderer.

The courtroom gallery quickly filled, and hundreds of people were relegated to collect on the lawn. I would later learn those who assembled outside enjoyed cuisine prepared in pioneer kitchens while being fed testimony by a town crier listening at the courtroom door.

A few minutes before 10 o'clock, Deputy Sheriff S. F. Parker escorted the villainous Dr. Sharp into the courtroom... Mrs. Sharp curiously lagged a distance behind. Upon reaching the defendant's table, Dr. Sharp stretched forth his hand. She ignored the gesture and claimed an empty bench several rows behind the rail.

"All rise," called the bailiff, as Judge A. E. House took the bench.

It was then that an 1845 courtroom scene came to mind, a story told to me by Wellington. He—along with his father, Leonard Wiltse—had served as jurors at the trial of *United States vs. Jefferson Lowe*, tried for the murder of Drury R. Dance. Public opinion was strong that the murder had been justified after Lowe said his farmhand, Drury R. Dance, had seduced Lowe's sister of fourteen years, who was keeping house for Dance. Lowe stated he had killed Lowe in justifiable homicide. Public opinion changed when Lowe confessed to those in his entourage that, armed with his rifle and concealed behind a tree, he had laid in wait for Dance as he approached with his arms full of piglets—

then he shot and mortally wounded Dance. The jury brought in a verdict of not guilty, and Lowe was generally congratulated on his acquittal. This had been the first indictment and trial for murder or any other crime in the courts of Delaware County. Another surprise came after the trial: Dance's widow married Sheriff Parker. I wondered what surprises might spring forth from the trial of Dr. C. C. Sharp.

"All that hast business with the court in the case of the *United States vs. Christopher C. Sharp* for the murder of Joshua F. Stout, draw near," said Judge House.

Prosecuting Attorney James Wilson called his first witness, Andrew Stone, to the stand. He was sworn in by the bailiff:

"Do thou swear that the evidence thou shall grant shall be the truth, all of the truth, and naught yet the truth, so help thou God?"

"I do," said Mr. Stone.

Attorney Wilson began: "Please give your full name and say to the court what thou do for a living."

"My name is Andrew Stone. I departed farming in 1854 and became proprietor of a general market—Stone's Grocery in Delhi. Mine wife Priscilla, and our youngest son Chester, on occasion, are also employed there... Chester hopes to take over the business some day."

"Is Dr. C. C. Sharp, the man on trial today for the murder of Dr. Joshua F. Stout, among thy patronage?"

"I have known Dr. Sharp for a year or longer. He places decrees for dry goods and other mercantile items and pays his account in full in the end of the month...only once, no-twice—perhaps a few times more, as I now recall, hath his account been carried over to the following month...when collections for doctoring were slow to join in, as Dr. Sharp explained to me. But such activity is customary, as many people in this room hast accounts owing at mine market. Many days, I admit, my liver moves as though I'm a banker instead of the proprietor of an establishment, from whose income I might not but pay mine own bills and feed and clothe mine family."

A few in the gallery hooted raucously with a tone of blame.

Judge House gaveled the courtroom back to order.

"Silence! Please keep silence throughout these proceedings or

I shall remove thee from the courtroom."

Attorney Wilson continued: "Please grant the jury thy assessment of Dr. Sharp's character... Did he threaten thou in any way when he was unable to pay what was owing on his account?"

"I found Dr. Sharp to be brash in character—however, ne'r did he intimidate or threaten me. I knew not the cause of the rumored disharmony 'twixt Dr. Sharp and Dr. Stout, though I became aware of a vileness growing 'twixt 'em, when I began to fulfill their decrees so the other would not pick up his order on the same day. What went on 'twixt the two beyond mine front door, I canst not say."

"Were there occasions when the two physicians were at the market at the like time?"

Mr. Stone described two occasions: The first occurred a couple of weeks earlier, when, upon provocation against Dr. Stout by Dr. Sharp, Mrs. Stone, fearing for property and life, fled the market in search of the aid of Sheriff Parker. In the scuffle that ensued, Dr. Boomer, who was awaiting fulfillment of his order, received a slash to his arm trying to protect Dr. Stout. Dr. Boomer ended the attack when he finally knocked the knife from Dr. Sharp's hand. I was not on hand to personally witness the attack, as I was making deliveries—Mrs. Stone relayed the incident to me later.

"The second time was March 10th. I was at the market with Mrs. Stone and our son Chester. Dr. Sharp was present to pick up his order when Dr. Stout entered the store. Dr. Sharp quickly stated his intention to kill Dr. Stout on the spot. With the attack imminent, Mrs. Stone sent Chester for the sheriff. Ere his arrival, Dr. Stout was twice *yerked*—stabbed—in the chest with the knife at the hand of Dr. Sharp."

Under cross-examination, Defense Attorney Timothy Davis suggested Mr. Stone was a purveyor of food, meat, and mercantile—and the hub of a *rumor mill* in the community. It was Mr. Stone who inflamed the quarrel between the two physicians, which led to the death of Dr. Stout, for which Mr. Stone should be brought to justice.

Attorney Wilson objected, bidding the statement be stricken

from the record, as Mr. Stone, a refined Englishman, was held in highest regard in the community and undeserving of the claim of incitement to violence, or charges already would have been instigated by Sheriff Parker.

Dr. Albert Boomer was called next to testify.

"Please state your full name and your relationship to the defendant."

"My name is Dr. Albert M. Boomer. Mi folk is o' Scots' descent. Ah was born in 1823 in Jefferson, New York. My father, Jonathan Allen F. Boomer, was a sailor in his early life—a drummer in the War o' 1812. Somewhere in mah history a'm related to Benjamin Franklin, or so I'm told. Ah met my wife in Illinois, and in th' year prior, we and our wee ones settled in Delhi. We ur staunch Methodists, and I see mah Christian callin' above any ither. A'm among those, most recently, to have established th' Delaware County Medical Society to assure good health care for all folk in th' county."

"Was it through this society that you became acquainted with Dr. Sharp?"

"I regret ah did not know Dr. Sharp thro' th' society—but only thro' word o' his Delhi medical practice. Not a disparaging word had I heard o' th' care he'd given to any who sought his help, whatsoever thair malady. For that reason, I consider him a colleague o' th' highest standing, though there was rumor o' some disgruntlement between Dr. Sharp and Dr. Stout, whom I've grown to know well through the society. Dr. Stout dismissed th' antagonism on Dr. Sharp's part as sparked by professional jealousy; we only spoke o' th' rumor on a single occasion, 'n' beyond that I'm without benefit o' knowledge.

"I should add that jealousy between doctors isn't uncommon. A physician kin graduate from an eastern college, which bestows a certain prestige; anither man kin have great charisma, which adds favorably to his patronage—and wealth. All kin be considered enviable by fellow practitioners. Bit I've ne'er known professional jealousy to produce a vileness such that sets aboot to murder another physician… It simply goes against th' Hippocratic Oath."

"Would thou say then thou hast a good reputation as a

physician in the Delhi community? Do you know of any who holds hostilities against thee?" asked Attorney Wilson.

"It is ma attempt to treat ithers kindly in a' ways 'n' manners. Ah dare say it should be mast egregious to me should I ever offend another physician—or any jimmy, for that matter."

Attorney Wilson walked to the jury box with the dirk knife in his hand, fully displaying the twelve-inch blade.

"Would thou tell us about the event the day thou were wounded by the defendant, Dr. Sharp, with the knife I hold in my hands."

Dr. Boomer removed his jacket and rolled up his shirt sleeve to expose the scar on the inside of his left arm, while recounting the day Dr. Sharp entered Stone's Grocery and of the unprovoked attack that followed.

"I only met Dr. Sharp in person a few weeks ago whin we both happened to turn up at Stone's store—mine stop was to pick up supplies fur my flint rifle... I'm an avid hunter, ye see, 'n' frequently shoot down as many as twenty-five birds in a single day. That day, noticing th' meager offering o' fresh fowl at the market, ah offered to supply Mrs. Stone wi' fresh birds fur their inventory."

"What, in thy estimation, Dr. Boomer, led to the attack by Dr. Sharp?"

"Dr. Sharp had stopped by the market—then, when Dr. Stout arrived, Dr. Sharp immediately, without provocation, charged at him wi' his sharp knife raised."

"Did Dr. Sharp say anything during the attack?"

"I shall dispatch thee!' was all 'twas said."

"How didst it happen thou were wounded? Was the attack intended for thou?"

"The attack, ah believe, wis intended fu Dr. Stout. Ah incurred th' injury to my arm in my interference wi' Dr. Sharp's ability to reach Dr. Stout."

"Will you tell us what happened next, Dr. Boomer?"

"Ah was able to knock the dirk knife from Dr. Sharp's hand— at that point, Dr. Sharp fled th' store. Dr. Wiltse 'n' Dr. Stout took me to Dr. Stout's office nearby to treat th' wound on my arm.

"What happened to the dirk knife?"

"Dr. Stout picked up th' knife wherein Dr. Sharp had dropped it, and placed the knife in a locked drawer fur safekeeping 'til Sheriff Parker could be located to hand it over to him. Sometime that night…an unknown culprit broke into Dr. Stout's office 'n' lifted it from th' drawer, or so I was told."

"Did thee bring a complaint against Dr. Sharp for thy injury?"

"No… ah hoped this would be th' end o' it. Ah didn't wish to tarnish Dr. Sharp's reputation over a single moment o' desperation. Ah read in th' *Delhi Argus Journal* our very own Congressmen in Washington bludgeon each other wi' canes over th' equality o' blacks 'n' whether or not our nation should abolish slavery. Should a Delhi physician then be required to report a beating of o' wife by her husband, an incident of molestation of a child by his very own father, or quarrel between farmers whose outcome in a pitchfork in th' back? If so, th' laws must be changed."

A conspicuous buzz spread across the courtroom.

"Order in the court!" Judge House said, pounding his gavel on the bench. "Consider this thy final warning—one more time and I'll clear the gallery."

Defense Attorney Davis redirected, suggesting Dr. Sharp had merely acted in defense on the day Dr. Stout was injured. "I have a submitted an affidavit stating Dr. Sharp was frightful for his life on March 10th, upon seeing the face of the man who, in private, had repeatedly threatened him. Any jealousy that existed was on the part of Dr. Stout."

Attorney Wilson called me to the stand.

"Please give your full name and tell the jury when you first became acquainted with Dr. Sharp?"

"My name is Dr. Alexander Wiltse. I first met Dr. Sharp at Stone's Grocery shortly after my family—my *épouse* Phebe, and our three enfants—emigrated from Ontario in the spring of 1855. Being a physician in a new country, I desired certification, and upon learning of the formation of the Delaware County Société Médicale, I made application. Following the conclusion of one such meeting, I stopped by Mr. Stone's Grocery for mercantile items for Phebe. On that day, it so happened that Dr. Sharp came into the store."

"Was yours a pleasant introduction to Dr. Sharp?"

"'Twas agreeable enough…though, hardly more than a few words were exchanged, as I recall."

Attorney Wilson raised the dirk knife once more for the jury to view.

"Was Dr. Sharp in possession of this dirk knife on that day?"

"Oui—he carried it in a leather case that hung at his waist… Said it had belonged to his father who had served in the navy. He held it in highest regard and should be sorrowful to ever lose it."

"You met Dr. Sharp again at the farm of Dr. Stout in September of that year, Dr. Wiltse… What was the occasion for that meeting?"

"Dr. Stout was kind enough to extend an invitation to me and my family to attend the annual prairie chicken hunt so I might meet other physicians in the region. We were privileged to accept."

"Was there a specific event that day, Dr. Wiltse, which in hindsight, might now be construed as an attempt on Dr. Stout's life. Wouldst thou describe that event for the jury?"

I testified that Dr. Stout had moved about throughout the morning to hunt for short durations at the side of each of his guests. At one point, Dr. Stout aligned himself at the end of the row of hunters next to Dr. James Wright and me. Suddenly, I heard the whiz of a lead ball fly by my head, and out of the corner of my eye, saw Dr. Stout reach for his jaw and fall to the ground. My inspection revealed he had received a small injury near the mouth. His brother-in-law, Dr. Acers, quickly came upon Dr. Stout and took him to the stone house for treatment."

"Were thou able to identify the origin of the firing?"

"It came from the right of Dr. Stout—mine eyes were immediately drawn to the grove of trees, though I saw no signs of any person, or of any movement at all for that matter.

"Did Dr. Stout indicate who might have had cause to shoot at him?"

"Dr. Stout dismissed it as *décharge accidentelle*—accidental discharge, and nothing more was thought of it."

"About what time didst Dr. Sharp arrive at the hunt?"

I testified Dr. Sharp arrived mid-afternoon. He had suddenly appeared, inserting himself at my side in the row of hunters without introduction by the host Dr. Stout, as had been the case with the other hunters at the debut of the hunt, which began shortly after sunrise. I recalled Dr. Sharp saying he believed his invitation had been lost in the mail.

"What was Dr. Sharp's disposition upon his arrival—was it anger? upon being overlooked with an invitation to an event wherein every other physician in the region was in attendance."

"Objection, leading the witness," Dr. Sharp's attorney cried out. "How can Dr. Wiltse possibly know the state of another's mind?"

"Let me rephrase," said Attorney Wilson. "How wouldst thou describe Dr. Sharp's attitude during the hours thou stood next to him at the hunt?"

"He seemed breathless, at first…explicable, as he seemingly had arrived on foot, and not by wagon as were the other *chasseurs*—hunters. Even so, Dr. Sharp settled in nicely and killed his share of birds within short duration with his flintlock rifle."

"How wouldst thee describe Dr. Sharp's ability with his rifle?

"He was an excellent shot."

Whispered gasps ricocheted within the courtroom walls.

"You were present on both days of Dr. Sharp's attacks at Stone's store—is that accurate?"

"Oui—the first attack wherein Dr. Boomer's arm was wounded was concerning. The struggle between Dr. Boomer and Dr. Sharp lasted but a few minutes, though seemed much longer. Mr. Stone keeps a children's puzzle on a board along the central aisle which was overturned during the attack—sadly, Dr. Boomer's blood sprinkled onto many puzzle pieces."

Audible shock rose to its highest pitch from the gallery.

"Order!" called Judge House, gaveling sharply from the bench. "Bailiff, I decree thee to clear the gallery heretofore upon hearing anyone making a *hurly-burly* louder than a mouse."

The bailiff took a step forward and sternly gazed at the gallery.

"You may continue, Dr. Wiltse," Judge House said.

"Many barrels and bins of legumes were overturned in the

mêlée before Dr. Boomer was able to liberate the knife from Dr. Sharp's hand—but not before Dr. Boomer himself had been wounded."

"Dr. Wiltse, now tell what you witnessed the day Dr. Stout was twice stabbed in the chest at the hand of Dr. Sharp, which ended Dr. Stout's life six days hence," said Attorney Wilson.

"'Twas as you've already heard others testify: There was no provocation by Dr. Stout. As Dr. Sharp charged, he made mention of receiving menaces against himself by Dr. Stout…and something about a woman of ill repute with whom Dr. Stout had become affiliated. All this was news to me, and I didn't know what to make of it, even as Dr. Stout lay in a pool of blood on the floor of Stone's market. I sorely regret not taking the first attack more seriously weeks earlier that led to the cut Dr. Boomer sustained to his arm… I believe the savage and brutal death of my dear friend Dr. Stout could have been prevented on March 10th."

Attorney Davis rose to begin his cross-examination. A shudder of fear ran down my spine.

"Dr. Wiltse—I find it interesting you mention feeling guilt over the loss of thy comrade Dr. Stout. I bid thee…is none of that guilt meant for *Dr. Sharp*, whom, you, along with so many other physicians, shunned since his arrival in Delhi? Didst it e'er occur Dr. Sharp was the victim of threats and intimidations when thy Dr. Stout was out of eyesight? Where was thou in Dr. Sharp's hour of need?"

"I was not aware such was ever the case, or I should surely have been his harbor in the storm," I said, aware my voice quivered.

"No further questions, Dr. Wiltse… You may return to your seat."

Attorney Wilson called Dr. John Acers to the stand.

"State your full name and tell the court the length of time you have resided in Delaware County."

"My name is Dr. John Acers. My wife Melinda and I arrived in the county in 1850, along with mine brother-in-law Dr. Joshua Stout, and his wife Lydia. We purchased adjoining land and hast found Delhi a prosperous place to farm and practice medicine. Several of our brothers hast also since located hither. Together we founded the village of Acerville."

Attorney Wilson continued: "Dr. Acers, you are considered a leading eclectic physician in the county dedicated to the betterment of society. Most recently—you helped found the Delaware County Medical Society. Please inform us about the work of this society."

"After a year's hard work, the By-laws and Constitution were recently approved. Any men engaged in the practice of medicine in Delaware County are invited—even urged—to join the society. Many area practitioners, heretofore, hast been country doctors, without accreditation, but in today's orb such hath become a necessity; hence, passing an exam is required ere membership approval. Delaware County accredited physicians subsequently offer aid to new applicants—studying for the exam, internships, e'en assistance locating a medical college, if a formal degree is the physician's goal. Our nation requires the medical field to progress to new heights in the care of its society, and meeting that challenge is our mission."

"Who are the society's founding fathers then?"

"Along with myself, as president...Dr. Albert Boomer, Dr. Joshua Stout, and a handful of others. Dr. Boomer hath completed tutoring Dr. Wiltse, who will soon undergo examination by the Board of Censors. Dr. Boomer also offered to tutor Dr. Sharp, who, within the past month, had submitted application for membership."

"Dr. Acers, were you aware of the ongoing quarrel between your brother-in-law Dr. Stout and Dr. Sharp?"

"Dr. Stout—Joshua—and I spoke of Dr. Sharp's increasing hostilities. Joshua played down Dr. Sharp's threats, considering 'em a condition of acrimonious bitterness. He felt they would lead nowhere, and he chose to shun 'em."

Attorney Davis stated he wished to cross-examine Dr. Acers, and approached the witness stand, stopping a foot away from the witness stand.

"Do you avow that *none* requesting membership would be turned away—is that a fair assessment, Dr. Acers?"

"That is correct. The society would ne'r reject a sincere request from anyone who sought medical accreditation."

"Even if the society president learned of a disconcerting claim against—say, *a brother-in-law*? What if the claim was about an unpleasantry in a physician's personal life, for example, an affair outside the bounds of the marital contract? With a woman of ill-repute? Would such a claim warrant a decline of his membership request?"

Dr. Acers appeared to stare across the courtroom at Dr. Stout's widow seated in the row behind the prosecution's table, then at a second woman in the room—dressed in black from head to foot, her pale face disguised behind a hatted veil. She was seated off the right shoulder of Mrs. Stout and was unfamiliar to me.

"Should I repeat the question, Dr. Acers?" Attorney Davis asked.

"*Not one!* would be turned away for any reason beyond his incapacity to pass the exam requirement," he finally responded.

Attorney Wilson called Deputy Sheriff S. F. Parker to give testimony of the evidence he'd found to support the arrest and trial of Dr. C. C. Sharp for the murder of Dr. Joshua F. Stout.

Sheriff Parker testified he had been summoned in the late afternoon of March 10th by Chester Stone, the young son of Andrew and Priscilla Stone, owners of Stone's Grocery. He arrived at the market within the hour of Dr. Stout's stabbing. Dr. Alexander Wiltse was in possession of a dirk knife—already entered into evidence by the prosecution—the weapon used in the attack against Dr. Stout. Dr. Wiltse told him the knife had been removed from Dr. Stout's chest area by the attending physician Dr. Albert Boomer, as Dr. Stout lay dying in a rear room of the market. The twelve-inch blade was covered with Dr. Stout's blood.

"A dirk knife is a long-bladed thrusting dagger, a personal weapon of officers engaged in naval hand-to-hand combat as well as das personal sidearm of Scottish Highlanders—which is ideal for close quarter fighting. I hast a book on weapons of all kinds, cause that's the job I'm in… I've seen every weapon ever made by man," he said.

Furthermore, Sheriff Parker stated he had interviewed Dr. Stout, Dr. Boomer, Dr. Wiltse, and others who witnessed the fight which ultimately led to the death of Dr. Stout. Of those men, several witnessed seeing Dr. Sharp previously carry the dirk knife on his person and heard Dr. Sharp state it had belonged to his father who had served in the navy. Sheriff Parker added that he found no discrepancies 'twixt any of their testimonies. On the day in question, Dr. Sharp prevailed upon Dr. Stout with his drawn knife, advancing upon Dr. Stout until he had twice stabbed the physician and he fell to the floor. After Dr. Stout died six days later, Sheriff Parker had gone to the home of Dr. Sharp, arrested him for the murder of Dr. Stout and took him to the county jail to await trial.

Coroner Simeon Ellis was called to testify. He stated that Dr. Stout, a previously healthy German adult male, had died at age thirty-six, on the sixteenth of March from a puncture stab to each of his lungs—wounds he had incurred six days prior. The cuts corresponded to the size of the twelve-inches dirk knife blade previously submitted into evidence. The blade tip damaged the airwaves and caused a bronchopleurale fistula in each lung. Leakage of air into the pleural cavities resulted in a pneumothorax, which eventually led to Dr. Stout's slow, painful death from suffocation.

Defense Attorney Davis called two friends and two clients to testify as to Dr. Sharp's character and dedication to the service of his community. Each confirmed Dr. Sharp had been a model physician and citizen in the Delhi community.

Under Attorney Wilson's cross-examination, none stated they were aware of threats and attacks against Dr. Sharp by the mild-mannered Dr. Stout—though all testified, on occasion, Dr. Sharp, had made ridiculing, degrading comments about Germans, in general, which may have contributed to a motive of retaliation against Dr. Stout, a full-blooded German and recent immigrant. Professional jealousy was also mentioned as a likely possible motive.

One man who admitted to being a long-time dear friend noted that Dr. Sharp may have had more personal reasons for the attack, but nothing that had anything to do with any hatred of Germans, or professional jealousy. "We never really know the losses others have incurred, particularly from a young age, and for which they may never fully recover," he said.

Attorney Davis chose not to put Dr. Sharp on the stand to testify on his own behalf and rested the case for the defense.

The trial had lasted two days. Prior to sentencing, Judge House asked Dr. Sharp whether he had anything to offer about why judgment should not now be pronounced.

Dr. Sharp rose and shouted that he had drawn his weapon in defense on both occasions at Stone's market, as was maintained by his defense attorney throughout the trail. He should'st not be found guilty of murder of the very one who provoked the entanglements.

Before Judge House charged the jury with deciding the fate of Dr. Sharp, he delivered these words to the accused:

"This is an enunciation in thy life, Dr. Sharp, where thou would to accept it as such, or not is thy choice. In this, thy valley of sorrow and disgrace, search thy heart for what has formed thee into a man that could commit such an egregious act as to take the life of another, e'en a fellow physician. Perhaps the role God gave thee on the day thou were born was not that of physician and healer. Perhaps thou hast not discovered your place in the world and responded to it. Only thou can discover what hath corroded and separated you from thy ideals. Fix thy relationships. Find what grants thou hope. Place your trust in others and bid them place their trust in thou. Teach what it is you lack: empathy. I bid thou work on these things, and thou may join out of this time of sorrow the better for it."

The jury did not deliberate long before returning a verdict of manslaughter. Judge House sentenced Dr. Sharp to ten years of hard labor at the Iowa State territorial penitentiary at Fort Madison.

I would ne'er forget that day in March 1856, when my dear friend and colleague Dr. Stout was murdered before my very eyes. I expected I would wonder what I could have done to prevent his death for many years to come.

The announcement of Dr. Sharp's sentencing in the *Delhi Argus Journal* appeared next to an announcement of the Chicago and Burlington Rail-Road Line—which had just run the entire distance from Burlington, Iowa to Chicago, Illinois. The line was expected to reach Delaware County by year-end.

CHAPTER TEN

Life at The Point

During the first week of July 1857, a drizzly rain began to fall. On a Thursday morning, as I set out for The Point a violent lightning storm ensued. Four months had passed since the murder of Dr. Stout. In the fierce downpour, I speculated how easily all evidence could have been washed away if his murder had happened in a rainstorm, perhaps even carrying off the corpse. Not all murder sees the full light of justice.

A thousand claps of thunder returned my focus to the road. I would later only recall climbing into my new four-seat buggy from Inger & Son, Carriage and Wagon Manufactory—another recent enterprise along Old Mission Road. Reaching the fork in the road that diverted me northerly to The Point, a bolt of lightning must have struck in the immediate vicinity, as it stupefied and prostrated me. My newly acquired black mare colt, a most handsome Canadian horse, took off running. In my hallucination, I witnessed an Indian brave take hold of the reins and bring my horse and buggy to a halt. The brave rode off before I could speak. Hours later, the event would seem an *apparition*.

'Twas then I named my mare *Boulon*— lightning bolt.

Continuing to feel off-center from the lightning strike, upon reaching the village, I dropped off my horse and carriage at the livery and walked to Bailey's store. There, I stood for a moment in wonderment at the signage in the window:

DR. ALEXANDER WILTSE
PROFESSIONAL CALLS AT ANY HOUR OF THE
DAY OR NIGHT

It had finally happened: my practice was among the six stores, one brewery, one flour mill, and three churches of Cass

Township.

Strawberry Point had been laid out in southwestern Clayton County in 1853 by W. H. and D. M. Stearns. The town's original founder initially called the place "Franklin." Another explorer who found myriad patches of wild strawberries changed the name to "Strawberry Point," which was then shortened it to "The Point." Two hundred fifty people now inhabited this place, even as the population of Clayton County had swelled to over four thousand. The immigrants largely came from the East: New York, Massachusetts, and Pennsylvania. But Canada, too.

These people would be my new *clientele*—though no patients awaited care outside my office on this morning.

Stepping inside the building, I felt the weight of the two medical books on loan from Dr. Ward stashed under my rain jacket. A week earlier, Phebe had given birth to our second daughter. 'Twas another difficult birth. At the height of her travail, I saw life draining from Phebe's face, and feared her fate would be like that of Louisa's. It was the premier moment when, Dr. Ward's book open before me, I turned to "Affections connected with Parturition" and followed the directives to safely deliver our enfant, Lucetta "Lucettie."

Joel Bailey was the proprietor of Bailey's store, though in name only. The surveyor, postmaster, judge, real estate developer, bondsman, commissioner, and most trusted and oldest living settler of Delaware County had suffered frostbite to his feet during the Christmas delivery of pigs to the Winnebago Mission School by Fort Atkinson. The loss of several toes turned him into a cripple, and ever since Mrs. Bailey handled all his properties.

She had designated the southeastern corner of the first floor of the two-story structure for my medical practice, complete with a desk and a chair inside the front door. A dense, grey cloth, draped from ceiling to floor curtained the examination area, and a narrow chest with glass doors held my instruments, medicines, liqueurs, patent medicines, and oils.

Opposite my desk was another, displaying the placard: R. ELVIDGE. I had yet to see him occupy the space since we'd joined forces in our endeavors to serve the community— *insurance and medicine to treat life's misadventures.*

A stack of newspapers had accumulated on Mr. Elvidge's desk. He subscribed to the *North Iowa Times, Clayton County Herald, Sand Spring Sentinel,* and *Delhi Argus Journal* to learn of Clayton County calamites. Then he called on those in the area to remind them that their financial hardships had been preventable through the purchase of insurance. He worked hard at the enterprise of sowing fear, bullying, and intimidation.

I laid the two books on my desk and removed my rain jacket, replacing it with a black physician's coat. A violent clap of thunder preceded a strong gust of wind that pushed through cracks around the door. I reached for the shawl Phebe had sent along, draped it across my shoulders, and walked to the metal box at the store's center to start a fire. I left the door ajar to watch that the flame didn't go out.

An editorial, "Quacks and Quackeries," beckoned to me from the top paper on Mr. Elvidge's desk. I carried it to my desk and sat in my chair. The room was cold; I pulled the shawl tighter around my chest. The article wished to call ill-attention to patent medicines…pills, syrups, compound extracts, and the system of inhalation.

> *There is nobody so easily humbugged as a sick person,
> and no humbug greater than the patient… If a lazy
> man would go to a physician every time he felt like
> leaving work…with a box of pills, a bottle of
> Sarsaparilla, Ague Bitters, Cherry Pectoral…he can
> play sick man to his own satisfaction.*

Would my new clientele at The Point consider me a *quack*, or a legitimate physician? I still could not boast of certification.

I checked the tenuous fire and added more kindling. The rain striking the window now resonated like frozen daggers. I found myself looking up as every buggy or wagon passed by the bay window. A moment later, I thought I might be feverish and placed a wrist against my forehead. I had no fever. 'Twas only the apprehension that had begun after Dr. Stout's murder. A reoccurring night dream had also pervaded my sleep…

> *a shadowy figure appearing in my office in the light of midday, a man with a vengeance in his heart over a child who had died while in my care... another of a prized horse I'd treated for strangles that could not be saved. The flash of a muzzle always awakened me from the dream.*

The fire had begun to crackle, and I closed the firebox door. Another short article "Railroad Management in Germany" aroused my interest.

> *Every railroad company is bound to have a double track on their lines, and no person may walk on a railroad track at any time under penalty of law. A barrier consisting of two strong planks is placed along the side of the tracks to keep off animals. Every fifteen to twenty miles along the route there is a station for a guard or watchman, who lives in the little hut, and whose business it is to be at his post, with a red flag in hand, at the approach of every train; and before a train is due, to patrol his bent to see that all is safe, and to remove obstacles that are sometimes placed on the tracks by miscreants. In case of danger, the guard hoists on a telegraph a red painted board, which can be seen by the engineer at a great distance, but if everything is alright, the two wooden arms of the telegraph are stretched in the air. During the night a deep red lantern is used as a warning of danger. At every crossing there is a gate, which is locked up as soon as the train is due, and anyone, either in carriage or horseback, desiring to cross, must wait until the train is passed. Germany now boasts of 5,000 kilometers of track, double that of France.*

The face of Mr. G. L. Tremain came to mind. He, along with Mr. Grannis, kept a good assortment of goods at their store. Upon learning Phebe and I had relocated to the area, Mr. Tremain promptly invited my engagement in the town's civic affairs. My principal mission: Lead the committee in formulating a plan to assure the railroad's passage through Cass Township. The Delaware County & Pacific Railroad Company had already filed a record for the purpose of constructing a railroad at the east line of Delaware County all the way to the Pacific Ocean—but railroads were known to change plans at the eleventh hour. The railroad brought great advantage to those whose market for grain was nearer than Dubuque. Without it, The Point would never grow to its full potential.

The committee also led efforts in the treatment of more vulgar issues: cattle rustling, gunfights, brawls, and land fraud. Horses and cattle taken by prairie banditti were often hidden in the timber along the Turkey River before being taken across the Mississippi River into Wisconsin and sold.

We proposed implementation of a law similar to one established at Colesburg—wherein, after a thief was found guilty of stealing stock, he was brought before a jury of three regulators to adjust the punishment of thirty-nine lashes with a black snake whip. After twenty lashes, if the thief promised to leave the territory, the other nineteen would not be administered, unless he returned. Before his departure, he was given a thorough bathing of bear grease to alert others of his cunning and thievery.

Heat from the firebox began to emanate into the room. I opened the door and placed a larger log on the flame.

My mind wandered…to the memory of the birth of our belle Lucettie, a month earlier. Arriving at our newly built 16 x 18 feet cabin, we had but the luxury of a roof, four walls, and a stone chimney, straw ticks for bedding, feather ticks for pillows—without furniture or curtains on the windows. Our cookware consisted of a few pots and pan and dishes brought from Ontario, and the Wiltse conch shell. Albeit, when I carried Lucettie into the light of the southern facing window on the morning of her entrance into the world, her face had an ethereal glow, and Phebe and I had everything we needed. We honored her with a name that signified *light*…and to remind of us the child we had lost—two in one.

The fire now burned with stamina, and I added another log.

An article, "The Damage to Wheat," supposed Wisconsin had

lost about a million dollars in stacked wheat destroyed in the field by the immense rains in recent weeks. Such negligent stacking was never seen in any other state. I sensed what felt like an electrical charge travel down the length of my back as I recalled last fall's slump in corn and wheat prices. Was America on the threshold of a *financial collapse*? If so, what would happen to the railroads crisscrossing Iowa?

I stared broodingly out the bay window facing Main Street. Just then the foggy shadow of a man passed by and the door flew open. He was holding a white towel to his bleeding head and urgently beckoned me to follow him. I grabbed my rain jacket, hat, and black bag and walked with him to a hardware store at the western edge of Old Mission Road.

Inside, the structure was in disarray with shards of glass scattered across counters and floors.

The man at my side identified himself as Mr. Searson, and pointed at Mr. Donahue, the store owner, seated in an armed chair next to the blown-out front window. Mr. Searson informed me that while mixing a compound for a customer—nitric acid, mercury, turpentine, and other ingredients—shortly after corking and shaking the contents in a bottle, the contents exploded. Bottles broke on shelves and sent splinters of glass throughout the room.

Upon closer examination, I found Mr. Donahue bleeding from puncture wounds and covered with chemicals—his entire face was gravely burned; one eye was severely injured.

Mr. Searson, who had also sustained cuts and burns on one side of his face, helped me get Mr. Donahue to my office. He appeared to be going into shock by the time we got him onto the examination table. I checked his pulse, then placed an opium pill for the pain on his tongue and helped him drink water from a glass to wash it down his throat. He gulped the water.

I laid him on his back, removed his shirt and pants, and elevated his legs to increase blood flow to his head.

"I'm going to remove shards of glass from your face, then apply axle grease to your burns—I need to create a clean seal. Do you understand?"

He stared blankly at me.

Using a tweezer, I began to pull the countless slivers of glass from his face, arms, torso, and legs—finishing by lightly brushing folds of gauze across the skin to catch the tiny ones. Next, I mixed a solution of axle grease, animal fat, and beeswax thinned with turpentine, and applied a light coat to his burns.

Mr. Donahue's left eye had been gravely damaged by the chemicals. I doubted he would ever see out of it again. After irrigating both eyes with a solution, I covered them with gauze held in place with white tape. I checked his breathing and pulse again before covering him with a blanket.

Next, I withdrew supplies from the medicine chest and invited Mr. Searson to follow me to my desk. Pushing the newspaper aside, he took a seat on the desk, dangling his legs over the edge.

He, too, appeared about to go into shock.

"Do you require something to dull the pain?" I said, offering him an opium pill in one hand.

He took the pill and swallowed it before I had a chance to pour him a glass of water.

"My wife hath taken the drug for diarrhea and moodiness… I shall now inform her of its use for pain," he said, closing his eyes.

Fearing he might fall from the desk, I removed him to my chair and, retrieving Mr. Elvidge's chair, elevated his legs.

"Thou are new to The Point?" Mr. Searson asked, sounding as if already in an altered state of consciousness.

I unwound the towel from his head and examined the cuts and burns on his face. His injuries were less severe than Mr. Donahue's.

Hoping to keep him alert as long as possible while I removed the glass shards from his face and neck, I engaged him in conversation.

"My famille came from Canada… We have been in Amérique about a year. I am affiliated with the Delaware County Médicale Société—and decided The Point could use a good médecin."

"It was our good fortune thou were in this place today… Mr. Donahue is burned badly, hum?" Mr. Searson said, mumbling his words.

"He will require médicaux care for some time, though I can't say with certitude I shall be able to save his left eye."

I asked Mr. Searson to open his eyes so I might irrigate them.

He obliged, wincing in pain as I poured the solution.

"If thou use an assistant, Mr. Wiltse, mine neighbor, Perry Dewey, is interested in medicine," he uttered, before reposing his head on the chair back and closing his eyes.

I checked his pulse. His skin was cool and clammy. His breathing, rapid. I tied him in the chair with towels as I continued removal of glass pieces while softly reciting the Physician's Prayer…

> *Close your eyes*
> *and reap thine healing sleep*
> *your body to repair*
> *much better than I*
> *with creams and ointments,*
> *your body knows*
> *how best to restore*
> *that which screams of injury*
> *and appears withered on the vine.*

—

Phebe was pessimistic about her kitchen, which remained without a grand wood-burning cookstove—though, also lacking a table and chairs. She promised her first splendid meal would be Canadian prairie chicken stew with yam biscuits. For that, she would need to grow carrots, peas, onions, yams, and herbs. Before she could grow a garden, a fence was required to turn away any kind of animal—from horse to sucking pig—from eating her plants.

And so it was with great delight that Phebe at last watched— from behind freshly installed cabin windows, enfant Lucettie in her arms, Vidella, Charles, and young Edwin at her side—the planting of the Osage-orange hedge around her garden area by contractors Samuel Knee and a German named Charles Bomgartner.

Almost immediately, I had taken a liking to Mr. Bomgartner, whom I noticed had a medical condition called a *roving eye*, along with a growth the size of a small pea under the eyelid. He wore a brown felt hat tipped toward the side of the misaligned eye, perhaps to help protect from the sun's glare—or perhaps, for ease of pulling over the face to nap, which he was accustomed to doing every afternoon.

Construction of our home now complete, I hired him as our farmhand, initially charging him with making a list of items to procure for the farm: stirring plow, hay rack, corn sheller, cows and hogs, milking equipment, even a pitchfork. Shortly he came across a notice of a public sale for 12 milk cows, 8 heifers, and a quantity of household furniture. I sent him off with an I.O.U. to purchase select items from the sale.

Additionally, I gave him responsibility for making a list of useful farm projects, and for hiring local chaps for the seasonal work of planting and harvesting crops.

Phebe created her own list for Mr. Bomgartner.

—

Uri took a second wife, Miss. Silvia Kelly, on July 14, 1857, which freed Mère Rachel and Père Philip to return to our farm. They had lingered at Uri's homestead to give concluding aid in the preparation of house, gardens, farm, and animals for Silvia's arrival. Their arrival came just in time to attend the Fourth of July celebration in Manchester—formerly Burrington.

The day-long event was the product of Dr. Joshua Stout, who had planned it in the months prior to his death. His whimsical idea of sending up a live ox in a balloon happened in the afternoon—'twas quite a sight to behold. Surprisingly, no ox was hurt or killed in the spectacle.

The *Delhi Argus Journal* recorded the day, thusly:

> *It began ushered in by the sun rising in the east, as*
> *usual. The services continued by the firing of thirteen*
> *crackers to represent the thirteen original States, after*
> *which the people formed a procession, headed by the*
> *Mayor, President, and Vice President of the day.*
> *Soldiers of 1812, immediately succeeded by the*

*regular elect aristocracy of the town, followed by the
military, fire and other companies, citizens, town
stock, etc., of Manchester, under the direction of the
Basswood Lumber Dealer, acting as Marshal of the
day. The rabble then trotted up the street to Franklin,
until they arrived at the speakers' stand, where a live
whangdoodle bore the concourse till satisfied. The
powder was burned, and blood spilled, if necessary.
No expense was spared to make it a day to be
remembered. Nourishment was furnished in
abundance to refresh the inner man, consisting of
regular and voluntary toasts, raw Dutch and Irishmen,
whisky pickled Yankees.*

Later, I learned the celebration had subversively marked the second annual anniversary, by many, of the lack of independence under the tyranny of President James Buchanan.

CHAPTER ELEVEN

Spinning Out of Control

Mr. Bomgartner, now employed as our farmhand, set about building a dugout stable and chicken coup, and embarked on the initial stages of turning the land into a cultivated farm. He carried a Hanover German .48 caliber percussion pistol and black powder loading musket. Killing on the prairie largely happened out of necessity—for food and to protect crops, livestock, and family. Cases of crime and jealousy between humans though oft times ended in violence with a knife, as was the case of the murder of Dr. Stout. Rare, was coming across a man's head split open with a hatchet. That was a far more personal crime.

I found the German Mr. Bomgartner an independent homme in purpose and judgment—much like his *roving eye,* which acted independent of the other. His labor was cheap at a dollar and a quarter a day. Père Phillip assisted him, whenever the job was a fit for his infirm body of fifty-seven years. Phebe kept track of the ten-gallon hat atop his head by day and by night as he moved among prairie, fields, and streams—as did Mr. Bomgartner.

On a Tuesday in early May 1857, Phebe at last discharged Mr. Bomgartner to The Point to claim her wood-burning cookstove which had arrived the previous day by stagecoach. Our maison was taking shape at last; not the massive, framed structure modeled after Abiathar Richardson's, but a fine home in the making.

Awaiting his return, she set about meticulously tending her garden in the cool of the morning. She had planted seeds procured from the Stearns' store at The Point, though her most prized heritage garden-tomato seeds she had transported from Ontario, along with a few flowers and herbs.

Vidella, Charles, and Edwin were at her side. Mère Rachel

watched over baby Lucettie, gently rocking her in the wooden cradle under the shade of an oak tree. At age 56, her hair had turne ashen on top with an undertone of yellow greige—a blend of gray and greige, the color of bark on a mature birch. The voyage to America and a strenuous year of pioneering had strained her. Like the oak tree, she, too, had begun to lean.

While Phebe worked, adorned with Louisa's beads around her neck, she taught the children parables from the Bible, supplanting her words with teachings passed down from her parents, Mère Hannah and Père Henry.

As garden lector she tied home to garden: "A garden and a maison naturally go together," she would begin if teaching the "Parable of the Mustard Seed," for example.

"The home should be attractive within and without. There is a growing problem today to make the home the most attractive place on earth. It is from holes in *société* that criminals and lawlessness come, the vicious and the degenerate. Good things develop in the home. Around the kitchen table good character is developed, fathers and mothers raising their children together. I fear the growing commercialization in our nation. Homes are made with blood, and sacrifice, and travail…you must have your whole soul into it. Cleanliness must come first before we can have godliness. People may wear patched vêtements, but that is no excuse they are not kept clean."

By the time Phebe's back commenced to ache, one by one our enfants began responding to another voice—the spirit that lay within each of them—beckoning them away from the rows of corn, squash, and other vegetables to passions too early to name.

While Charles had shown an early interest in planting and growing things, he departed for the creek to sail the boat Uri had helped him craft. His voluble, articulate recitations of math, reading, and the sciences—Phebe's parables, too—could be heard carried upon the thin winds that danced across tender heads of yellow grain, field to field. He seemed determined to rid himself of his stammer, for which his Mère and I had considered submitting him for "the cure." He also faithfully sought out plants from which medicines could be made, healing plants, that Louisa had pointed out to him.

Vidella's head oft seemed in the clouds, and at some point, she set off to explore the woods and prairies—with Edwin in tow and Cloudy in his arms. On one such occasion, she discovered bees-trees, and summoned Mr. Bomgartner, who removed them to bee boxes quickly assembled, and placed them near a flowering apple tree a few yards from the spot where the chamber pot was emptied. It was an uninhabitable place anyway, he said, ascribing that as the reason for the location.

Phebe told me of these things and others in the evenings after a Bible reading and a prayer to prepare us for a good night's rest.

One evening she confessed to wondering whether her mother was living, and would she ever see her family again?

—

I continued to divide my time between Delhi and The Point. At the July 1857 société médicale meeting, emotions remained raw over the brutal murder of our colleague Dr. Stout. Within a month of his trial, the *Quasqueton Guardian* announced Dr. Sharp had escaped from prison at Fort Madison. Then, Sheriff Parker heard of him in Tennessee, where he had married a girl of sixteen of highly respectable parents. The sheriff subsequently submitted a requisition to Tennessee Governor Andrew Johnson, who granted the necessary papers to arrest the fugitive, and return him to his quarters at Fort Madison. Mrs. Stout, hearing of it, had him charged for bigamy.

Further stirring our emotions, Dr. Acers' shared a ghastly report of an incident from a week earlier. He had accompanied Sheriff Parker to the home of the Delhi jailer, Mr. Kellogg, who was found dead in his bed, brained with an axe around 3 AM. The sheriff took Mrs. Kellogg into custody, but evidence lacking that she had done the act, she was let go.

"What is to be done if sufficient evidence can't be obtained to warrant what we know to be true about the cause of injury and perpetual wink of our fellow citizens? The long blonde hairs found towards the axe handle were clearly those of Mrs. Kellogg. Investigation of crimes by authorities must be enhanced, even as we physicians toil to improve our profession," Dr. Acers said.

My mind revisited the night in Uri's stable… *Would the sheriff have been called if the deceased was Indian—doubtful*, I thought. *Surely, there had to be a grave somewhere on Uri's property.*

On another note, Dr. Acers reminded us that the Delaware County Seat would transfer by year-end from Delhi to Manchester, when société médicale meetings would also transfer to a building to be determined.

He also read the list of names of the physicians who had signed the society's Constitution and paid the $1.00 fee: J. W. Bobbins, W. H. Finley, W. A. Morse, J. M. Banning, and A. A. Noyes, and others. Additionally, he noted that Dr. Albert Boomer was absent from the meeting, as he had just been appointed County Agent for the sale of spirituous liquors.

He took a vote about whether to invite Dr. A. B. Ward to speak on "The Consummate Need for Credible Hospitals in the State" at a date convenient to Dr. Ward, the same presentation he'd given at the Bremer County Medical Society, where he was an esteemed member. None objected, and I offered to extend the offer to speak to Dr. Ward.

Finally, he urged Delhi physicians to take a leadership role in securing a rail line through their towns. Unfortunately, the Dubuque & Pacific Illinois Central train route had swerved three miles to the north of Delhi. He now personally backed the Great Northwest Railway Company's petition, asking for an election to determine whether the people of Delaware County would give aid of $250,000 in construction of the railroad across the county. The vote was scheduled by year's end.

At the meeting's conclusion, I spoke privately with Dr. Acers to inquire as to the well-being of Mrs. Stout and her young son.

"Has she need of another hired hand on the Stout farm? I know of those looking for work."

Dr. Acers confessed that he and his family themselves had recently found need to seek room and board with Mrs. Stout— after his framed house, said to have been "the meetest in the county," burned to the ground a month earlier. The event happened after ordering his hired man to build a fire in the yard, as his folks were ready to make soap; seeing an hour later, the order not obeyed, Dr. Acers commenced to start a fire himself. Somehow the home caught fire and could not be saved. He would rebuild the home—with brick.

A long pause followed as sizable tears welled up and threatened to drop from his eyes.

He added, most offensive to him was that the fire had destroyed most of the copies of the book he had written some years before to prove the Bible is not inspired. That loss was almost as difficult as when his village of Acerville had failed.

Finally, Dr. Acers whispered his report of Mrs. Stout… *She had met with the "other woman" after Dr. Sharp's trial…who admitted Dr. Stout and she had first met when he treated her for a stubborn cough. In his desire to offer her comfort, it just happened… They fell in love.*

—

Stepping through the front door of Stone's Grocery, I noticed the bell strangely clanged like a stiff cowbell. Then, I became aware the market's whole interior had undergone substantial change.

Above the long wooden counter at the store's rear now hung a large sign:

DEALER IN DRUGS, MEDICINES, PAINTS, OILS,
DRY STUFF, GROCERIES, HARDWARE, BOOTS,
SHOES, STATIONERY,
AND TOILET GOODS
TRADE FOR MILK OR EGGS!

A half-dozen hundred pounds of sacked flour and sugar lay piled on the floor next to the counter.

The legumes bins had shifted to the left wall.

A section dedicated to calico, yarn, clothing, flannel, and shoes was arranged along the eastern wall. Above, notions, pins, needles, and thread hung another sign.

Perishables were in another designated area.

BACON — 2.5 CENTS A POUND
FLOUR — $1.25 A HUNDRED
EGGS – 3 CENTS A DOZEN

A section advertised "Men's Clothing, Tats, Tools, Nails, and

Miscellaneous Stuff."

KNIFE — 35 CENTS   BOOTS — $2.60 A PAIR

SHIRT — 80 CENTS   PIPE — 42 CENTS

Horse collars, saddles, harnesses, snowshoes, traps, and hunting supplies dangled from the ceiling.

An upsized scale next to the roll of brown paper and ball of string on the counter—where a calico cat now groomed himself.

Rows of glass jars, holding an assortment of items from pickled pigs' feet to herring to beans, sparkled on shelves from beams of sunshine piercing the new larger western windows. The otherwise dimly lit store was now bright and cheerful.

Mr. Stone appeared through the rear doorway. He still wore the full attire of a modern merchant.

"Mrs. Stone shall arrive shortly, whose memory is better inclined toward those specific to Mrs. Wiltse's liking—or may I fulfil your order," he said cheerfully.

Even though we had long ago become close friends, he addressed me professionally as Mr. Wiltse, and Phebe as Mrs. Wiltse.

I handed him Phebe's list. He took it and laid it aside to resume working on a previous order.

As I turned away, I caught sight of a new woven circular rug covering the spot where Dr. Stout had lay gasping for air. Gone was the *arôme de vinaigre*.

I walked to the pickle barrel to peer at the puzzle board, expecting to hear Mr. Stone's gasp.

I only heard paper being torn from the roll on the counter, the twirl of the bobbin as he pulled a length of string, and the single crisp snip of a scissor.

"In the spring Mrs. Stone convinced me we should travel to the Mississippi River where we connected with a shipment of new market stock," he said, pulling food stuffs from shelves, bins, and drawers. "Thou may wish to bring Phebe to the market…we now offer tea from China, dress goods from France, and dishes from England, and much more."

"Oui—though she rarely accompanies me on voyages to Delhi…as we now happily reside at The Point, and there is a fine mercantile there."

My hand brushed the back of the chair where Dr. Stout had sat that day. I again took the seat across from him and recalled the camaraderie we'd shared—Dr. Boomer, Dr. Stout, Mr. Stone, and myself—enjoying coffee and tartes seated around the puzzle. I recalled then hearing the clang of the bell, and out of habit had turned to see who had entered the space. Tears filled my eyes.

I'm sorry I didn't protect you, my friend. I'm so very sorry. Wasn't it pretty to think this couldn't happen.

I looked up as a woman entered the store carrying a letter and sizeable package. Inexplicably the bell remained silent, *hung up in the mechanics*, I imagined.

The woman walked past me without noticing my frame slumped in the chair.

Hot tears continued flowing down my cheeks. I reached for a handkerchief in my pocket, wiped my eyes, then relieved a built-up accumulation in my nose.

"Mr. Stone," the woman began, "I have received a letter from my sister, and I would have thee read it to me. Plus, I have a package, please see to its safe delivery to the name as I've addressed it."

Mr. Stone accepted the package, and placing it on the counter, pulled the letter from its envelope and began to read out loud. The woman's sister had written to tell of the birth of her tenth baby and to express worries about the economy.

When Mr. Stone finished, the woman departed, and he refocused his attention on my order.

"The store is exceptionally calm today, Mr. Stone," I said.

He ceased his labor, and I felt a sympathetic stare fall upon my shoulders.

"At first, people came in to see the place of Dr. Stout's tragedy… I'm glad that episode is over. It might remain hard for thee to sit at the puzzle board."

I nodded and stared at the floor as tears dripped down my cheeks.

I heard the sound of Mr. Stone resuming his work, though it was in his nature to try to improve the mood.

"Have thou noticed, Mr. Wiltse, that Silver Lake, the pride of Delhi, nearly two miles in circumference, is slowly and mysteriously disappearing? We are dismayed at the possible loss of such a treasure."

I dabbed at my eyes before turning in the chair to address him.

"I was unaware…as we speak, Cousin Uri prepares for the annual boat race on the lake in the spring. He is counting on winning the first prize—a handsome ten-dollar bill."

"Uri hopes to impress his new bride, with certainty. Whilst Miss. Silvia Kelly comes from good stock, should I have been consulted, I cannot say I recommended the union."

I turned away, a signal he had overstepped the bounds of appropriate commentary.

"I am weary, Mr. Stone, and wish to return home to my Phebe in time to hear prayers with my children before bed. Haste, please, I beg of you."

Once more, I heard paper torn from the roll, the twirl of the bobbin, and snip of the scissors.

"I have thy decree content now, Mr. Wiltse—and I must report, even with the sale of your drugs, thy receipts hast grown considerable."

—

The bubble of speculation burst in September 1857, creating a financial panic across the country and the world. Within three weeks banks closed and railroads defaulted on their bonds. A sharp increase in unemployment and a money-market panic on the European continent followed. Autumn harvests, however, proved bountiful—though dealers had no money and could not sell the grain, even at fifty cents a bushel. The farmer's wife was compelled to give two pounds of butter for a yard of calico.

At the same time, America moved closer to a violent civil war, a second revolution as great as the one that had severed the connection with the mother country, England, in 1776.

Another harsh blow followed. Iowa Governor James W. Grimes, before leaving office in January 1858, had pardoned Dr. Sharp for the murder of Dr. Stout. Murder, according to the definition of the Iowa legislature, was the unlawful killing of a human being with malice aforethought. Apparently, Gov. Grimes thought Dr. Sharp's crime of *passion* was without penalty. Even when murder is brought to the full light of day in a courtroom, it did not necessarily mean justice prevails in the eyes of the community at large.

The image of the murder in Uri's stable once more reared up in my memory. *What justice had there been for that victim?* 'Twas another reminder to me to search for an unmarked grave on Uri's homestead.

—

That summer Phebe's garden grew heartily amid the earthly stress of a financial panic and an impending civil war. As the vegetables matured, increasingly she looked forward to making Canadian prairie poulet stew on her grand cookstove. I begged an invitation from Dr. Boomer to hunt for prairie chicken at his farm, and within the week, he and I waited for birds to take flight amid wave after wave of booming sounds—loud, deep, and resonant— arising from his damp, foggy prairie.

Rifles at the ready, Dr. Boomer sent out his dog to stir the prairie chickens from the prairie floor. Waiting, we found ourselves again commiserating over Dr. Stout's senseless death. Dr. Boomer said he had learned more about Dr. Sharp's family history. He was raised in Ohio—and had come from good stock; the Ohio Sharps were strong Union supporters. Dr. Sharp was a Southern sympathizer, as we knew well.

"Would that explain Dr. Sharp's desire to one day murder a colleague?" Dr. Boomer asked.

Admittedly, neither of us were well acquainted with diseases of the psyche, though I reasoned, if a woman had displayed an ungovernable temper…sullen, wayward, malicious, defying all domestic control, or in want of restraint over the passions, she would be diagnosed with "hysteria," and sent to an asylum for the insane.

"Why had we not acted so when witnessing these tendencies in Dr. Sharp?"

Dr. Boomer gave no reply as he stared at the field void of birds. "The birds were lax to cooperate," he said, "seemingly preferring to hunker down until they find sun enough to warm up and dry off."

Our conversation moved to a reoccurring subject: Bennett Medical College in Chicago. The building was complete although a civil war might delay its opening. I conveyed to him my continued interest.

Dr. Boomer added that civil war was likely unavoidable and would surely ensue as soon as Abraham Lincoln was elected president. He hoped to be among the first volunteer physicians to fight for the just cause of freeing Negro slaves in the South. After winning the war for the North, he would become a prohibitionist.

"Will ye enlist, Alexander?"

"It would be a strong burden on my dear Phebe."

"As we speak, mah home is ridden with diphtheria…three o' mah ten children are very ill. Charlotte wull bear up well under th' strain o' thair care in mah absence."

The morning sun finally burned off the fog, and Dr. Boomer again sent out his dogs. By noon, he had shot a dozen birds. I managed to kill two with my Parker.

Departing his farm, he handed me his birds to deliver to Phebe.

"I shall give these in exchange for Phebe's prairie chicken recipe for mah wife."

—

I delivered the three-pounds birds to Phebe and watched her carry them outside the cabin to preserve her kitchen from the unnecessary disarray of dismembering the meaty breast from the entrails and feathers. Making the *roux* for the dish was easy, she said: Mix equal part fat to equal part flour, cook until it forms a ball in the pan before slowly adding liquid—fresh cow's milk, preferably—stirring constantly to the desired consistency, then add an onion base, thyme, and other herbs. Finally, add tender peas, which Phebe had dried from her spring garden, and integrate pieces of bone-in prairie chicken meat into the sauce, topping it all with spoonfuls of yam biscuit dough before placing the pan in the baking oven 'til the biscuits are brown and crusty.

An hour later, Phebe pulled the saucy, flavorful stew from the oven and placed it on the table centered between the place settings. Since a boy, I had particularly enjoyed this dish, then made by my Mère. I retrieved the ancestral conch shell from the kitchen windowsill, where Phebe preserved it out of reach of our young children. I blew it mightily. Although old—it was perfect. Tears filled my eyes as I remembered those who had sacrificed so much for my family to come to this great country.

Like Uri, our family had done well for ourselves in America.

—

The following spring the *North Iowa Times* began to report the whole nation had filled with young grasshoppers—just hatched, from an eighth to three-fourths of an inch long. They had amassed some two inches thick on railroad tracks, delaying departures forty minutes and longer. Fear and supposition grew in the following weeks that they would eat crops and other plants, state to state, and create unprecedented human famine. The Hudson Bay Company in Canada reportedly ordered shipments of pigs, flour, and other dispositions to sustain supplies and fulfill orders.

As it turned out, what grasshoppers there were had grown fatigued in their attempt to traverse wide bodies of water like the Red River and were consumed by countless fish where they landed. I was happy I hadn't succumbed to Mr. Bomgartner's suggestion to forego planting my fields that spring, for the crops in Clayton and Delaware Counties proved bountiful in the fall, and there was plenty of feed and cornmeal to deliver to the mill at The Point.

From tales of grasshoppers came rumors of acts of aggression leading to the onset of a civil war. An alleged Negro-led insurrection in Kansas also turned out to be a hoax.

Meanwhile, Phebe continued to pass on valuable life lessons to our enfants. To Charles and Edwin, she admonished: "When you marry, be sure to get a femme who is clean and a clean housekeeper. There is no maison so poor that it cannot be kept clean. And when you have children, be sure your wife teaches these things. The training you give a child goes with them throughout their whole life."

—

A bright light went dark in late fall when my mother passed away. Mère Rachel met Phebe in the kitchen at dawn appearing as healthy as one who would surely live to see another day. Around noon, Phebe looked up from her work in time to see Mère Rachel collapse to the floor, without letting out so much as a whimper. 'Twas the result of an attack of the heart or brain, I ascertained. Baby Lucettie, tied about the waist in her high chair at the table, was the last to see her *grandmere's* face. Phebe said…she had a peaceful glow, as one suddenly called up to stand before the throne of God.

DIED

The dear mother of Dr. Alexander Wiltse of
Strawberry Point, RACHEL DUNHAM WILTSE,
passed from this world to the next on November 19th.
Rachel Dunham Wiltse was 57 years, four months, and
17 days. She was born to Joseph Wiltse and Drusilla
Howland Wiltse in Yonge, Leeds Upper, Canada, and
leaves behind a husband Philip, and numerous
children in Canada. She emigrated to America 3 years
prior with Dr. Wiltse, his wife Phebe, and 3 enfants.
Throughout her ensuing years in America, she
demonstrated a strong pioneering esprits to the end.
She was a dame of great faith, oft stating, "My God
shall lead me whatever the circumstance." She had
but one regret: "Never did I take a stagecoach ride."
Rev. S. C. Churchill of the Manchester Circuit
officiated at the home of Dr. Wiltse, with burial at
Cass Township, Clayton County cemetery.

I mailed a letter to my eldest sister Carolyne in Ontario to let the family know of our mother's passing. I would await her reply, though the winter was upon us when mail service by the way of the river was suspended.

During our evening prayers before bed, I chose to delay telling Phebe of my search for an unknown grave on Uri's property. I had found such a mound but wished to first speak with Uri.

—

Recovery from the nation's depression began in early 1859, when Mr. Elvidge and I placed our first joint advertisement in the *Clayton County Herald*. Mr. Elvidge surprised me by incorporating the sale of compounded drugs with his offerings— seemingly uncontrite of any infringement it might have on my medical practice.

WILTSE & ELVIDGE

Wholesale and retail druggists, Strawberry Point,
Iowa. Dealers in all kinds of Medicines Liquors,
Patent Medicines, Paints, Oils, etc.
—Dr. Wiltse will attend to professional calls
at any hour of the day or night.
Office in Bailey's store on Main Street.

CHAPTER TWELVE

War Of The Rebellion

Lloyd Bartings, a young German man in his mid-30s, had stopped by my office in the fall of 1859, complaining of uncontrollable shaking. I observed him for well over twenty minutes as his limbs danced of their own volition. His speech was slurred, and he displayed involuntary outbursts of swearing. He said his symptoms escalated year to year. So profound was his affliction, I was certain it would lead to a slow, miserable death, *like being stalked by a murderer.*

I searched in nosology—a list of diseases—of the 170 ways people were dying: abscess, canker, carbuncle, cramp, eruption, hemorrhoids, spasms, tetter, thrush, and worms—which did not normally kill. More people likely died with these things, not of them. Most deaths were from simple vitamin deficiencies. Deaths by black tongue, chlorosis, jaundice, rickets, scurvy, and perhaps even dirt-eating could have been cured with a simple multivitamin or a more steady, sensible diet. A second subset of mortality was due to cancer, heart disease, and apoplexy, or from tuberculosis, cholera, and infectious diseases. Sooty wood-burning stoves and tipped kerosene lamps caused homes to catch fire, which took many additional lives.

I found no disease specific to Mr. Bartings' disorder, although I planned to call on him with regularity to record the progress of his ailment. He lived alone in his cabin in the wetlands. Unfortunately, the winter route in 1859-1860 proved mostly impassable by wagon and ox-team, or by foot in my tall gumboots, forcing me to wait for spring.

Largely, my new clientele at The Point consisted of those suffering from mid-winter ague—chills, fever, and sweating at regular intervals, common to those living near wetlands. Frostbite, too, was common among people of all ages. I dispensed colchicum to others with gouty arthritis. For a dame who'd fallen while hanging laundry on a rope strung across the confines of her home, I plastered her broken left wrist. One elderly woman I diagnosed with disease of the urinary system—diabetes mellitus. Drinking the urine was the way to detect diabetes; hers was exceedingly sweet. Dr. Ward's medical book recommended the patient eat only the fat and meat of animals or consume large amounts of sugar—I suggested the former. She had cracks in her feet that became pussy sores and kept her bedridden and in pain. I monitored her progress. My fee of two dollars she paid in produce, a little salted meat, and pickled vegetables from her garden.

When I finished treating humans, frequently I was directed to stables, coops, and shallow coverings among the trees to treat cattle for 'the slows,' brucellosis in sheep, or coccidiosis in chickens and pigs.

Foremost in my mind on this February morning was the birth of our twins. Phebe's labor continued for twenty-eight hours, alarming me to the point, wherein, trembling but resolute, I withdrew a surgical knife from my bag in preparation for a cesarean section. Better to lose one, than two—or all.

Baby Sophia arrived on the early afternoon on February 20th, healthy and with the creamy smooth complexion of a newborn lamb. I listened for the second heartbeat that had grown increasingly faint during the birth. Before the sun broke on the horizon of the new day, as Phebe slept in an exhausted state, I reached my hand into the womb and gently withdrew the second enfant, feet-first, from the chambre. Swaddling the bluish newborn, I carried her to the kitchen where I tried with everything that I knew to save her. Around dusk, while gently rocking her in my arms, I felt her *esprit* release and rise, as a whippoorwill alights from the forest floor and disappears into the foliage of a birch tree at the river's edge…departing without ever opening its translucent eyes or singing its première night song.

For another hour or so, I regarded her long, dark eyelashes as they lay upon her soft cheeks. I caressed the folds of her wrists and fingers and toes. Twice I kissed her on her forehead—once for me and once for my Phebe before bathing her in perfumed water. Then I dressed her in one of the baptismal gowns Phebe had sewn and carried her to the corner of the Osage-orange hedge outside our bedroom window. As Phebe slept, I buried the second twin in a warmed blanket in the icy snow. A flat stone shaped like a half-moon marked her grave.

Such action might have been thoughtless, I told myself, but I simply could not ask Phebe to bear the loss—one, who for now seemed wholly content in giving all her attention to baby Sophia. We would talk about the loss of *the other* when Phebe was stronger. She would be alright though she would never have more children.

—

It was afternoon by the time I reached my office in Bailey's store, and I was *chilled to the bone*—or, as my Dutch ancestor would have said: *Ik was tot op het bot gekoeld*, or in Canadian French: *J'ai été refroidi à la bon*. Such were the exchange of languages that boomeranged in my brain.

I saw signs Mr. R. Elvidge had been here recently. His desktop held rifled papers from the Franklin Health Assurance Company, notes, pencils, and sundry other items were strewn about—'twas a different mess from the previous week. I had come to realize potential clients didn't readily seek out his service. While insurance was a new way to spend a pioneer's hard-earned cash, people had rapidly learned to work the system. *Calamité* in life was guaranteed. Having insurance coverage when calamité hit—home and property, and death, especially from cholera—became a game of chance. Only southern states offered insurance for death or damage of slaves.

I lifted a newspaper from Mr. Elvidge's desk and walked to my chair, scanning a headline: "U.S. Depression Recovery Continues." I was reminded no coverage was available for some calamities.

My desk sat five feet from the iron firebox. I could tell Mrs. Bailey had been in the structure tidying up. My first clue was the dripping mop and other cleaning supplies left along the back wall. The second clue: the blazing fire in the firebox. She found out I came into the office on Mondays and Thursdays.

I waited to unbutton my winter coat and remove my gloves. My eyes were drawn to the announcement of a remedy for cancer on the front page.

Cancer Cured

A cure for cancer has been found by a Dr. Fell of London six or eight years ago, by placing a piece of sticking plaster over the cancerous area, with a circle cut from its center a little larger than the cancer, so that a circular rim of healthy skin next to the cancer was exposed. Then a plaster made of chloride of zinc, bloodroot, and wheat flour was spread on a piece of muslin the size of the circular opening and applied to the cancer for twenty-four hours. Upon removing the muslin, the cancer is found to be burnt into it, appearing the color and hardness of an old shoe sole, and the circular rim outside of it appears white and parboiled, as if scaled by hot steam. The wound is dressed, the side rim soon separates, and the cancer comes out a hard lump, and the place heals up. The plaster kills the cancer so that it sloughs out like dead flesh, and never grows again.

Such remedies were often proven false. Why then claim a cure for that which is known false? *Fame and money*, I imagined. My homemade brew of laudanum and brandy—an anti-cholera medicine—remained popular and a steady source of income, and it worked.

If only a remède could be found for heartbreak.

—

I became an American citizen in the spring of 1860 and felt it was my patriotic duty to participate in seeing justice carried out. Sometime during the previous year, a man, Andrew Ostland, had been cruelly murdered in Dubuque. N. A. Johnson was arrested for the murder, and after a two days' trial, the jury of a dozen men returned a guilty verdict of murder in the first degree. Judge

Wilson decreed that on May 18th, between the hours of 10 AM and 2 o'clock PM, N. A. Johnson was be taken to some convenient place within the corporate limits of the town Delhi, and there be hanged by the neck until dead.

On the appointed day, several thousand people—men, women, and children—assembled at the site of the newly constructed gallows. A posse of citizens, summoned to act as guards, formed a hollow square around the site at the northwest corner of the Court House Square. On one side of Johnson walked the newly-elected Sheriff Eddy; on the other—the priest, followed by the Hon. Joel Bailey, and other county officers. The prisoner ascended the scaffold with a firm step. After making his final confession to the priest, his hands were tied behind him and the black cap drawn over his face, shutting from his sight forever all mortal scenes. There was no disturbance, no tumult. No one attempted to interfere. With one blow, Sheriff Eddy severed the rope, and the doomed heavyset Swede fell. Death ensued immediately, his neck being broken by the fall. This was said to be the first execution in Delaware County.

I heard it said by those standing nearby, "Mr. Johnson surely deserved hanging, a good honest hanging."

I looked into the faces of the children standing at the sides of their mothers and fathers.

What did they think of such brutality? What impact of the day would they carry throughout their lives?

The hanging came at the time when the state of Iowa was debating capital punishment on whether the gallows was a "divinely ordained" institution necessary to deter crime, or a terrible wrong. Both made their cases from Scripture.

On my way home, it felt as though I had participated in murder.

—

Phebe grew increasingly bad-tempered with each passing week. I reasoned it was from the required care of a newborn who deprived her of sleep and much-needed rest. Plus, the death of Mère Rachel had elevated Phebe's household responsibilities.

Père Philip, who bore much on his shoulders from the demands of Mr. Bomgartner, sought to relieve her of her garden duties, only to be chased away by her uncharacteristically, uncharitable insults.

I asked Dr. Boomer for advice, one husband to another.

"Phebe has not been herself since the birth of Sophia… She appeared happy and content at first but has succumbed to an ungovernable *tempérament*…more sullen with every passing day."

"Ye need to secure qualified hulp fur a time," he said. "And yer wife kin require an asylum fur a period o' rest."

In his tone I thought I heard…*remember the lesson of Dr. Stout.*"

A few days later, Dr. Boomer brought by a young girl named Gilda, and presented her to Phebe as an aide…"Just 'til Sophia begins to sleep through the night," he said.

Phebe swiftly disappeared with Sophia to our bedroom, closing the curtain 'round her. I followed. From outside, I heard the sound of Sophia nursing.

"Do ye wish Gilda to remain?" Dr. Boomer asked in private.

"For now… We'll wait to see if Phebe will chase her away."

"Remember, Phebe may require an asylum fur a period o' rest," he whispered again while preparing to leave.

His words swarmed 'round in my head and made me feel quite ill.

—

In November 1860, Abraham Lincoln, a giant of a man, or so I was told, was elected President of the United States. *Hurrah for Lincoln!* the *Elkader Journal* headline read. The vote of the county was: Lincoln: 2,089; Stephen Douglas: 1,572, John C. Breckenridge: 14.

Within a month, South Carolina seceded from the Union, followed by ten additional states, and establishment of the Confederacy. Then came news of the Confederate bombardment and fall of Fort Sumter—and commencement of Civil War.

The Wiltse family was well acquainted with the *boucherie* and *sauvagerie* of war. I knew well the story of Philip Maton de Wiltsee—then spelled with two *ees*—a Walloon Huguenot soldier of fortune who had first set foot in America in 1623, arriving from Holland on the ship *Netherland*. He had served under Prince Morice in Austria against Spain and was employed by the Holland West India Company at Fort Orange, the original Dutch settlement in New Netherland.

Philip's family was part of a detail of eighteen families sent to settle the area to build Fort Orange—which eventually became the city of Albany. For several years, the Indians were all as quiet as lambs and came and traded with all the liberty imaginable. On a day when Philip had taken sick, a horde of Delaware Indians fell upon the fort and massacred every adult man in the settlement—totaling thirty-two. That almost ended the life of my first ancestors in America.

Unbeknownst to anyone until many years later, the two boys, upon hearing the victims' cries and seeing the slaughter of their family and others, had fled and hid in the brush. Later, found by Mohawk Indians, they were taken up the Hudson River to Quebec and given into the hands of Jesuit Fathers Le Jeune and Jean Brebouf. There, they received a good education—even mastering the French, Latin, and Huron languages—though the priests made no mention in public of having any white children in their care.

During a visit to Brantford with the priests in Ontario, the boys, then ages 16 and 19, decided to make a break for it. They quickly learned of the location of their mother and younger siblings, who had long ago returned to Holland, and found them there. In 1656, Hendrick again came to America, bought land at Newtown, Long Island, and eventually enlisted as a soldier at Fort Orange. Several years later, he found himself with the opportunity to accompany a band of Mohawk Chieftans to a council held at Quebec, serving as an interpreter.

Four Wiltses—the spelling changed again—enlisted and fought in the French and Indian War of 1760 and the War of the Revolution in 1776: Hendrick, at 50 years of age; his son Daniel, who had enlisted two years earlier; along with Hendrick's son William; and Hendrick's grandson, Samuel.

After the American Revolution was fought and won between 1765-1783—the Thirteen Colonies defeating the British—the first European settlements transpired in Ontario, when 5,000 United Empire Loyalists—including many Wiltses who had remained loyal to King George III and the British Empire—left the United States of America to become Canadian citizens.

Benoni Wiltse, my grandfather, arrived in Canada in the spring of 1792, relocating from Hopewell, Dutchess County, Province of New York. Soon his two brothers, James and Jeremiah, and half-brother, John, arrived—and in consequence, the settlement became known as Wiltse-town. He later served in the British Army in the War of 1812.

Most recently, Uriah Wiltse and Leonard Wiltse Jr. had fought in the Mexican American War between 1846-1848.

This much I had learned about war, whether fighting against Indians, the British, or Mexico. War meant thousands of deaths— even a war anticipated to last only a few months. Those who returned home alive would limp or shuffle along the remainder of their days in shock, anger, or disillusionment, never to feel safe or whole again.

Eleven generations hence the arrival of Philip Maton de Wiltsee in America in 1623, once more our family faced war: 18 free Northern states pitted against 15 slave Southern states, father against father, and brother against brother.

—

President Lincoln's initial call came for 75,000 troops from Iowa. The men and boys came out by the hundreds from loyal Clayton County, more than was required. My assistant Perry Dewey was among the first to enlist, along with his friends John Carpenter and Leroy Parker. Cousin George Wiltse, Leonard Jr.'s eldest son, also left home to serve about the same time.

Uncle Sam swiftly rejected the application of Mr. Donahue, the man I had treated for injuries following a chemical explosion. The Union army and navy stated they required two good eyes of those who served their country. Mr. Donahue, by then, was under the care of the oculist and surgeon Dr. McTaggert, a physician at McGregor, whom I endorsed in his advertisement in the *North Iowa Times*. Mr. Searson, on the other hand, had significantly recovered from his injuries sustained in the explosion, enough to enlist. He decreed he would serve our country for the two of them.

Not long after, Dr. Acers announced all Delaware County Medical Society meetings were canceled until the war's end.

The annual boat race on Lake Delhi, too, was cancelled. Uri would instead have to fancy himself giving Silvia rides on the Turkey River on his bateau built of cement plaster and wood, and flying kites on Sundays with my children on the beach.

As for me, I would continue to strive to bring the railroad to The Point, working energetically with other committee members appointed in towns along the line of the proposed road, to secure aid to what we called the Narrow Gauge project.

Most importantly, I would diligently provide care designed to release my Phebe from her bad temperament.

A constant vow of mine was to play my accordéon more.

And so, the year was marked by the commencement of the Great Rebellion and Civil War in the United States of America.

Major General Ulysses S. Grant aptly remarked there were three great parties in the United States: The Republican, the Democratic—and the Methodist Church. What would my Methodist denomination do about the impending war with its one and a half million members? The slavery issue had already split the Southern M. E. church into two bodies.

I braced myself, knowing when our soldiers finally came home, they would return shot to pieces, body and soul.

—

In the weeks that followed, I found myself absorbed with the George Ostrander murder in nearby Auburn, which had occurred in October. Sheriff Welsh requested I accompany him and the coroner to the scene. I learned Mr. Ostrander had been married before, which made wife No. 2 jealous that she should not inherit property or land in the event of her husband's death. Meanwhile,

Mr. Ostrander flirted with femme No. 3—then asked wife No. 2 to separate from him and leave, which she refused to do. The evening followed when Mr. Ostrander walked to a neighbor informing him Mrs. Ostrander, wife No. 2, had been kicked by a cow while she was milking, and he feared she was near death.

We found the deceased woman lying on the bed in the house, with her infant child trying to nurse from its dead mother's breast. I examined the woman whose skull had been crushed by a heavy blow, and the right side of her face, over the right eye, crushed to a jelly with an eye protruding from its socket—a ghastly and sickening spectacle. In the yard nearby was found a bloody axe and a pool of blood. The little son told Sheriff Welsh that his mother was in the yard milking when his father came up behind her and struck her on the head with the axe and she fell. The lad had cried out, "Pa, you have killed Mamma."

Mr. Ostrander appeared surprised, as he evidently had not been aware the boy was nearby. It is probable the second blow on the side of the face was struck to give the appearance the unfortunate woman had been kicked by the cow.

The fiend then bore the body of his murdered wife to the house, laid her on the bed, and hurried to the neighbor. The blood of his victim on his coat sleeve made a crimson stain on the door as he entered his neighbor's house.

Mr. Ostrander was arrested for the murder and taken to the Dubuque jail. I awaited his trial, where I would testify.

This was believed to be the first murder ever committed in Fayette County.

—

In the fall of 1861, I had occasion to speak with Uri about the mound I had come across at the edge of Bear Creek, a few yards from Louisa's tomb—a mound large enough to accommodate an adult homme. The explanation of what had occurred hardly seemed worth pursuing any longer, as five years had passed since I had come across the violent scene in Uri's stable. Part of me still longed to know the truth: *Was Uri a murderer?*

I found him in his pasture tending to his white Yorkshire pigs. I had neutered the male piglets before they were three months old. The hogs seemed happily consumed with rooting for acorns among the fallen red oak leaves. Uri was on his knees in the muck, checking the hairless beasts for St. Anthony's Fire, a parasite infection, I presumed. A small bucket of garlic cloves sat on the ground nearby.

Seeing my approach, he stood, wiped his hands on his cavalry trousers—then seemingly thought better of shaking hands with me and withdrew his hand.

"I don't want to infect you…difficult to tell how pig diseases transfer."

"Has disease gotten the whole herd?" I asked, scanning for the sign of raised diamond-shaped red tissue on the animals.

"No, just a few—which I need to separate," he said, pointing to a small, fenced enclosure nearby. "This one is likely goin' ta die—nothin' more I can do."

"Where will you bury the corpse?"

"I've got a spot—an animal cemetery, or sorts. Seems like pigs, deserve a proper burial, like humans and dogs. They've kept me and my wife fed with meat."

Surprised, I looked 'round me for the site.

"Nothin' to see, really…after a good rain, prairie grasses cover the mound pretty quickly," he said.

"Is that how you buried the Indian?" I blurted out. "You know, the one you fought within the stable… There were signs of a violent struggle—you remember, the night we arrived from Ontario. I've always wanted to ask what really happened, Uri."

He untethered the ring-nosed hog he'd been inspecting, and the barrow squealed and ran away.

"I suppose I should have expected your question… It's just been so long ago. I'll tell 'ya only 'cause it will help clear my conscience—then this will be the end of your questions about that night in the stable."

"*Ouais*, Uri," I agreed.

We retreated to sit on the trunk of a tree downed by the wind.

"It was late when I came home after a meetin' of us who'd served in the Mexican War," Uri began. "I went to the stable to feed and water my warhorse… The animals were on edge, pacing in their pens. I saw a shadow move in one corner and set alight a lantern. The *thing* was too grand to be a rodent or cat—but bigger than a skunk or raccoon. I thought it might be a panther or bear, and I picked up a hatchet with one hand, the lantern in the other, and skulked toward it. That's when I was attacked...I thought I was goin' ta die. I never knew anyone fight with an Indian and live to speak of it... He must have been there to steal my cow and her calf. If he'd just left when he saw me that would have been the end of it. My lantern fell and a small blaze broke out at my feet as we began the most vicious battle I'd known in my life, including the army. It ended when I heard my hatchet crack his breastbone and he dropped to the floor by the door."

Uri's voice now trembled. I thought this was perhaps the first time he'd spoken of the event to anyone.

"Uri, what did you do next?"

"I put out the fire, then sat for a long time staring at the corpse... He was just *a young boy*—about my age when I joined the army. The next morning, I rode off to speak with Père Leonard, who returned with me and we buried the Indian. He convinced me it was not necessary to report the death to authorities; I had acted in self-defense to protect my property. This was the law founded by pioneers. We gave the Indian a decent burial, at least... I'm thinking you discovered the mound."

"You must have worried every day that vengeance might be at your threshold at any moment," I said, "for you, and your Louisa."

"Yes, for days and months I waited for Indians to arrive on horseback to carry me away; Louisa, too. But over time, I realized no other person was aware he was here to steal my animals. He was missing from the clan, but none knew how or why."

So, there it was... I had finally heard Uri's story and I felt no better for the knowing.

—

In the early spring, I began calling on Lloyd Bartings at his backwoods cabin. His *chorea*—involuntary dancing—had advanced to near constancy. I increased the prescription for laundunum, as small doses did little to give him relief enough to sleep. I never found mention of his malady in medical journals. I learned he had a daughter in Colesburg who finally agreed to accept him into her home, as he required care day and night. She had found his disease distressing and his swearing off-putting. His care would be burdensome, she said, though I assured her his time was short.

The elderly woman with the disease of the urinary system—diabetes mellitus—died within a week of a foot amputation. Not from the disease, but from infection. I did all for her that was available to me.

CHAPTER THIRTEEN

Secrets Kill

What was to be done about Phebe, I did not know. My foremost thought was to send her and baby Sophia off for a long visit to her mother and father in Nillville, Floyd County, Iowa—though, simply put, neither could arrive at the residence of Mr. Henry and Hannah Wiltse wearing tattered or worn pioneer clothing. Phebe would require new dresses, bonnets, and footwear—the same for Sophia. This was the first I realized my secret about Sophia's twin had the potential to destroy that which I held most dear: The joy I beheld in my beloved Phebe. My tainted act made me a pigeon for this. Secrets kill. They kill your joy.

A few days hither, I delivered Phebe to the dressmaker Amanda Hall. She had attended *couturière* school and after receiving her apparel size chart, worked for a tailor in the region, Mr. Thomas Hogan. Phebe sparkled at the sight of a fine piece of French cloth Miss Hall put forth for examination. Lifting a corner with her fingers, Phebe marveled at its texture, stating: "It would make a very fine evening dress, indeed."

"Not a more handsome or less expensive article of such quality in the area—the cost, a mere $5.00," Miss Hall noted.

By the end of the visit, on the counter lay yards and yards of French cloth, ribbons, laces, embroidery, corals, and gold—along with cloth for baby clothes—beyond that which any others in my family had known. Such extravagance would be difficult to pay from my daily receipts. As the value of a dollar remained in flux, most clients paid for visits and medicaments in poultry, eggs, and deer meat.

A few weeks later in the spring of 1860, Vidella, Charles, Edwin, Lucettie, plus Gilda, and I said *au revoir* to Phebe and Sophia at the M. O. Walker's Line of Stages depot at The Point.

Both looked fashionable—Phebe, in particular, in her long torso stiffened with constricting corset, trimmed with braids and cords, and voluminous skirt supported by a cage crinoline, a wire hoop.

Phebe's final words to me would echo in my mind long after her departure:

"*Parlez-moi de votre chagrin*, Alex, *prenez votre temps*—Tell me about your grief, Alex—take your time.

"*Laissez toutes vos armures à la porte*— leave all your armor at the door.

"*Je veux laisser le mien derrière moi, aussi*—I wish to leave mine behind, too."

She bent over to kiss each of our enfants on the forehead and gave a peck to my cheek before stepping up into the stagecoach with our Sophia in her arms. Phebe rapidly realized she required my assistance getting her and her large, unruly skirt inside the cabin. Finally, she removed the wire hoop and handed it to me, asking that it be attached outside the coach for the duration of the trip. I gave it over to the driver who hung it from a hook at the coach's rear.

Through the window, Phebe added a final request: "In my absence, try to find some timberland, or ask Mr. Bomgartner to do so… My cooking stove was built to hold a large fire."

An instant later, puffs of dust from the wheels fell upon my suit of broadcloth and soon clouded the stagecoach from view. The stage line schedule noted their arrival at Nillville would be in five days' time. I sorely did not wish for either of them to go. My Sophia was the sweetest cherubim, my little lamb. And Phebe…the pain in my chest informed me she had taken with her—my heart.

—

Chaos erupted at The Point as our men and boys departed for the army. Women were left to take over running the farms, plus organize sewing circles in anticipation of aiding with supplies— caps, uniforms, blankets, and other items—that would be needed in in battle and hospitals.

Union men would also require encouragement. Nearing age

thirteen, Vidella informed me she had joined a letter-writing campaign, and she requested I post a letter to a Mr. Clinton G. Ennes from Ohio, a name on a list given to her by a committee member from The Point. I agreed to post it during my trip into town that afternoon. There, I found a letter from Ontario had arrived from sister Carolyne, who stated our Ontario family was most grieved to learn of Mère Rachel's death. She advised me of her plan to visit Iowa after the ice had fully gone out from the Williamsburg Canals.

With Phebe gone to Nillville, our children required much more of my time… They would dearly miss their Mère. Charles, age 12, invited me to listen to his recitations, requesting I remain silent and patient, should his words come out haltingly. I helped Lucettie learn the 7s in the multiplication times table—and Mr. Bomgartner enticed her to the idea of having him construct a dollhouse. Lastly, I encouraged Vidella to teach Gilda the preparation of French food—first a *soufflé*, perhaps.

I found myself suddenly wishing to reduce the length of my light brown hair to collar length, with the side hair covering only my ears; and my beard I wished to imitate that of President Lincoln's. I asked Gilda…was she familiar with cutting hair and trimming beards?

She responded: "*Oh, ja, ich schneide hare*—Oh yes, I cut hair."

And, of Mr. Bomgartner, I requested his aid with the garden, along with care of the livestock, crops, and all his other projects. Within a short time, together we located a piece of prime timberland in Section 14 near our farm, as Phebe had requested.

—

Admittedly, I found the South's swift military response to the outcome of the presidential election bewildering. Had southern states seceded simply because a northern candidate had won the election? Abraham Lincoln was perhaps as surprised as anyone of his victory, having received only forty percent of the vote of the three Republican candidates.

Lincoln's success was likely due to the Lincoln-Douglas

senatorial debates in 1859, when he hammered upon Douglas' refusal to admit the "immorality of slavery." The *Clayton County Journal* noted that after the Missouri Compromise, forty years prior, the slavery extension question had hardly been spoken of—but the Civil War being waged by the South was indeed over the issue of slavery.

The battle to take Fort Sumter began April 12th at the entrance to the harbor of Charleston, South Carolina. The fort held no strategic value to the North, as it remained unfinished, and its guns faced the sea rather than Confederate shore batteries. Notwithstanding, it held enormous value as a symbol of the Union, and the loss of the fort was heartbreaking to the Union.

—

Though the nation was now fully engaged in Civil War, no cost was spared in preparation for the Buchanan County Fourth of July celebration in 1861. Dr. Ward invited my family to commemorate our nation's independence with him and his family at Independence; 'twould be a full and complete program, he said.

We met at sunrise on the western edge of town. I watched Dr. Ward negotiate his careful descent from his buggy. He now walked with a definitive limp—and had picked up a noticeable cough.

We stood in silence for the national salute of thirty-three cannons, one for each state—Kansas had been added to the Union in January.

"Where is Phebe?" Dr. Ward muttered, no longer able to contain a cough. I held my response, waiting for him to discreetly discharge that which he had coughed up into a cloth he pulled from a pants pocket.

"She has departed to visit her parents in Floyd County…to present our enfant Sophia," I said.

"I am surprised thou and thy other children didst not accompany her…'twould be a long journey for a mother and a new baby alone," said Mrs. Ward.

"The man at the stage line ticket window assured me the route was well stocked and every effort had been made to forward passengers with comfort and dispatch… Phebe's father will meet them upon arrival at the depot. Months ago, we learned my mother-in-law is gravely ill with consumption, another reason 'tis a timely visit."

"I thought Phebe was giving birth to *twins*, a miscalculation surely," Mrs. Ward added, while encouraging five-year-old Griffy from his hiding place behind her skirt. He was acting shyly towards Gilda, I presumed.

I felt my face blush. A moment later, I said: "I believe I failed to present our nanny, Gilda."

The young girl managed a curtsy while holding Lucettie, nearing age 4, in her arms.

"Gilda shall reside at our maison until Phebe's return… Dr. Boomer highly recommends her services."

Dr. Ward looked at Gilda quizzically.

"Does she speak French, Dutch—any English? How's she able to communicate?"

"Only German—a little Anglais. She is brilliant and will learn more words in time. She and my hired hand, Mr. Bomgartner, enjoy their conversations in German, and she has introduced *choucroute*—sauerkraut—to our meals, though I admit sour cabbage will take some getting used to."

A sizable crowd began to press 'round us heading toward the west side of the river. We followed, coming to a stop at a two-hundred feet tall pole, where, at its top, the splendid United States flag with thirteen stripes and thirty-three stars floated in the breeze.

About half-past ten o'clock, festivities began with martial music and a brass band, under the direction of the marshal. Dr. Ward pointed out that Oxbow had sent a delegation headed by a marine band and carried the U.S. flag.

The bands started to march down Main Street. At a grove of trees, we gathered for a reading of the "Declaration of Independence," which elicited a most enthusiastic applause. Next came an eloquent address of the Rev. Mr. Smith, "The Mission of America," whose treatment of such a theme revealed the state of the popular mind: *when few predicted the country was about to be plunged into a terrible struggle for its very existence.*

A glee club sang "The Star-Spangled Banner" that was followed by more band music, a series of toasts by state and county dignitaries on the value of immigrants and pioneering, railroads and manufacturing, to the nation—and poetic recitations on the value of home and country.

Then, all were invited to a public dinner with edibles provided by the public, for twenty-five cents per ticket. Tables numbering four hundred proved insufficient and elicited a rush to locate more. The avails of all this entertainment would go toward securing a Town Bell to ring across the land, reminding us of our patriotic duty to defend the Union in the days ahead. A sign posted at a collection box stated:

> *Come one, come all. Let patriotism, mingled with rational pleasure, be the order of the day and the evening. May it ever be the Day of Independence.*

In the afternoon, we attended a performance by the Dubuque amateur minstrels and witnessed balloon ascensions—four were sent up. None with oxen. Noteworthy to our children in the evening were the blazing rockets and Roman candles sent up along Main Street.

My patriotic heart for my new homeland was filled with great enthusiasm and national pride. There was no celebration like it in all of Canada.

—

Through newspapers collecting on Mr. Elvidge's desk, I kept abreast of battles being fought and of losses to Union and Confederate soldiers. The Battle of Shiloh in Tennessee on April 6-7, 1862 had proven to be one of the bloodiest with 13,000 out of 63,000 Union soldiers killed, and 11,000 of 40,000 Confederate soldiers killed. My heart ached to learn whether Cousin George or Mr. Dewey had sustained injuries—or death.

Not until mid-year 1862 did the first letter arrived from Mr. Dewey, written and mailed from Camp Union at Dubuque, where he had been assigned to the 21st Iowa Infantry Company B. He wrote that had undergone training "to turn Iowa farmers into soldiers for the war." His commander's comment did not speak well of the intelligence of the very builders who had turned Iowa prairie into vast farms, businesses, and towns, he wrote. Hundreds of volunteers had arrived at the camp in the weeks that followed, with not nearly enough food, blankets, or barracks for all. Citizens hastily responded with donations of tents and blankets.

Mr. Dewey added that some evenings he went into Dubuque. On one such occasion, he heard anti-war sentiment from businessmen concerned about the Mississippi River trade being damaged by Union soldiers. This gave him cause to inquire: "Has the Union already lost the war?"

He also bemoaned the financial hardship and physical strain his service to the country would put upon his wife Matilda, who must run their farm in his absence. He was paid twice monthly and mailed every spare penny to her aid, and that of their two young children.

I most appreciated his closing remarks:

> *Thank you, Dr. Wiltse, for the time to serve as your assistant, if only a few months before my departure. Because of your training, I shall continue to teach my fellow soldiers to boil the water they drink. I shall write again as I have time. I am very fortunate to be literate—and daily assist others with writing to loved ones at home. I long for battle and worry there won't be much fighting by the time I arrive on the battlefield. For now, my unit guards a Missouri railroad depot with a muzzle-loading, bayonet-tipped rifle-musket issued by the infantry.*

—

At the time of Cousin George's enlistment, he declared himself measuring "5' 7¾" tall with blue eyes, dark hair, and a dark complexion. That was partially true. He had also lied about his age, stating he was 18 years old—when, in fact, he was only 17.

Lying did not bode well for one named *George Washington* Wiltse.

Assigned to Co. D 21st Iowa Infantry, at the time of his letter, he confessed to being *somewhere in the south*, but wouldn't say where, lest the mail be intervened by the Confederates and they should learn of his regiment's position.

His premier glimpse of slavery had been ghastly, he wrote— the sight of black men, women, and children working in cottonfields from morning to night, most rail-thin, residing in shanties, a dozen people in each, all treated like property… 'Twas the likes of which no Northerner would abide.

He added: "I realized then the Big Lie being perpetuated by the South was that slavery was the cause of the Civil War—when, in fact, the war was being waged by the South to protect states' rights to maintain the social order of white supremacy that had begun with the Colonial Era."

—

During this time, I found little time to make sick calls with Dr. Ward. However, during one brief visit, he invited me to accompany him to a meeting of the Oxbow Union Club at the Minton Schoolhouse in the township, wherein a resolution was adopted condemning the bitter partisan spirit which was becoming dangerously vindictive and malicious when eulogizing and endorsing the president, the administration, and the war policies. Further, the resolution urged upon all loyal, true Americans, without regard to party, to unite in supreme effort to save the Union.

I informed Dr. Ward that a similar atmosphere existed at The Point.

He invited me to join him when hundreds of family and friends gave the troops a rousing feast and send off—John Ford, John Leehey, and a host of others, those whom Dr. Ward knew well. Their only preparation for war had been, for a month prior, meeting three evenings weekly at the headquarters of the Buchanan County Light Infantry for the purpose of the drill.

Disappointingly, when it came time to depart from the

Independence train depot, the conductor led the soldiers to open cattle cars, rigged with rough board seats, where the hot sun could play upon them and clouds of dust would cover them over. Their destination: unknown.

—

In early August 1862, President Lincoln, suddenly aware of the threat of a prolonged war, realized the need for more volunteers. He asked Congress for passage of a draft, the first in American history, calling for 300,000 men to either volunteer or be drafted for a period of three years. Iowa's new quota was 10,500 men between 18 and 45 years old. The names of those subject to the draft were published in newspapers, alphabetized, and broken downwards to outer townships.

At age 39, I registered for the draft—and awaited the call to serve my country.

—

In the early morning of September 5, 1862, I found my father, Père Phillip, slumped over as he tended the garden, his ten-gallon hat still atop his head. He had passed away from a broken heart, having never recovered from the death of Mère Rachel three years earlier.

Urgently, I posted a letter to Phebe, hoping this should spur her return home. *Would this be the event to bring us together in heart and mind once more?*

DIED

The dear father of Dr. Alexander Wiltse of Strawberry Point, PHILIP MARK WILTSE, passed on 5 Sep 1862, a few weeks before reaching his 63rd year. He was born to Benoni Wiltse and Rachel Marks in Yonge, Leeds Upper, Canada, and leaves behind seven children, five of whom reside in Canada, and many relatives in Clayton and Delaware counties. He emigrated to America in 1855 with Dr. Wiltse, his wife

Phebe, and their three children. A man of unassuming demeanor and quiet servitude, he died early in the early morning tending the family garden alone. He was faithful in worship at the Methodist Episcopal Church at The Point. Dr. Wiltse says of his father, "No father loved his son more, or a son his father; he was a man to emulate in every manner." He was preceded in death by his wife Rachel, and infant son Daniel. Rev. S. C. Churchill of the Manchester Circuit officiated at the home of Dr.

Wiltse, with burial at Cass Township, Clayton County cemetery.

—

Dr. Albert Boomer was due to muster into Co. F 27th Infantry on September 16, 1862. His wife Charlotte, seven children and I planned to see the regiment off at Dubuque, at least until his departure was delayed for the purpose of burying a third child—three smitten from diphtheria in three consecutive weeks.

I felt a tug in my heart to follow my dear friend onto the battlefield, but it was impossible with Phebe and Sophia in Nilesville.

CHAPTER FOURTEEN

Letters From The Battlefield

Dr. Myers and Dr. Rawson were new members of the Delaware County Société Médicale. On a day prior, I had consulted with them over a sizable and growing tumor on W. E. Little's vertèbre. Removal of the growth was foreseeable, though none was willing to commit to surgery. We departed, leaving Mr. Little in the same condition as we had found him. I imagined he likely felt much the same as a victim struggling to take his final breaths as another looked on, doing nothing to save him.

The memory lingered well into the next afternoon when I brought my mare and carriage to a stop outside the post. The postmaster handed me four letters—one from Captain Clinton G. Ennes addressed to my sweet Vidella. I considered pulling the pocketknife from my pocket, slashing open the envelope, and reading the note. It was inappropriate for him to dare to write so freely to a young girl of only fourteen years. Only the look of shock that I imagined on Vidella's face later prevented me from doing do such a thing.

I continued on to Bailey's store, leaving my mare and carriage hitched outside the door. Inside, I quickly realized Mr. Elvidge had moved out—entirely. His desk was void of all things insurance-related. Newspaper subscriptions though had continued to accumulate, and Mrs. Bailey had stacked them neatly on one corner. Checking the firebox, I estimated she had left within the hour.

I placed the letters on my desk and poked at the coals, adding two thin logs to the fire.

Among the correspondence was one from Mr. Dewey—this time arriving in a handcrafted envelope made from a book page he'd fashioned for the purpose. Slicing it open with my knife, I mused about his thick head of black hair…he had enough hair for two Welsh men. I wondered how he marched fifty miles a day in all kinds of weather and could care for it properly. Washing it and his bushy beard would take a length of river.

His letterhead was also interesting, as he had sketched a beautiful snowy battlefield—though 'twas a clinical portrait of war, without any bloodshed, loss of limbs, or intestines spewed from the explosion of cannonballs.

He began by stating that the 21st Iowa Regiment had departed Camp Franklin in Dubuque on September 9, 1862, by barge and boarded the sidewheel steamer the *Henry Clay* that delivered them to St. Louis, Missouri. There, they boarded railroad cars usually used for freight and livestock, and started west. Along the way, more regiments from Missouri and Illinois joined them. The brigade, under the command of General Henry Fitz Warren, experienced its first battle in early January 1863 at Hartville, Missouri—seemingly a chance meeting of the two armies. The Confederates, led by Brigadier General John Sappington Marmaduke, outnumbered the Federals by over two to one. The battle ended with Confederates withdrawing to the south. Federal soldiers then traveled to Lebanon before returning to Houston. Union casualties were an estimated 7 dead and 64 wounded; Confederates: 22 killed and 125 wounded. Currently, Mr. Dewey's regiment was on its way to meet up with the 22nd Iowa, 23rd Iowa, and 11th Wisconsin regiments for the Vicksburg, Mississippi campaign.

I found Mr. Dewey's words descriptive and leaving me with the feeling I was standing next to him as he told of the sounds of mini-balls flying by his body…the smoke and dust…screaming men…the blood and smell of gunpowder…and the sight of black powder on hands and faces. Commanders were killed. There would be a lull in the fighting then rebel forces would attack again, almost on top of 'em, muzzle to muzzle.

The number of deserters, those who took unauthorized "French leave," increased sharply after their first battle. While agreeing no conscript should have to serve longer than nine months—"I could not see myself sneaking off to the mountains in the dark of night," he wrote. He added he had been promoted from Third Corporal to Fourth Sergeant.

In closing, he confirmed he and his comrades were drawing full rations and had plenty to eat...squirrels were in abundance and provided meat on occasion to make *chicken* pie. All that was missing from the feast was a nice bottle of wine.

He inserted a postscript, pleading with me, should his mother come to my office for treatment of milk sickness, that I not mention the number of killed or wounded in battle, lest she worry unnecessarily for his safety.

I immediately responded to Mr. Dewey:

> *Fourth Sergeant Perry Dewey,*
> *I have received your letter of 12 September, two weeks after your post. As you might divine, I follow the newspapers closely for word of battles involving Co. B 21st Iowa Volunteer Infantry and am relieved to hear of your survival at the Battle of Hartville. I had almost given over in despair.*
> *I found your letter most interesting and exhort you to write as often as you are able, s'il vous plait—please.*
> *Perhaps you are interested in knowing what is new at The Point. Our children have been sleighing for a week and have had the coldest weather ever experienced. Today it has moderated and is again snowing—which will make for more splendid sleighing.*
> *Also, the Freewill Baptist Church, erected at a sturdy cost of $4,000, has already proved beneficial in the holding of numerous church conventions...the activity of the Good Templars, and by other towns in the county. 'Twas a good investment of time and money.*
> *And I took your advice and opened a pharmacy at The Point, where sick persons can get medical advice or medicine, cheap.*
> *I can also report your mother, Mrs. Dewey, is growing stronger by the day—the cow that ingested white snakeroot has been destroyed, which prevents other family members from drinking the milk. I continue to treat her with brandy, charcoal, strychnine, and bloodletting. I shall explain further about bloodletting as there was not time to cover this in your training*

prior to your departure. There are many ways to bleed a patient and it's often done repeatedly over a short period of time. A single bloodletting generally consists of 12 ounces, about 6% of an adult's total volume of blood. Other principal treatments for the maladie include specific diet instructions, rest, baths, massage, blistering specific areas of the body, sweating, enemas, purging through use of diuretics and emetics, and prescriptions such as anti-inflammation creams or herbal pills.

Still another remedy I shall pass on to you (with humour) is for snake bite, though it requires whiskey, which, I fully realize, you will not have at your disposition. Do you recall a Mr. Baker from The Point? He informs me he was bitten by a rattlesnake while working in his garden last autumn. Feeling a sting to his finger, he withdrew his hand to find the snake holding on by its fangs. He happened to have a half-pint of whiskey on hand, which he consumed rapidly, then procured another half-pint, which he also drank. Mr. Baker affirmed the problem stopped. While I am not aware drinking whiskey to be a remedy for snakebite, you may wish to give it a try.

Your promotion to the rank of Fourth Sergeant speaks well of all that I know you to be. I shall check in with your wife Matilda and daughter to assure their every need is met in your absence. Everyone at The Point prays for your safety.

God go with you.

Kindest regards, Dr. Alex Wiltse

Cousin George's first letter told of the battle at Milliken's Bend on June 7, 1863, on the Louisiana side of the Mississippi River, about 10 miles northwest of Vicksburg. The Union's Gen. Grant had placed the strategic Mississippi River city of Vicksburg under siege. Confederate leadership believed Gen. Grant's supply line ran through Milliken's Bend, and Major General Richard Taylor was tasked with disrupting it. Taylor sent Brigadier General Henry E. McCulloch with a brigade of Texans to attack Milliken's Bend—which was being held by a brigade of newly recruited Negro soldiers and left it vulnerable.

McCulloch's attack struck early on the morning and was initially successful in hand-to-hand fighting. Fire from the Union gunboat *USS Choctaw* halted the Confederate attack, and McCulloch later withdrew after the arrival of a second gunboat.

He added: "'Twas a shock to my system to fight with a regiment of blacks… It proved Negro soldiers will fight hard for their liberty. At the start of the war, I wasn't sure whether I was against the war. I hoped I was against slavery, though I questioned if I had lived in the south would I not embrace the cause of southerners whose economic survival depended on slavery? On the battlefield was where I reconciled that my Methodist heritage informs me 'tis against God's commandments to place a price on another man's life and to force him into labor. I wonder why this idea hasn't taken root in southern Methodist churches. It's my understanding that colored pastors aren't even allowed to shepherd a colored congregation. Do whites believe God cares for one man over another simply based on the color of one's skin? The idea seems absurd.

"One more thought he noted: "I feel I was deceived when I enlisted…never was I told as a soldier I would be called on to make routes, construct bridges, quarry stone, burn brick and lime, cut and carry wood, hew timber, construct it into rafts and float it to the garrisons, make shingles, saw plank, construct mills, drive teams, make hay, herd cattle, build stables, construct barracks, hospitals, and the like, which takes more time for their completion than my period of my enlistment will allow."

Finally, he alerted me that epidemics of dysentery, typhoid fever, pneumonia, mumps, measles, and tuberculosis were rampant among soldiers. He himself had fallen ill prior to a battle at Milliken's Bend, Louisiana. After first attending to the wounded and dead, he got himself to a division hospital for treatment and was out of commission for a brief time. He urged me to quarantine any man returning from the war.

I wrote a short response:

Dearest Cousin George,
I am sorry to hear of your illness and am certain the
division hospital will provide as good a treatment, or

nearly so, as that which I could provide in your situation.

It is with considerable relief to learn of your survival at the battle at Milliken's Bend. I find your comments about the African Americans insightful. I, too, find myself occupied with the reasoning behind the Civil War. It appears on the surface white Americans believe they are smarter and more civilized than Negroes, and 'tis their God-given right to subjugate the colored. As Christianity is central to my life, how can one say you love God and not your fellow man, whatever the color of their skin?

Religion has become a central theme in the American Civil War experience. It has given Americans at war a vocabulary through which to understand life and death, a rationale for fighting (or not fighting) for one's country, a moral compass, and an institutional means of providing relief to soldiers in the field and people suffering on the home front.

Additionally, I report bad news from the home front. You may not be aware but after the birth of Sophia, ma chère Phebe entered into a phase of moody temperament, upon which I urged her to take Sophia to visit her parents in Floyd County. As you know, Phebe has longed to be reunited with her family since our arrival in America, and now my mother-in-law suffers from consumption. Phebe and baby Sophia departed several months ago, and I dearly miss them both. I wrote and exhorted their return following the death of my father, Philip, on 5 September 1862—but there's been no word from Phebe as of today. Keep them in your prayers, as we pray for you.

Take care of yourself as you fight heartily for the future of a united America.

Warmest regards, Cousin Alex

Surprisingly, Dr. Boomer found the time to write, albeit a brief note. He stated that duty had taken his regiment first to

Jackson, Tennessee to guard the railroad from Corinth, Mississippi to Memphis 'til June 2, 1863. He had full charge of the regiment on occasion, until such time his service as surgeon should be required on the battlefield.

I was most excited to learn of the "surgical kits" being dispensed by the government containing tools for general surgical procedures, including tourniquets, knives and scalpels, capital saws, tenacula, and artery forceps; also trephining tools for cutting the skull to treat hemorrhages, sub-dural abscesses, and depressed fractures of the skull. The main trephine tool was a T-shaped trepan with a bladed cylinder at one end. Other tools for trephining were the Hey's saw, and the elevator for scooping and lifting small pieces of bone. He assured me these kits would soon be made available to every surgeon in the country.

He added appalling news of an event that began in Nashville and soon become commonplace—that of "public women" descending upon the camps by night. Officers were quickly forced to put into play disciplines to keep the men focused and away from brothels. The women, he presumed, were the wives and mothers left destitute by their men going off to fight in the war.

My response was also brief:

> *Dr. Albert Boomer—*
> *I am appreciative you took the time to write, and I read your note with great interest. I am certain you shall gain innovative medical practice from your time on the battlefield. I vow to put into practice anything that you deem worthy of transmitting to me here at The Point.*
> *I have one update from Delhi: 'Tis rumored Mrs. Dr. C. C. Sharp #1 relocated to Keokuk after the trial and travels by train to visit her married daughter in Burlington, plus another in Garnet, Kansas. I find I continue to fear for her life. Dr. Sharp has proven himself a vengeful man, fully capable of killing.*
> *Kind regards, Dr. Alex Wiltse*

I laid my three return letters aside for posting and withdrew the *Clayton County Herald* from the stack on Mr. Elvidge's desk.

The "Ostrander Murder" case in West Union again made the headline. George Ostrander had been initially charged with murdering his wife in October 1861. I had accompanied Sheriff Welsh and the coroner to the scene. Numerous delays in the trial occurred over the next two years. I finally testified as to the severity of the injuries sustained by Mrs. Ostrander, whose skull had been crushed by a heavy blow, along with the right side of her face, and over her right eye, resulting in her death. On October 24, 1863, the jury found the defendant guilty of murder in the second degree, and Ostrander was remanded to the Penitentiary of the State of Iowa at Fort Madison to be confined for life.

—

Newspapers largely contained reports of Civil War battles, the missing, and the dead. I recalled the day I had learned Samuel G. Knee, 29, part of the 12th Iowa Infantry, had been taken prisoner at the battle of Shiloh in April 1862—well over a year ago. The U. S. Government ardently sought his release. Most prisoners died not of ill-treatment, but of disease. I wondered if he was among those at the famed Andersonville Prison. Samuel and Mr. Bomgartner had built our house. During that time, I learned Samuel had come from Pennsylvania, settled in Colesburg, and engaged as a carpenter the same year that my family and I had arrived. More recently, before enlisting, he had vied for the position of Colesburg postmaster. With winter now soon upon the nation, I wondered if he was being given adequate rations? Did he have a blanket to keep warm? Would I ever see him again?

I searched the paper but found nothing about the release of Samuel Knee.

Nearly one-third of the total Union-Confederate forces engaged at the Battle of Gettysburg on July 1-3, 1863, had become casualties: General George Gordon Meade's Union Army of the Potomac lost 28 percent of the men; General Robert E. Lee's Confederate Army of Northern Virginia suffered loss of over 37 percent.

President Lincoln later toured the battlefield, where 51,000 men lay dead or wounded, along with horses and abandoned artillery, such that he found only a narrow trail on which to ride his horse. The Confederate Army had been defeated, but victory has no charms for men when purchased at such cost.

It was rumored that hours after delivering the Gettysburg Address, the President suffered weakness, fever, and headache on the train back to Washington, and within a few days developed widespread pustular lesions. I surmised it was "army itch"—scabies, rampant among soldiers. His absence from newspaper articles for a month led me to believe the rumor was true.

Now into the third year of the war, I had come to view President Lincoln as a gentle human being who grew into the job of leading a divided nation in its eighty-fifth year in the bitter struggle over slavery and the economic challenges it represented. Periodic newspaper photos of the President reflected the intensity with which he grappled with the issues. How quickly he had grown old.

His policies on slavery had also evolved; passionately he now sought for passage of the 13th Amendment to outlaw slavery, issuing the final Emancipation Proclamation on January 1, 1863. It freed all slaves in territories under the Confederate states. Most people believed emancipation would end the war.

I found myself bemoaning the fact I had not gone to Council Bluffs in August 1859 when Mr. Lincoln visited Iowa. But, in retrospect, Mère Rachel had passed a few months earlier, and my mind remained in a state of confusion at the loss; then came the death of our newborn twin, Annetta—followed by the passing of Père Philip. But I'd never really regained solid footing after the murder of Dr. Stout in 1856.

Iowans had first learned of Mr. Lincoln as the great political debater in his memorable contest with Stephen Douglas during the 1858 Illinois senatorial campaign. A few months later, a newspaper noted that "Mr. Lincoln went west for a little rest." As it turned out, his trip was to also consider seventeen plots of terrain he held as collateral for a $3,000 loan to a friend. It was quite by chance then that Mr. Lincoln met up with Iowa's

Grenville Dodge, responsible for much of the railroad construction in the western and southwestern United States, during which time they discussed placement of a Transcontinental Railroad. It was due to this chance meeting that the eastern terminus for that railroad was placed in Council Bluffs. Congress had passed the Pacific Railway Act the previous July 1862.

The most wonderful things come from the most innocent acts.

I stared out my office window at my Boulon and carriage on Main Street.

How I longed for *an innocent act* to appear that would return my Phebe and Sophia home.

—

Many evenings at day's end, I arrived at my dugout stable in total darkness to the sight of Mr. Bomgartner emerging through the stable door with a lit lantern in hand, walking in my direction…reaching for the reins of my carriage. 'Twas no different on this night, as I wearily stepped from the black carriage onto the icy ground. Winter had befallen Iowa once more. The landscape reminded me that Christmas, too, was on the horizon.

The glow of the lantern flashed a deep loyalty in Mr. Bomgartner's eyes as he aided my descent.

"Be careful of your footing, Dr. Alex. The snow melted earlier but refroze after the sun retreated from das afternoon sky."

"*Bon soir*! Mr. Bomgartner. How was your day's journey?"

"You shall finden out as you enter your haus," he said, pulling his brown felt hat from his head to expose his considerably reduced head of hair.

"Did you fall down the stairs?"

He shook his head and grinned.

I recalled my words inviting Gilda to cut my hair and trim my beard to mimic that of President Lincoln's. *So, this is how well she cuts hair*, I thought.

"Before I forget—I've made an appointment for you, with Dr. McTaggert at McGregor. I believe he can help correlate movement of your misaligned eye with the good eye… *Ça te plait*—if you approve, an early Christmas gift.

Mr. Bomgartner seemed stunned.

"*Ja*—I am beyond words," he said. "*Danke*, Dr. Alex."

Grabbing my black bag from the carriage, I warmly patted his arm. Every step to the cabin felt heavy and reminded me how dreadfully I missed Phebe and Sophia. *Why had Phebe still not written?*

I opened the door and stepped inside to the overpowering odor of sausages and sauerkraut that hit me like no other odor. Mr. Bomgartner had told me no matter which animal he shot on the prairie with his Hanover German .48 caliber pistol, Gilda turned it into German sausage—and layered it with sauerkraut.

My children ran to greet me. I huddled them in my arms far longer than normal, noticing Charles and Edwin had new haircuts that rendered them quite odd-looking.

The room, too, had changed. 'Twas Gilda who likely arranged making cut-out paper ornaments of trees and wreaths with the children and stringing them on sections of the walls. Handmade cards made from scraps of paper and cloth sat on windowsills. Five child's stockings hung by the fire.

"Do you carry a letter from Mère—when will she return?" Edwin implored.

"Soon, my child…very soon, of that I'm certain."

"Are you alright, Père?" Vidella said.

"I am very happy to be home with all of you…and believe I shall make one of you very happy."

I released them from my arms to withdraw a single envelope from my bag.

"I believe you have been waiting for this, my sweet girl," I said, handing Vidella the envelope.

She squealed in glee and grabbed it from my hand.

"Oh, Père! a letter from Capt. Clinton G. Ennes…addressed to me! I shall surely need to write a response this evening and leave it on the table for you to post on the morrow?"

The children followed Vidella, hoping to hear her read the letter out loud. She shooed them away and withdrew to her bed to read alone.

I sat at the table and Gilda brought me my dinner.

"What das you think of das haircuts? Ich cut Mr. Bomgartner's haar, too" she said. "Ich cut yours—tonight?" she added, removing my hat and running her fingers through my brown hair.

Famished and melancholy, I waved her off to allow me to eat.

I first bowed my head, clasped my hands, and in silence prayed:

> *Wherever you are tonight ma belles, Phebe and Sophia. You are loved and missed greatly. I am blessed... We are blessed, blessed, indeed. I look forward to your safe and swift return, soon. May God bless us all.*

CHAPTER FIFTEEN

Bridging

Dr. Ward had alerted me of the imminent construction of the first bridge to span the Little Wapsipinicon River at Oxbow. On a spring day in 1864, I invented a reason to travel there to gaze upon Oxbow's civic progress. The visit would be a welcome reprieve from thinking only of war and death.

At the western end of Main Street, I spotted the tall, magnificent wooden structure adjacent to the Minkler & Nichols grist mill. I flicked the tasseled snapper above my Boulon's head to indicate she should pick up the rhythm, keeping my eyes focused on the bridge—while, at the same time, watching for Dr. Ward's buggy and mare hitched next to the mill where Dr. Ward had his office.

I felt the beats of my heart increase as, foot by foot, the dirt road rose to meet the floor of the wagon bridge. Then, in an instant, I was upon the oak planked floor and felt the rumble of the bridge reverberate up through the wheels, undercarriage, and bench seat. Guard rails built of heavy timbers, to my right and left, extended beyond the floor high above the river. Another forty feet to my right lay the dam built of vertical logs, placed side by side, bank to bank, and beyond that, an opening in the trees along the eastern riverbank exposed the Everett and Bacon steam sawmill, from whence came the logs for the bridge. Then, I felt renewed stability upon reaching the first of two sets of pilings supporting the bridge's 280-foot span. Looking left—the river narrowed and flowed southward, coursing its way to the Gulf of Mexico via the Mississippi River.

The heavily timbered west side of Oxbow was unknown territory to me. Dr. Ward had spoken of a huge lime quarry to the south—the proposed site of a Catholic church. A grocery store and livery, too, had sprung up. A bridge would bring changes to Oxbow. People on both sides of the river would have access to the same goods and services. Catholics on the west side and Protestants on the east side would be required to merge into one community.

Turning my unit around on Walnut Street, the words of Mr. Damion, who resided along Otter Creek, came to mind. During the previous spring, from his cabin he had witnessed huge masses of ice being hurled against the pilings of the modest Otter Creek bridge built the previous year. The ice slid up against its pilings, he said, then broke with a dull, leaden thud with an explosive sound like that of heavy ordnance, followed by the sound of the foremost breach made in the crib. When boulders at the shoreline base began to tumble out, the whole structure became askew, 'til suddenly the rest of the piers gave way—and the bridge came down with a terrible crash.

The land through which the Wapsie flowed at Oxbow was for the most part sandy, according to Dr. Ward, and therefore, drifted readily with every spring overflow.

Bonne chance, sawmill bridge! I thought. *You shall need every bit of luck—and more—to survive.*

I halted my unit beside Dr. Ward's mare tied by lark's head to a post at the mill. Deafening was the sound of water plunging over the wooden rungs that turned the grist stone wheels, and the blizzard of fine flour dust filled the air and fell like snow upon my dour gloomy wool coat, grey hat, and tall black boots.

At the base of the wooden stairs, I scrutinized a professionally printed posting tacked to the mill wall.

WANTED!

*Information pertaining to a Bound Girl, sixteen or
seventeen years in age, who has fled my care and
control. Anyone giving aid in the form of food,
shelter, or travel bears full responsibility. Contact me
with information as to her whereabouts. — A. Canfield*

I climbed the narrow stairs to the short landing on the top floor, pushed opened the door, and, without knocking, entered Dr. Ward's cove.

Dressed in black jacket, the physician looked up from a

wooden arm chair where he was seated opposite a small desk. His eyes appeared moist with tears. Between his long fingers was a penned letter.

Before he could utter a word of salutation, he began hacking phlegm from his chest, a fit lasting far longer than it took Mr. Bomgartner to consume a pint of *bière*.

Finally, his lungs rattling, he decried in his typical booming voice: "I'm in mourning, Wiltse… Received word Private John Ford of Co C 9th Iowa Infantry, who had his left foot amputated after Vicksburg in May 1863, hath now died.

"I bid thee, what's his wife and young daughter to do without him? In the bloom of manhood, and in the full usefulness and efficiency of the noblest efforts for his country, he hath laid down his life as a sacrifice for liberty and the preservation of this republic. I followed him in the newspapers in battles in Missouri, Eastern Arkansas, Tennessee—Sherman's Yazoo Expedition, too… He is now among the thousands buried in Vicksburg, Warren County, Mississippi.

"Wish to god I knew who hacked off his foot…the physician likely knew naught about surgery. Controlling blood loss is imperative. Probably bled him to his perpetual wink.

"And is our nation thankful for the rendering of his life? I hope sufficiently we are. 'Tis an unholy rebellion underway."

"We suffer with such losses at The Point, too… Do you favor being called up to serve your country?"

"Some physicians might not but keep behind to care for the infirmed and women and children—thou should'st not feel insecure about thy job in this war—as long as ye do it well, Wiltse."

I nodded in agreement before moving the conversation to the heart of the consultation that I sought.

"'Tis for both professional and personal reasons I've come to you today, A. B," I said. "First, to inform you that a Mr. Little from Manchester has a tumor on his vertebras that grows month by month. Dr. Myers and Dr. Rawson from Delhi invited me to consultation—and none wish to engage in its suppression, for we could not assure Mr. Little's survival…though the tumor will surely kill him, too, eventually."

"Only say the day thou would like for me to travel to Manchester, and I shall render my meetest diagnosis," he said.

"Thank you…and of a personal nature, my visit has to do with my Phebe. With great sadness I inform you that this past February Phebe and I lost one of our twins—Annetta, though I tried all that I knew to save her. Phebe became distraught to the point I sent her and the surviving enfant, Sophia, for an extended visit to her parents in Floyd County. 'Twas many months ago—and she has written not a single word. I wonder some days if she will ever return."

"I am sorry for thy loss," Dr. Ward said, pausing before continuing. "Let me tell thee the story of Jacob Minton to show cause for what thou should do. Mr. Minton befell Oxbow about 1852 and constructed his log house in the south part of the township. He then involved himself in civic matters and was regarded well by all the early pioneers—Everett, Patterson, Myers, Conable, Wright, Clark, and others. Recently, he masterless his wife and children and went to Indiana—thence Texas, where he married a woman who departed from this township the same time as he. His first wife hath continued the management of the place, with the wholehearted support of the community, and I report she is successfully raising her children to good standing.

"The reason I tell thee this story—*hold onto thy family*. Go and fetch thy dear Phebe and child…and return them home with haste. And I bid you, give her honest reply to all things she wishes a reply to."

A tenuous knock on his door interrupted our conversation.

"Enter, 'tis open."

Miss Lucy Dean and sister Hattie entered through the haze of flour dust, both acting rather shyly on this day. They carried a long, brown-bound paper package in their hands.

Miss Lucy first directed her comments to me.

"We have walked from the cabin of Madam Fairbank, who saw thy unit parked next to Dr. Ward's mare. She sent us to inquire if young Edwin accompanied thee on thy trip…. And Madam Fairbank said to deliver this pie-plant to Dr. Ward for all the good thee do."

The girls walked to the desk and lowered the package into Dr. Ward's hands.

I responded: "I should guess that Edwin is assisting his sister Vidella and other women from The Point with assembling caps, uniforms, and blankets to send to hospitals for the care of the wounded on battlefields. Surely Edwin's rabbit, Cloudy, is at his side."

"I am eager to see Edwin and Cloudy…'tis been since last fall," Miss Lucy added.

"Perhaps I can arrange for you to come to our farm one day soon. I shall check with your aunt for a day you are available. Both sisters shall be invited, of course—though only upon the return of my wife, Phebe, who is off visiting her parents for an uncertain duration."

"Thank thee, Dr. Wiltse," Miss Lucy said.

Dr. Ward stood to speak: "And please thank Mrs. Fairbank for the pie-plant."

The girls curtsied and departed back out into the wheat-dust blizzard.

Dr. Ward continued toward the door, displaying the limp I'd come to expect.

"You can join me, Wiltse, in a sick call—unless you have other business in Oxbow. We shall call on Henry Axtell who was leading a colt when it wheeled around and kicked him with both feet, one foot striking him under the chin and the other on the temple, knocking him senseless, in which condition he remained for five or six hours. He was in a precarious condition for a day or so. I should welcome thy observation of his infirmity."

He grabbed his black bag from the bureau top by the door, and I followed him down the stairs.

At the bottom, I pointed to the WANTED poster.

"Do *Iowans* hold slaves?"

"Tis a young lass who bartered for her passage on a ship to come to America and has now fled from her duty to serve her master for three years. In such cases, she likely came to a realization the repayment was more than cleaning and cooking—I should not get involved, Wiltse—'tis but another form of slavery."

I found a corbeau perched atop my black carriage roof, *cawing* as if in agony.

"What is't, now with thee and the crows, Wiltse?" Dr. Ward said. "Do thou carry birdseed in thy hat?"

—

I read in a copy of the *Delhi Argus Journal* of the dedication ceremony at the Soldiers' National Cemetery in Gettysburg, Pennsylvania on November 19, 1863. The bodies at the Battle of Gettysburg the previous July had deteriorated quickly, and thousands had to be quickly buried in shallow graves on the field where they fell. The field soon returned to grass, stripped of the smoke of cannon fire and blood that had hitherto covered the landscape. President Lincoln put his feelings into a succinct two-minutes address:

> *The world will little note, nor long remember what we say here, but it can never forget what they did here. It is for us the living, rather, to be dedicated here to the unfinished work which they who fought here so nobly advanced.*

His words, although brief, once more left me breathless.

—

The hope of the committee that worked tirelessly on the Narrow Gauge railroad project was to lay rail north from The Point to Fayette County, plus construct an engine house with three stalls to accommodate three engines. How I longed to hear the puffing, wheezing, and panting and the rumbling of wheels arising in the valley from the approach of an imposing 4-4-0 locomotive. My optimism of seeing our soldiers coming and going from The Point depot, however, had long ago evaporated, much like steam lifting from a far-off engine on the horizon.

Newspapers claimed the turning point of the Civil War had been the battle of Antietam in September 1862, when the

Confederates were prevented from winning their premier battle on Union territory. Europe, France, and Great Britain—enduring cotton shortages—watched in the wings, eager to legitimize the Confederacy. Troops from both sides faced-off across a massive cornfield. Union troops, significantly outnumbering Confederates, fired at the Confederate's left flank and the carnage began. Confederate troops ferociously fought off offensive after offensive to prevent being overrun, turning the cornfield into a massive killing field. As night fell, thousands of bodies littered the sprawling battlefield. Both sides regrouped and claimed their dead and wounded. Just twelve hours of intense and often close-range fighting with muskets and cannons resulted in over 20,000 casualties, including an estimated 3,500 dead.

Two years later, the war raged on.

Letters from Perry Dewey and Cousin George arrived sporadically in the summer of 1864 with news of battles waged across Mississippi, Texas, Arkansas, and Alabama. Mr. Dewey again sketched drawings—one a rendering of tents raised a couple feet off the ground in the woods by placing it on a square of logs, with a small fireplace at its entrance, where he noted: "We cook rations, boil coffee, and warm ourselves after a night on guard in heavy snow." He also reported learning of smallpox epidemics in the Confederacy since the Battle of Antietam… The disease was winding its way through camp after camp.

I wrote that Mr. Bomgartner had encouraged my venture into raising sheep, stating there is always room for them on a farm, and they consume and turn into money food otherwise wasted. He proposed that I cultivate eighty acres, chiefly raising grain—planting one field with spring grain; one spring wheat. One-fifth of the farm should remain pasture. One-fifth prairie. With only one sheep to every five acres, their products would be clear gain. In the spring they would run on the sod, which is to be planted; after that they can go into pasture and will eat what the cows will not. A run onto stubbles in the autumn would not be felt when there is plenty to feed, with the addition of a little grain. The most profitable sheep were the coarser woolen breeds, whose lambs sell for higher prices, and when fattened—sell for as much as a yearling steer. His research was compelling. I demanded he procure a small herd for our farm.

To Cousin George I added a note about the Probate for my father, Philip Mark Wiltse, which had appeared in the *Clayton County Herald* in the fall of 1863. He had few possessions in this world, save for a gold watch—passed down from Benoni Wiltse. My sister Carolyne declared the watch should remain in my care. She had arrived in Iowa in the spring and took up residence at Uri's homestead, where Uri's wife Silvia and Carolyn lavished their attention on baby Warner, Uri and Silvia's first child. The boy had curly blonde locks, like Uri—or so I was told. My family would meet the child upon Phebe's return.

—

About the same time, at the end of what had been a rather unremarkable day, I returned home to find the newly elected Clayton County Sheriff John Garber on the porch with my thirteen-years-old Charles standing beside him.

Upon closer examination, Charles was confined by balls and shackles.

I had met Sheriff Garber the previous July when he asked me to complete a certificate of death for a man named Schutte at Guttenberg, Iowa. Schutte had gone to the home of his former wife, a Mrs. Heller, and there was set upon by her two boys, who attacked him with an axe and knives, and chopped him almost to pieces. I noted the cause of death on his certificate as "multiple stabbings."

"Good day, Dr. Wiltse," Sheriff Garber said as I approached.

"Why is it you have my son in chains?"

"He was caught stealing a horse—you know what they doth to horse thieves? I rescued him from a mob after hearing his surname was *Wiltse*."

"Whose horse did you steal, Charles…and *why*?"

"I w-w-wish to go r-r-retrieve Mère. Why, Père, have you n-n-not g-g-gone after your f-f-femme? W-w-we shall h-h-hardly r-r-recognize her or S-S-Sophia if they are g-g-gone any l-l-longer. D-d-do *you* not l-l-long for their r-r-return?"

Charles stammered more when he was angry or upset.

"S'il vous plait, remove the chains… I shall be responsible for my son and any costs related to the theft," I said to Sheriff Garber.

"I can let the boy off this time… Next time, you shall see him in court."

He removed the shackles from Charles, who disappeared in embarrassment through the cabin's front door.

"I should'st keep a close watch on both thy boys, ere they go down a road from which others decide their fate," he added.

I bid the sheriff *au revoir* but did not choose to follow Charles inside. There would be ample time to speak with him in coming days. I knew what I must do next.

The most wonderful things come from the most innocent acts.

—

Two days later preparations were complete for the 85-miles voyage to Nilesville. My four children—and Gilda—boarded at the wagon's rear, where food, bedding, checkers, and such were positioned for their comfort and entertainment. I directed Charles to sit on the bench next to me and handed him the reins to the bœufs. He tapped the near ox on the head with the tip of the whip, and the wagon moved forward.

"How do you imagine the crops will bear in the autumn?" I inquired.

"F-f-fields have had a-a-adequate rain; the n-n-normal number of green worms, and h-h-hail did not touch our c-c-crops beyond the s-s-s-s-spring s-s-storms," Charles said.

"We are blessed in that."

"Yes, we are b-b-blessed, Père."

The familiar northerly trail took us to The Point where we stopped so I might tack a note on my office door, directing anyone in need of a physician's care for the next week to contact another.

Charles and I rode much of the first day in silence, save for the rises and falls of laughter coming from the other children and Gilda. My mind was chiefly consumed with thoughts of our impending arrival at Père Henry and Mère Hannah's homestead.

Surely, I would find their farm as fine a place as they'd left behind in Ontario. A *grandiose* mansion. A stable full of show cows and horses. Two or three hired hands. How many of their other nine children had emigrated to America with them, I did not know.

My mind thought back to my last conversation with Père Henry while still in Ontario. On that day, he had persisted with more questions…about the death of a patient. *Had his mort really been beyond my control?* Then his tone again intimated I wasn't a good provider for his Phebe and our children. What more could I say in my defense? Nothing was to be gained by rehashing the past. Within the year we left for America.

Charles stopped the ox-team whenever we reached a cool stream to allow them to drink and rest. Around noon we broke for lunch. As the sun commenced to sink on the horizon, he found a tranquil site near a grove of trees about fifty rods from another creek.

Seeing the smoke from our campfire, a man, who identified himself by the surname of O'Conner, called on us. 'Twas on his property that we sought shelter, he said. The man was not over five feet in height—and most unusual in appearance, wearing a shirt with torn-off sleeves and collar and without boots or shoes on his feet.

I explained the purpose of our voyage, and he heartily welcomed us to stay the night. Gilda invited him—using her Germano-Anglais words—to abide with us to eat the *wienerschnitzel* she had prepared, raising the pan of flattened veal to his nose. She topped most every dish with sauerkraut.

I sensed he found the smell off-putting and declined.

"Mrs. O'Conner is awaiting my arrival for cabbage stew at our cabin just beyond the crest of the hill," he said.

I believed his statement to be a lie… He had no femme. Phebe would never allow such a ragged appearance, no matter the circumstance.

Early the next morning we resumed our journey. Charles had shown himself adept at driving the oxen, and I found myself without worry that we should end up going off a cliff or become entangled in briars.

Lucettie, age 7, had tired of playing with her dollhouse in the rear of the wagon and begged to sit on Charles' lap.

Continuing to play out in my head was my impending reunion with Phebe. I would first warmly greet Phebe's parents and any other family members. Phebe would greet her children, even before she and I exchanged an embrace. I would inquire of her health, and she would utter a polite response within the short distance of her parents' ears—her way of signaling that we, as husband and wife, would speak more intimately when alone. Nonetheless, I would search her eyes and the lines on her brow for a signal of her temperament and readiness to return home. I wondered again if she knew of the loss of our twin, Annetta? What had she told Père Henry and Mère Hannah as the cause for the drawn-out separation from me and her children these many months? Sophia, approaching her second birthday, would surely be at Phebe's side. She would not recognize me as her Père, of course, so I would need to gently approach her to get reacquainted. I imagined lifting her into my arms to gaze upon her cherub face, listening for her sweet babbling sounds. The scene reminded me once more of the day I'd last looked upon the face of Annetta… My eyes filled with tears and my chest heaved at the very memory of the loss.

Lucettie moved onto my lap as Charles navigated the oxen to a T-intersection near NEW HAMPTON—the town's name chiseled into an enormous boulder. We laid over on our second evening just beyond the village. A Mrs. Sullivan swiftly arrived at our bucolic site. Her husband, she said, was away fighting in Co. G, 22nd Ohio Infantry. The most recent letter she'd received was after the broil of Bull Run in August 1861. She feared his imprisonment by the Confederates somewhere in the deep south, though she reported someone informed her he had fled to Canada.

"I'm tired of war, why can't we compose peace with the Confederacy?"

She shared the same question as myriad women who were left to work the farms in the absence of their men. Her appearance was haggard, her long dress and apron soiled, with a few strands of curly black-greyish hair, tied up with a length of narrow plain cloth since before sunrise, broken free to intermingle with the sweat on her brow and cheeks. Her hands showed callouses and cuts and wear beyond their years; her fingernails permanently outlined in black from toiling in the soil morning 'til night.

Mrs. Sullivan invited my children to play with her daughter and two sons and bid us tarry for as long as we wished. She said my oxen were free to eat from her prairie grasses and posset cool water from the artesian well that flowed from aquifers under the ground of her farm.

I noticed her wrist appeared inflamed. She admitted to a run-in with the bull days earlier and wrapping it in milkweed for the pain.

"It might be broken," she said.

Edwin took the cue and retrieved my black bag from the wagon. Examining her wrist, I explained I was a physician from Strawberry Point. As suspected, her distal radius was fractured. I cleaned her hand and lower arm with chlorine and applied a blister.

"You may remove the blister in four to six weeks. Aspirin made from the bark of willow trees is helpful for pain. Nature will take its course in time," I said—before inquiring of other maladies on the farm, human or animal.

Mrs. Sullivan asked me to follow her to a shallow enclosure near the Little Cedar stream that flowed diagonally across her farm. For the next hour I castrated a dozen pigs.

Before our departure, she pointed us in the general direction of the Henry Wiltse farm.

On the morning of what I hoped would be the final day of our voyage, Edwin, age 12, asked permission to join Charles and me on the bench. 'Twas then a seat full, as their bodies neared the size of an adult male.

Edwin seemed eager to talk of doctoring, as always.

"Tell me, Père, of other plants useful as remedies…. And it appears chronic maladies or faults in the constitution, either inherited or acquired, is the source of death for many people."

He had been reading the books on loan from Dr. Ward, I suspected.

Before I could formulate a response, Charles, a year older than Edwin, interjected himself into the conversation.

"Why Père do you not t-t-teach me the ways of a d-d-doctor? I, too, wish to follow in your s-s-steps… Is it because of my s-s-stammer that you ignore my r-r-requests?"

It was no surprise Charles inquired of these things; I had long anticipated his question. It was time to *let the monkey out of the sleeve*, so to speak.

We spoke of these—and many other intimate things throughout the day's journey. Speaking so was a way to bridge many places where bridges are very necessary.

Curiously, Charles also wished to speak of the Civil War. "Did the southerners really believe the South could separate from America—in a way that Italy had broken away when most of the states of the Italian Peninsula and the Kingdom of the Two Sicilies were united under King Victor Emmanuel II of the House of Savoy?"

At this moment, I was duly impressed with the lessons taught at Miss Amalia's school.

At sunset, we arrived at an unimposing farm just beyond a hand-crafted sign NILESVILLE. At the top of a short winding lane stood a log cabin of middling size. A slender femme of medium height, holding a young child in her arms in the front yard stood, seemingly staring off into the distance.

I held the reins of the oxen tightly in one hand and cracked the whip above their heads with the other to get them to pick up speed.

The woman began walking toward us as my ox-team moved us up the long lane.

I thought I could hear my Phebe's thrill cries.

I turned my head toward my other children in the wagon's rear.

"Look children! I believe 'tis your sweet Mère and our Sophia."

The children screamed in unison, "Hurry, Père, hurry!"

"Step Up!" I called out to the oxen.

With excitement and trepidation, we lurched forward.

My mind was fraught with questions…

Where does one begin to restore that

which is broken between lovers?
Who initiates words when both
are drowning in a frothy, tumultuous sea,
with sorrows too deep to articulate,
unsure exactly of one's footing?
'Tis well if words flow evenly like an August river—
and everything gets said in good time;
more difficult if hurt and loss and disappointment
are held back, like waters from deep
within the earth's center, held in place
by glacial rocks since the beginning of time.
And how does one know when brokenness is restored?
And what becomes of the two vessels then, if lost at
sea?

CHAPTER SIXTEEN

Final Casualty of The War

Somehow life finds a way to go on even under the most difficult conditions. Sometimes all any man can do is to take small steps forward and be satisfied it is progress. There are always setbacks, too—most difficult when a country is *already walking on one's gums*, so to speak—exhausted by war. Who could have anticipated the unparalleled, appalling, and unspeakable murder that lay ahead?

With the coming election of November 1864, President Lincoln found himself with shrinking northern war support. His adversary was the former Union commander General George B. McClellan. President Lincoln's name wasn't even on the ballot in many southern states—as had been the case in 1860.

In Clayton County, endorsement for Lincoln was also under debate. His many calls for troops which had necessitated the draft, were highly unpopular. Some called for a county convention, stating "all those opposed to the re-election of Lincoln and the continuance of this war for the sole purpose of freeing the Negroes at the expense of the lives of hundreds of thousands of white men and imposing upon us a national debt too onerous to be borne."

That was not my sentiment. Many evenings I found myself staring at the picture of President Lincoln on our cabin wall, wondering how the daunting burden of guiding our shattered country through four years of war could be carried by one man.

In the end, President Lincoln was re-elected by a landslide—even carrying the states of Tennessee and Louisiana, strongholds of the Confederacy. Soldiers voted from the field giving President Lincoln over seventy percent of their votes.

—

The *Burlington Weekly Hawk-Eye* continued carrying details of battles. Gen. Lee's army stubbornly held out. In early June 1864, a nine-months siege began in Petersburg, Virginia. The city was a hub of railroad lines that supported the Confederate Army. The Union's Gen. Grant dug in on the southern and eastern areas below the city, extending his lines westward constantly and cutting off the railroad's supply lines. It was thirty miles of trench warfare at its worst, especially for Lee's worn-out army. Ultimately, the Union assault on Lee's armies failed to capture the Confederacy's vital supply center and caused them to suffer appalling losses. By February 1865, Lee had less than half the soldiers of Grant's 110,000 as Grant continued to order attacks and cut off rail lines. On April 2, Union forces launched an all-out assault that crippled Lee's army. That evening, Grant evacuated Petersburg, and a week later, on April 9, 1865, Gen. Robert E. Lee surrendered to Grant at Appomattox Court House.

The end of the nightmare of Civil War had finally come. The evening of Good Friday, April 14, 1865, Washington, D. C. celebrated the war's end by illuminating every one of its public buildings with candles. Candles also burned in most private homes, causing a city paper to describe the nation's capital as "all ablaze with glory."

Even so, the war had simultaneously made President Lincoln one of the most loved for preserving the Union and abolishing slavery and hated men in America.

The next day the nation awoke to a shocking headline.

***Burlington Weekly Hawk-Eye*, April 15, 1865**
President Lincoln Assassinated by
John Wilkes Booth

President Lincoln was assassinated last night while at Ford's Theater in Washington to witness the play of the "American Cousins," by Laura Keene, and occupied a private box of the second tier. At about half-past 10 o'clock, near the close of the Third Act, a man dressed in a dark suit and hat entered the box in which were seated the President, Mrs. Lincoln, Miss Harris, daughter of Senator Harris, and Capt.

Rathbone of Albany. Immediately upon entering the door, he advanced toward Mr. Lincoln with a six-barrel revolver in his right hand and a large knife in his left hand. The assassin fired at the President's head, the ball entering at the backside and coming out at the right temple. Mrs. Lincoln let out a shriek, which was followed by an announcement the President of the United States had been shot.

Laura Keene and the director of the orchestra recognized the assailant as John Wilkes Booth, the actor and rabid secessionist, who on former occasions had played in that theatre. He was an Englishman who came to this country and amassed quite a fortune in his profession. He had often rendered himself obnoxious in theatre circles by the expression of his disloyal sentiments. His brother Edwin is intensely loyal and feels deep mortifications at this sad event.

The alarm was sounded in every quarter. Calvary men were sent out in all directions, but thus far in vain.

About the same time, a desperado called on Secretary Seward's pretending to be the messenger from his physician, but being refused admittance by a negro servant, he forced himself inside and attacked Fred Seward, son of the secretary, knocking him down, then passed onto Secretary Seward's room, where after cutting down two male attendants, he cut Mr. Seward's throat. He has thus survived the attack.

The wildest excitement prevails in Washington, Vice President's house, and residences of different Secretaries are closely guarded.

President Lincoln, the sixteenth President of the United States, died this morning at 20 minutes after 7 o'clock, attended by his wife and children, the members of his cabinet, Vice President Johnson, and others.

Andrew Johnson was immediately sworn in as President of the United States of America.

Arrangements are underway to convey the body of the

President to Illinois.

E. M. Stanton, Secretary of War

It appeared the plotters aim was to paralyze the country once again by striking down the head, the heart, and the arm of our country. I wondered why had an election in our democracy brought us to war and the death of our highest elected leader, and what was to become of our nation?

News of the President's death came like a thunderbolt to The Point. Citizens were bathed in tears; a few exclaimed Lincoln's assassination had been but a casualty of war, and it would have been better in the end to have let the South leave the Union peaceably and try her hand at making a nation.

This marked the moment in time that I understood the meaning of *democracy*. Since the origin of humans, everyone had done what was right in their own eyes. Violence rose. Political crisis. Cultural chaos. Only God could put a stop to it. Democracy is of God where all men are treated equally under the law. This truth sets mankind free. Commitment to truth leads to good. The Christian faith is a strong ally of democracy.

Within days, I wrote a strongly worded editorial that I submitted to the *Sand Spring Sentinel*, stating we should be indebted to President Lincoln for the Proclamation Emancipation which had extinguished one of the greatest of national evils: American slavery. I called for punishment of all assassins and traitors, whether of high or low degree. I chose words to stimulate all loyal citizens to renewed sacrifices and more patriotic efforts, to the end that so fiendish a rebellion may be speedily crushed out and ended forever.

—

The ice on the lakes and rivers in the winter of 1866-1867 formed to a thickness of three feet or more. When the break-up came in the spring, the masses of ice in varying sizes crashed down streams like floating islands of death.

Sadly, I would learn during my April visit to Dr. Ward that the ice took out the new Oxbow bridge—along with the grist mill and Dr. Ward's office. Fortunately, he had time to move his belongings to his home as the ice congregated at the dam and water rose and overflowed the riverbed.

A new mill would be built in the coming months.

—

Following Confederate Gen. Lee's surrender in April 1865, newspapers began listing the names of deceased soldiers for whom commanders held personal effects—pocketbooks, discharge papers, watches and suspenders, knapsacks, blankets, boots, and final payment owing from the government. They were available for claiming by relatives.

For weeks we waited for the return of our soldiers to The Point.

Perry Dewey and Cousin George–and friends John Carpenter, and Leroy Parker—finally mustered out of the army on July 15th at Baton Rouge, Louisiana. George showed off his musket and accessories for which he had paid the government $6.00 to retain.

Dr. Boomer continued writing notes to me; a recent one expounded on the new approaches to medicine he'd gleaned from treating soldiers on the battlefield: "We observed the benefits of boiling stitches, covering wounds with clean cloths, and adequate hospital ventilation."

I responded with news that Mrs. C. C. Sharp #1 had died from the effects of a poison contained in a mince pie eaten just before her departure on a train from Burlington, Iowa. She was returning to her home in Keokuk after visiting a daughter. An investigation by the Des Moines County sheriff was underway.

Dr. Boomer was among the last soldiers to muster out. In August 1865, greatly weakened from exposure and over-work and impaired in health, at age 39, he was forced to retire from the army—reportedly to die. He had served admirably in the 27th Regiment, Iowa Infantry, F & S and achieved the rank of Assistant Surgeon.

'Twas a great relief to me when word came that Sgt. Samuel Knee, who after being held a prisoner of war at Shiloh for these many months, had been released—though he promptly re-enlisted and rose in rank to Lieutenant Colonel, before mustering out in

November.

—

With his return from war, I surmised Capt. Ennes would request Vidella's hand in marriage. I gave my blessing to the union. At age 16, she had blossomed into a beautiful woman—and fit well enough into the dress worn by my Phebe.

Vidella declared: "Wearing the dress of my Mère on her wedding day will bring my marriage to Capt. Ennes happiness and good fortune, such as my parents have known."

"Finding the person who's right for you requires a very subtle alchemy," I said.

The word *alchemy* reverberated in my mind. Was not alchemy then also able to *reignite* the fire of *passion* from a union decades earlier?

Since Phebe's return to The Point, she had remained cool and distant. Now, I began to imagine a drug—*a love potion*—that could remove memories of loss and tragedy from one's mind and revive the deep love that existed before *a man did the unthinkable thing that took it all away.*

I searched in Dr. Ward's medical books for the four imbalanced body fluids, called humours: yellow bile, black bile, phlegm, and blood. *Melancholia*—that which enveloped Phebe in a black veil—was caused by too much *black bile in the spleen*. I saw no advantage to subject my beloved to the prescribed treatment of bloodletting. Instead, I would encourage treatments of exercise, baths, diet, music—and drugs.

The basic ingredients in my love potion would be those found in "Lydia E. Pinkham's Vegetable Compound," used as a treatment for a variety of female sickness: unicorn root, life root, black cohosh, pleurisy root, and fenugreek seed. I reasoned adding donkey's milk would encourage a healthy immune system, reduce blood pressure, and maintain a woman's beauty. The stamen of saffron flowers would act as an antidepressant. Blister beetle was a powerful aphrodisiac. The fat of a snake would aid in reducing any inflammation, and poppy extract, would encourage sound sleep. Opium—God's gift for all that ails 'ya—

would ally to also control coughing and diarrhea.

My alchemy supplier provided many of the items. With mortar and pestle, I crushed, ground, and mixed them. The final step was to add a good wine of high alcoholic value—wherein Mr. Bomgartner was of great assistance in securing the required quantity from Cincinnati, Ohio. I generated enough potion to fill a large vat.

In the months leading up to the marriage, I encouraged Phebe to drink a small glass of the potion before bed each evening.

Phebe and Gilda collaborated extremely well on all the preparations for a feast, which included French, Dutch, and German cuisine, plus making the two-tier wedding cake. They cooked for weeks with a surprisingly subdued posture between them.

Surely, my alchemy is working, I thought.

I had long desired to have my hair cut and beard shaved to resemble President Lincoln's and decided now was the time for the new look to make me more desirable to my Phebe. I sought out the new barber at The Point for the transformation.

The wedding day arrived, officiated by Andrew Stone, who, in addition to running Stone's Grocery, served as Justice of the Peace. Upon his arrival in the morning, I offered him the potion, then a second glass—and a third. He seemed uncharacteristically free with his remarks and salutations throughout the ceremony, and the rest of the day and evening.

I grew more confident the potion contained the power I desired.

The wedding guests included Wiltses, physicians, friends, and neighbors, numbering about forty-five. They ate nearly every lick of food and consumed large quantities of German beer and my compounded wine.

That evening, I played my accordéon with the German band Gilda had chosen for the festivity—playing my instrument better than ever. I sang and danced 'til late into the night. 'Twas more merriment than I could remember of any another nuptial in my life.

In the end, the potion overtook even me.

Early the next morning, the wedding couple rose and left for

Birmingham, Ohio, where Capt. Ennes would continue, after a short honeymoon, to serve as a vessel master on the Great Lakes.

I awoke *round as a shovel handle*—very drunk—though very pleased at the rush of memory flooding my mind of our eldest daughter's wedding day.

I searched for Phebe with my hand across our straw bed. She was gone. From the kitchen, I could hear her scolding Gilda about *le désordre of* the kitchen—then, raising her voice, she declared pleasure with herself for not imbibing in the wine in the weeks and months leading up to the marriage—or all the wedding preparations would never have gotten done.

"And surely, the wine would have inclined me to sleep in the morning after," she said—louder. Her words were clearly meant for my ears.

I heard Gilda acknowledge she had gratefully drunk the glasses of wine Phebe left unattended all those many prior months.

I wandered into the kitchen in time to hear Gilda add: "I and Mr. Bomgartner had *ein* fine time at wedding dance, too," with a new twinkle in her eye.

My mind returned to thoughts of Phebe and the *love potion*. Suddenly, instead of defeat, a feeling of triumph overcame me.

While remaining emotionally reserved, she had continued to demonstrate *un amour éternel*—endless love; after all, hadn't she chosen to return home with me from her parents' homestead and remained at my side all these many months?

In an instant, I knew the next step to take. I would ask for her forgiveness in a long-overdue note and leave it on the short bureau in our bedroom for her discovery—along with a box of three combs to put up her long, beautiful auburn hair.

> *My Dearest Phebe,*
> *I realize I have hurt you. Please forgive my insensibilities. I can be so unfit at times, acting like a bull who got into a china shop.*
> *I meant to give you these combs to wear at Vidella's marriage. I pray you will wear them in good health, remembering they come from the one who has adored*

you since first we met.
Let us work to put this thing behind us so the suffering
may pass, s'il vous plaît.
Lovingly, your Alex

Surely, this act would put all things right between us—where the love potion had failed.

—

Dr. and Mrs. Ward arrived at our farm for a weekend visit in the fall of 1866, with Griffy, age 9—and Miss Lucy, age 11, and her sister Miss Hattie, age 13. Mr. Bomgartner soon enticed our visitors—along with Charles, age 15, Edwin, age 14, Lucettie, age 9, and Sophia, nearing 5 years—with a tour of the honeybees by the apple tree.

It pleased me that Mr. Bomgartner was acknowledged around The Point as "a man who had a way with bees."

The layered movable-frame hive sat on four short stilts a few meters from the spot where the chamber pot had once been emptied. The ground, Mr. Bomgartner explained, remained permanently fouled, but the bees found the setting agreeable.

"Don't worry dass sie shall sting you," he added, giving puffs of his smoker he held in one hand while lifting the outer cover with the other hand, exposing the first frame. "Just remain das very calm."

Mr. Bomgartner puffed more smoke into the air as dozens of bees lifted and swarmed among the bodies. The children appeared rapt and stood unflinching still.

Giving another puff of smoke above the box, he invited them to step closer to peer inside at hundreds of bees crawling on the flat frame.

"Each hive hat only a single queen bee. Her job is to lay all the eggs für das colony. She places each egg deep into das bottom of a honeycomb cell, then checks das cell and measures das diameter mit her front legs. Upon finding a clean cell, she lowers her body into the cell and releases an egg. If das cell size is proper für the worker bee, das egg will be fertilized with semen before it leaves her body. If das cell size is larger, intended für the drone—a male—das queen lays an unfertilized egg that will become a drone. They are important to colony life, but das thousands of workers das maintain the hive.

"Which be the queen bee?" asked Griffy.

Mr. Bomgartner searched the frame for the grand bee.

"I don't see her here. Sie must be deeper in das hive," he said— adding, "Did ye know it is said bees need to be told when the owner dies, and das hive must be draped with a shred of black cloth, so they don't evacuate das hive.

"Where is the Papa?" Miss Lucy asked.

"Yes—*a Papa is required*," Miss Hattie insisted.

"There is no Papa… Need only the queen für das colony to thrive… See how well they work together."

Miss Lucy and Miss Hattie stared into the busy hive.

Mr. Bomgartner continued: "When ich die, I shall be proud if das bees would accompany my cortege to das funeral tent, clamoring at the ceiling and floral sprays, while mourners remain immobile in das seats."

—

The next morning, our group of twelve boarded our wagon pulled by ox-team, to travel to Uri's homestead for an afternoon of sailing on his cement bateau. Uri's second wife, Silvia, had died of pneumonia the previous January—when snowdrifts were so deep and menacing that for days, I was unable to even drive to the village for supplies, much less call on Uri in his hour of sorrow. Their son Warner, age 2, would also join us on the outing.

Phebe had packed a picnic lunch, and at a palatial sandy-pebbled bar, we stepped from the wagon to spread blankets beneath the canapé of the cottonwood trees along the Turkey River.

There, we enjoyed *cassoulet* composed of white beans, *poulet* legs, and pork, plus cheeses, and bread; our beverage—a drink free from alcohol made by taking three gallons of water at blood warmth, three half-pints of molasses, a tablespoon of the essence of spruce, and like quantity of ginger, mixed well together with a gill of yeast that she let stand overnight.

Lunch being consumed, Uri brought out his home-crafted kites. Flying kites was a unique experience for Griffy, Miss Lucy, and Miss Hattie. Observing the wonderment of happy, smiling children—who held tightly to a tenuous string attached to a framed box encircled by brightly colored paper floating high above in a cloudless blue sky—was quite enough, more than enough to persuade even me from out under the black cloud that had hung over me since the death of President Lincoln. Uri, too, seemed happier, at least for these few hours, diverging from his mourning the loss of Silvia.

Edwin helped Miss Lucy with her kite, providing instruction of how to catch currents of air to keep it aloft. Once more they were inséparables. Would the tides of life carry them in alternate directions when Miss Lucy began her study of *la couture*, dressmaking—and Edwin, his medical studies at Upper Iowa University. It was not clear to me at this juncture which direction the wind would blow them in the future. Privately, I wondered if their lives had been too easy, thus far—the worry of most parents, I imagined. Would they be too cavalier in their adult choices? Would they face the future naively, thinking no ill-wind could possibly blow so hard they could be knocked off their feet? Had Phebe and I protected them too much from the world? What skills had they acquired to keep love and marriage alive?

I noticed a difficulty that Griffy and Miss Hattie were having with their kite, and encouraged them to relinquish more string from the spool in his hand. The fluttering kite made several dives then rose high, and higher above the water, where it fluttered much like a large butterfly.

Phebe, Mrs. Ward and young Warner watched from the blanket as Charles, Edwin, Lucettie, and Sophia ventured to the river's edge to wade and splash in the water.

I overheard Phebe say: "The magnitude and destructiveness of the war has been unprecedented, Maria…do you think there shall be a corollary effect on the number of marriages and children to come? Shall our men and boys be so depressed that they will take no heart in rehabilitation?"

"'Tis true, they hath known the terrible anarchy of war—far more damaging than any other, I should imagine," Mrs. Ward said. "Yet it is proven from every other war, they shall rebound over time. As for the south, backward and primrose going ere the war, it may take longer. 'Tis purely an agricultural country, non-industrial by nature, which shall continue to slow their forward-thinking progress. Slavery was a factor of prime import—we shall see if their slaves indeed remain freedmen, or if they chose to hold onto the past. Reconstruction will be in some ways as depressing for them as war."

I noticed Phebe pull a comb from her hair that I had left for her and finger it thoughtfully. I remained unsure whether she thought our union was unfit for rehabilitation.

"I saw a good brick house at the corner of 10th and Iowa Streets at The Point for sale," Phebe added. "I believe I shall ask Alex to procure it. 'Tis often after dark when I return to our homestead after church and anti-alcohol meetings. I fear for my safety…after a pack of twenty wolves recently chased my carriage for many miles.

The remainder of the afternoon we took turns boarding Uri's boat—its grand cloth mainsail open above our heads, and large rouge hand-painted HO! at its top—gliding for hours back and forth on the river as freely as birds bound only by currents of the wind.

—

With regularity, I made calls to the homes of soldiers Perry Dewey, John Carpenter, George Wiltse, Leroy Parker, and others. I found each in various stages of shock from witnessing the unthinkable shams of war. Their physical afflictions included gunshot wounds, diseases, syphilis and gonorrhea.

I found Cousin George at his parents' home, Leonard Jr. and Louisa Jane Wiltse, in Clayton County. At the time of his enlistment, George had the appearance of a man much younger than his seventeen years, with eyes full of optimism and gusto. Now, his thin face bore deep wrinkles on the brow and cheekbones, and he seemed to look past me as I spoke. Overall, he had suffered the effects of dehydration from marching day in and day out without adequate drinking water. Fainting spells kept him close to home. His seven siblings hovered 'round him—a soldier like his father—gawping in pride.

"I've come to encourage George to attend the Fourth of July celebration at The Point," I said. "No celebration is planned at Elkader, so our crowd is expected to be large. An oration shall be delivered by President Bush of Upper Iowa University when our patriots shall be given commendations and shown the community's gratitude for winning the war. The Fayette cornet band will play a discourse of glorious *rémanences*—afterglow— of revolutionary times. Military exercises and balloon ascensions will happen in the afternoon, fireworks in the evening."

I added: "I expect Miss Emily Twombly twill be in attendance."

"I shall attend with my unit, of course," George said, "though my strength wanes quickly. If you see Miss Twombly, do not mention me in your greeting…'twill be a good while, I expect, 'til my health returns."

He thanked me for coming then looked away.

—

The Civil War behind us, I set about making application to Bennett Medical College in Chicago. The entrance requirements were to be 21 years of age, and submitting two letters as to my "good moral character"—provided by Drs. Ward and Boomer. To graduate, I would need to complete two courses of lectures, but four years of "honorable practice" could be substituted for one course. A course of lectures lasted six months. I would need to pass "satisfactory and honorable exams" in each department. Most importantly, upon graduation as an Eclectic Physician and Surgeon, I would depart with a much sought-after "surgical kit." W. E. Little, the man with the large adipose growth over his *vertèbres* remained in the forefront of my consciousness.

A bill allowing Negroes to immigrate to Iowa finally passed both houses, which incited another mass migration. Thousands of travelers trekked from the south to the prairies of Iowa. Even though they usually traveled in numbers, the chances of being set upon and robbed were always present—as was the chance for murder.

On the morning of May 4, 1866, a man whom newspapers called "an Irishman" went looking for a stray horse along Camp Creek. Instead, he found a dead Negro wearing a Union Calvary overcoat. The Irishman ran to a nearby home to spread word of his horrible discovery. None in the community, where the death had occurred, recognized the corpse. In the days he had laid on the ground awaiting removal by the coroner, wild boar had mutilated the body. The coroner eventually ruled the unknown man had been dead a week-to-ten days and was "killed by blows with an axe by some person unknown."

It came as a shock to me, that, while the Union had fought so stridently, so passionately for four long years to free Negroes from slavery, apparently there were those who did not wish to have more of them in Iowa. This attitude was another continuance of the bonds of slavery.

And thus, began a new wave of murders across Iowa for authorities to investigate.

CHAPTER SEVENTEEN

A Time to Heal

The former President of the Confederate States of America, Jefferson Davis, had been imprisoned at Fort Monroe, Virginia for two years—then was released in May 1865. He would never be tried for treason. Neither did he ever officially surrender; nor was he held responsible for causing 1.5 million deaths. In war time, a soldier who kills an enemy under the rules of war isn't considered—a *murderer*.

It was unclear exactly who should be credited with the war's *la victoire*. President Abraham Lincoln had put the nation back together, liberated the slaves, and showed the rest of the world a virtuous democratic country, one that had held together during the most difficult times.

Congress changed the way President Lincoln fought the war. Republican reformers like Representative Thaddeus Stevens of Pennsylvania, a strong believer in racial equality, pressed the president to emancipate and eventually enlist black men as soldiers.

The common Union soldier fought for lofty causes: The Union and emancipation of slaves, intensely aware of the issues at stake and passionately preoccupied with them. Somehow their insensibilities informed them they were playing roles in a transcendently important struggle on which the future of the American nation would pivot. Each was willing—perfectly willing—to lay down all his joys in this life to help maintain this government and support the U.S. Constitution, and to pay that debt. And so many paid with their lives: over 350,000 Union deaths, with nearly as many wounded.

African Americans, it seemed, may have overcome more than any other, relinquishing prejudices to serve as soldiers, laundresses, cooks, and laborers. Their participation challenged the prescribed notions about race and gender and pushed the boundaries of Negroes' roles in America. Half of the south's population was enslaved. Their cause for liberty transcended class, education, and social position.

As far as America's new Commander in Chief, President Andrew Johnson, he was said to be an old-fashioned southern Jacksonian Democrat of pronounced states' rights views, who, during the secession crisis, had remained in the Senate, even when Tennessee seceded, which made him *un héros* in the North, and a *traître* in the eyes of most Southerners. So he, too, had done his part for the Union's cause.

His first act in office was an Amnesty Proclamation that mirrored President Lincoln's. The Confederate states would be required to uphold the 13th Amendment, which abolished slavery; swear loyalty to the Union; and pay off their war debt. Then—and only then—could they re-write their State Constitutions, hold elections, and begin sending representatives to Washington. Under the plan, Confederate leaders would also have to apply directly to President Johnson to request *une grâce*—for grace. Then, reconstruction could commence in those states.

I followed newspapers for news of President Lincoln's assassin, John Wilkes Booth. Newspapers, even in the south, expressed dismay and sympathy over the assassination. Booth allegedly was shocked they described him as "a common cutthroat," rather than a *hero*.

An epic manhunt transpired involving nearly 1,000 Union soldiers. It appeared Booth had broken his leg when he jumped from the balcony to the stage at Ford's Theatre—supporting the idea that Confederate sympathizers had likely aided his escape. The bounty for the capture of Booth and his accomplices rose to $100,000.

It was believed Booth and one other crossed the Potomac and Rappahannock Rivers into Virginia. Posing as wounded Confederate soldiers on their way home from the war, they took shelter in a barn on a Virginia farm. A tip led Union troops to the farm early on the morning of April 26. Booth signaled his intent to fight back. The troops lit the barn on fire. When Booth finally emerged from the burning barn, a Union soldier shot him in the neck, and he died shortly.

I thought of my Charles and his attempt to steal a horse when he had felt desperate to retrieve his mother from Floyd County. Had the father of John Wilkes Booth been too absorbed with his own acting career to prevent his 26-year-old son from going down a path anarchy? And Mrs. Booth—surely, she was devasted beyond all belief upon hearing the news her son had killed the President of the United States, while reportedly she had stated knowing her son harbored Confederate sympathies, hated abolitionists, and thought they were trying to destroy the country he loved.

—

In March 1870, the habitants of Manchester resumed a match of shooting prairie chickens. People from across the county were invited to come and enjoy a drink from the crystal springs that bubbled up from the rocky ledges, relax in the leafy shade of the oaks, and consume a bountiful dinner from the well-filled baskets in farmers' wagons flanked with watermelon and sweet cider. Three thousand attended, and five hundred and ninety-nine birds were taken.

There, I first met Mr. E. C. Huntington, editor of The Point's first newspaper, *The Press*—the first I knew a newspaper editor who promoted the community's collective support without renunciation: "Lose your newspaper, lose your commercial edge," he said—adding that a good newspaper was as important as the railroad coming to any town.

It became normal fare for Mr. Huntington to often incorporate articles in his newspaper that first appeared in other papers from across the state:

> *Andrew Thompson, indicted for murder in Clayton County, was tried in the District Court of Fayette, convicted, and sentenced to be hanged on the 9th of September following; but his trial was reviewed by the Supreme Court, and his sentence was changed to*

imprisonment for life. He did not remain in jail long, however, for, stealing a case-knife, when his food was brought to him, he managed to saw off the iron bolt that fastened his door, and escaped. One hundred dollars' reward is offered for his apprehension.

A disgraceful Bull Dog and a Wild Cat fight will take place at the Slaughter House on Tuesday of this week. The bet is purported to be $100. About 400 people are expected, at 50 cents each, to get in the enclosure.

Two little girls of George Durst went into a barn near The Point a few days ago and set fire to some hay with matches. Both children were taken from the charred timbers and attended by Dr. Wiltse, who pronounced them dead from fire and asphyxiation soon after.

The number of armless and legless soldiers now borne on the pension rolls: Number have lost both legs: 42; one leg lost: 4,627; one or both arms lost: 5006; one arm and one leg lost: 31.

I found Mr. Huntington's use of words delightful, when, for example, promoting an announcement about our M. E. Church:

The wicked story has been started at The Point, at the Methodist church sociable, 25 cents paid in cash entitles the liberal party to the privilege of kissing any lady in the garden he may select. The probability is that this church makes money at its social.

Phebe and I encouraged our children to attend our church's attempt at matchmaking, though Charles, age 17, had his sights set on Anna Grannis; Edwin, age 16, and Miss Lucy would also attend together. Lucettie, age 12, had not entertained a suiter, but Vidella, whom Lucettie adored, had written a letter from her home in Ohio urging Lucettie to marry by age 16, as she and her Capt. Ennes were exceedingly happy. "You're a grown woman by 16," Vidella wrote.

Two carriages would be necessary to transport us to the social. Charles had gone into town weeks prior and purchased a

Frisian horse and borrowed a second carriage from a neighbor. Red prairie fire crabapple flowerets ornamented the headstall of both horses. My Boulon—with its black star on the forehead, both hind legs white, and long black tail—looked particularly regal.

At the appointed hour, our women, dressed in their most fashionable dresses—and we men, in our finest cloaks, shirts, and pants marched through the front door of our maison. I offered Phebe my hand as she stepped up into our black buggy, and tucked my body on the front seat against hers; Edwin and Miss Lucy climbed into the rear bench seat. A crack of the whip and we rode off into the late afternoon sun amid nuances of sunlight filtering down upon us through the trees. Phebe spoke enthusiastically of the *coming about* of our children; of her flourishing garden; and of sundry subjects of her choosing. I listened and silently rejoiced. Her *tempérament* seemingly had returned to such as first we met.

Upon our arrival at the church's west side, we entered through an iron gate into the small *roseraie* where the Reverend and his wife, along with Perry and Matilda Dewey, welcomed guests. Arm in arm, Phebe and I led the way to the table of refreshments and strawberry pie—greeting young and old, those we'd come to know so liberally.

By the time the sun reposed on the horizon, the numbers had grown to forty or more—though disappointingly, I saw no Cousin George or Miss Emily Twombly. John and Mary Carpenter, too, were absent, I was told, they were attending to the baby girl recently born to the couple. Leroy Parker was also absent and none knew of his current whereabouts.

The moment arrived when the gents were invited to stand before the dame of their choosing. The small cluster of people shifted, marked by nervous giggles and some tomfoolery. Lines formed. Conversations moderated. Phebe and I watched as our children faced off with their partners. Behind each suitor, one or two others awaited their chance for a 25-cent kiss.

I turned to face my Phebe.

Grasping her hand in mine, I asked, *"Puis-je t'embrasser—* may I kiss you?"

I watched her facial expression turn from blushing coyly to

uncertainty to submission.

"You may kiss your femme," she said.

I cupped her face lightly in my hands and pulled her close, feeling the warmth of her soft lips press against mine. Her body grew limp in my strength. In my mind's ear, I heard an accordéon gently playing "Considérez les Lillies."

Slowly releasing Phebe and taking a step back, I bumped into a gentleman who not been there moments earlier.

"I hawp its another's turn fur a kiss," he said, holding a quarter between two fingers of one hand.

"Dr. Boomer—'tis you?"

—

Uri Wiltse's third marriage to Elizabeth "Libbie" McConkey happened on July 19, 1870 at Winterset, Iowa. The details of how they met remained unclear to me—as she resided two hundred miles from Forestville. But at age 46, Uri was rightly viewed by single, young women as a prosperous, steady landowner; his homestead of 160 acres was worth about $4,000. And he, having turned his wild prairie into a fine residence and well cultivated fields, likely felt he had conquered a kingdom. Nevertheless, he came with an encumbrance: Silvia had passed away in 1864, and alone he had reared Warner, who was now 8 years old.

I wasn't surprised Uri had remarried, though I was astonished he had chosen to marry a woman who, from the outset, had declared her keen interest in *writing*. On Christmas Day, she called for interviews with the warden and prisoners at the penitentiary at Fort Madison, and her first article subsequently appeared in *The Press*.

> *Elizabeth Wiltse and Mary Rogers, a minister of the Gospel in the Society of Friends, were allowed a Christmas visit to the Penitentiary at Fort Madison recently, carrying a letter of introduction from the esteemed townsman, D. H. LeSeuer.*
>
> *Christmas was allowed a holiday, meaning they did not have to work that day. Christmas dinner included*

chicken, some apples, and other things, for which they heartly enjoyed.

I also met the chaplain—and recognized one of the guards as an old friend, who had no complaints about living with the growing number of convicts at the prison, only a few of whom, he said, were dangerous.

The Warden confirmed the number of prisoners at 220. Those sentenced to life: 14. A growing number are added each month. The cells, as far as I could see, are a pattern of cleanliness, and of those to whom I spoke, stated they had no cause of complaint as to how they were fed.

A fire had occurred the night of 19 May 1868, and considerable rebuilding was required. The hospital building is now 104 feet long by 40 feet wide. The dining room 40 feet by 80 feet, big enough to seat 400 people.

A Sabbath school, proposed by Governor Merrill, was organized May 1869 as a means to rehabilitate the prisoners. The number of those in regular attendance: 170.

For some time, Warden Martin Heisey had been trying the experiment of governing the convicts by the power of kindness, punishment being a last resort. He said, "Since the addition of a Sabbath school, the inmates were more pleasant, cheerful, and obedient."

While the warden has entirely dispensed with the whipping process as a mode of punishment, he still may choose another option of putting a man in a dark cell without any seat, bed, or anything upon which to rest, but for the dirt floor, feeding him only bread and water, until he promises faithfully and unequivocally to reform his conduct, leaving the length of his stay in the solitary cell entirely up to the prisoner.

—

The most recent action of the railroad committee was drafting a letter to be sent to the Davenport and St. Paul Railway, proposing a railroad line between intermediate points that commenced at Fayette, then to Brush Creek, Strawberry Point, Delhi, and some six points beyond—a good practicable route of about one hundred miles. The expense of grading and bridging would probably average between three thousand and five thousand dollars per mile. There were but four bridges of any note on the entire route, and neither was very expensive. The advantages of an inexhaustible supply timber along the route couldn't be overestimated. Further, the route ran through the great manufacturing interests of Iowa, and if extended to St. Paul, would reach Minnesota's great manufacturing interests. This enterprise had the greatest likelihood for success.

Phebe enjoined with a few of Libbie Wiltse's enterprises. She kept abreast of the liquor debate heating up in Iowa and across the country. The Liquor Dealership Associations of the State of Iowa published advertisements acclaiming the liquor trade to be a legitimate enterprise representing two million dollars in revenue to the State of Iowa—and therefore, was entitled to protection under the laws of Iowa. Further, they deemed the Prohibitory Liquor Law on the statue book an act of infringement of the rights and liberties of the people inconsistent with the spirit of the Constitution of the United States of America. They proposed striking the law from the statue.

To head off the backhanded efforts of the Liquor Dealership Associations, Phebe also joined the Women's Suffrage in Iowa in anticipation of passage of the 19th Amendment to the Constitution to give women the right to vote. After that, she worked to start a library at The Point, and to acquire formalized text books for schools. I was proud of the work she did; Phebe was finding her own voice.

—

In the summer of 1870, our family was pleased to attend the marriage of Cousin George Wiltse and Emily J. Twombly at the Methodist Episcopal Church at The Point. George had regained much of his strength; the twinkle in his eye was because of his beloved Emily.

George's wedding reminded me that five years had passed since he mustered out as a soldier of the Civil War. However, I continued to read newspaper accounts of the Confederate flag flying over public buildings in the south and heard talk of building memorials to Confederate military leaders. One article announced the women in Columbus, Georgia planned to hold a "Decoration Day" to honor the dozens of Confederate soldiers buried in Linwood Cemetery.

A part of me wondered whether the South had really won the war, and the North was merely slow in grasping the fact.

My journey had taken me on a different route…and I was preparing to graduate Bennett Medical College. Edwin, too, had commenced his formal medical education at Upper Iowa University at Fayette; then he would attend Bennett. I was enthusiastic that we, father and son, would both have medical degrees. Perhaps, one day Edwin would have a son, and a third Wiltse would become a physician.

CHAPTER EIGHTEEN

The Broken

The spring of 1871 Dr. Ward invited me to accompany him on three medical requests. First, to investigate complaints of negligence of a child of about eight years of age; second, to treat a farmer who had caught his hand in the cylinder of a threshing machine, which would likely require amputation of the hand; and a third, he said, would be a most familiar circumstance—involving another murder.

A Township Trustee had first alerted Dr. Ward of a malnourished boy weeks earlier. His mother had died when the boy was a year and a half old, at which time the father, John Link, placed his son into the care of a neighbor, Mr. Richards—said to be a very gentle man. Mr. Link remarried two years ago, and the child was returned to his home. From time to time, Mr. Richards called at the Link's home to check on the child, and on a recent occasion, when Mr. Link and his new wife sat at the table to eat, Mr. Richards said he witnessed the naked boy crawl from under a bed to eat victuals that Mrs. Link had placed in a metal pan in the corner of the kitchen.

The Link's farm was fourteen miles west of Oxbow in Bremer County. Along the way, Dr. Ward informed me no advance notice had been given to Mr. or Mrs. Link of his directive to investigate the child's well-being in the home.

Dr. Ward brought his mare to a standstill in the dirt yard centered between a two-story framed house, a stable, and a fenced-in chicken coup. The only animal in sight was a Guernsey cow grazing in a field beyond the stable. A scraggly St. Bernard dog gingerly approached the carriage, seemingly more curious than threatening.

We leaped from the carriage and headed toward the covered porch at the front of the house. Dr. Ward, with black bag in hand, gave three short knocks on the door, and waited with me at his side.

A curtain at a nearby window moved and a man peered out through the glass pane. Within a few seconds, the door opened.

"What's thy business?" the man said gruffly.

"I would to speak to Mr. Link."

"Speakin'—what's thy business?"

"I'm Dr. Ward and this gentleman is Dr. Wiltse."

"Ain't no one hither bid for a doctor."

"I hast been summoned by Bremer County authorities upon complaint of an unkept child on the premises. May we join inside?"

"'Tis not a convenient time for yer visit...am jess about to milk mine cow."

"I warrant thee this shall not take a instant of thy day, Mr. Link...it's important I also speak with Mrs. Link—if she can avail herself."

My body jerked, causing me to fall against Dr. Ward, as the large dog surprised me with a touch with his big nose against my back.

"The dog won't bite...hasn't a brain in his pate," Mr. Link said.

A minute later, Mr. Link hesitantly backed into the room leaving the door wide open, as though inviting us inside.

Dr. Ward and I entered the home where a steaming bowl of food sat on either end of the table at place settings with a spoon, knife, and tin cup.

Mrs. Link regarded us from where she stood at the small cookstove. Nervously, she wiped her hands on the full-length apron covering her plain dress. A deep crease formed upon her brow.

"State thy business then be on thy way," Mr. Link said.

"As already stated," Dr. Ward began, "I am hither to address multiple complaints of an undernourished child on the premises. I must be allowed to see and thoroughly examine the child for my report, which I am bound to submit to county authorities within three days' time."

The couple stared at the other from across the room.

"We know naught of such an inquiry," Mrs. Link said. "Mr. Link hath a son, who's naught but trouble to us both… he is foul-mouthed, lazy, and a no good rut of da litter."

"I implore thee, 'tis important that I be allowed to examine the boy," Dr. Ward stated again.

"He's in the next room," she added, pointing toward a cloth-draped doorway. "But be warned, the stench shall get thee."

Dr. Ward pulled aside the drapery and led the way into the adjacent room that smelled of filth. I walked to the window and pulled back the curtains to allow light into the space. The only furniture was a single bed and straight-back chair—no sign of a child's things…a ball, a jump rope, or a book of games or rhymes. Even so, I sensed another was present. Dr. Ward enjoined me in crouching to view under the bed, and there, we found the boy. Dr. Ward beckoned him to come out, and after some persuading, the child, wearing only a shirt collar around his neck, crawled out, cowering as though fearing one of us would strike him at any moment.

Dr. Ward helped him stand then sit on the bed.

"Don't be afraid," he said. "What's thy name?"

The child stared past us, in much the same way as had the men who returned from the Civil War.

Dr. Ward examined his body that was black and blue from head to foot, obviously from beatings. We also discovered a large cut on his head, and his feet showed signs of being frozen, as did other parts of his body.

"How didst thou get these bruises?" Dr. Ward asked, as we attended to his injuries.

The boy spoke not a single word, not so much as even a sigh, though such injuries would make another child scream in pain.

"Other visitors from Bremer County will arrive after me," Dr. Ward said. "Tell 'em what caused thy bruises, as they shall surely further inquire into your well-being."

Dr. Ward and I re-emerged on the other side of the drapery.

"I've completed my examination of thy son, Mr. Link. The final piece of my report shall be my interview with the two of you. Say to me whom hath laid a hand on this child, Mr. Link— or 'twas it thee, Mrs. Link?" said Dr. Ward.

Mr. Link leaned over his plate at the table, his chin against his chest, and kept silent—as did Mrs. Link, who turned her face away toward the stove.

"We shall see our way out now," Dr. Ward said, turning to depart.

Reaching the carriage, I asked: "What happens next?"

"The Trustee shall secure a warrant, arrest Mr. Link, and bring him before Squire Leonard, who shall promptly fine him fifty dollars and require him to grant bonds to pay for the health of the child. If he can't grant the required bonds—and doubtless he shall object—the child will be taken from the home. I shall write my report against the chances of the boy's recovery in the home. I expect the citizens of the county shall be so outraged they shall rise up and threaten to lynch Mr. Link."

Hardly another word was spoken between the two of us for the rest of the afternoon about the *State of Iowa vs. Mr. and Mrs. Link*. Left to muddle in my thoughts, I remembered similar cases over my years as a physician. I would be more circumspect of the care of children in future home visits.

—

Dr. Ward wasted no time in reaching his next client. We approached the farm of Robert Wright, passing fields of harvest underway, presumably the labor of his charitable neighbors and friends. The harvest would surely be completed by end of day.

Mrs. Wright met us upon our arrival in the yard cluttered with horses and wagon units and delivered us straightaway to Mr. Wright in bed. He held one hand bound in a bloodied towel in an upright fashion on pillows. His eyes informed me of his acute pain; the faces of the children encircling his bed spoke of their aggregate concern for their father.

Dr. Ward introduced me as "an esteemed physician from Strawberry Point," noting I would act as a second attending physician, having over fifteen years' practical experience, and a recent graduate of Bennett Surgical College.

He removed the bloodied towel wrapped around Mr. Wright's hand. 'Twas apparent the tissue and muscles were so torn and mutilated as to require immediate amputation. Within a short time, we moved Mr. Wright to the kitchen table, under close scrutiny of Mrs. Wright and their children.

Dr. Ward sent them to the parlor for the duration of the surgery.

He and I took turns rigorously washing our hands and forearms in a solution of chlorinated lime in a basin at the sink. We had begun this surgical protocol after reading in a *medical* journal of a Hungarian obstetrician, Ignaz Semmelweis, who, in 1861 linked a higher rate of mortalities from sepsis of mothers, who, after giving birth, were treated by physicians with unwashed hands—some who'd just finished performing a series of autopsies. Then, in 1867, Scottish surgeon Joseph Baron Lister introduced spraying the surgical field with disinfectant carbolic acid, resulting in a drastic reduction in surgical mortality. Most physicians of the Delaware County Société Médicale had begun to follow these protocols, but not all—some didn't believe hygiene was linked with mortality rates.

I set about cleaning the wound area with iodine and bromine and applied a tourniquet, tightening it above the wound to reduce bleeding. Dr. Ward laid out his tools: scalpel, straight forceps, large amputation saw, scissors, probe, tenaculum, tourniquet, bone brush, amputating knife, and a Catlin knife.

Ready to commence, Dr. Ward addressed Mr. Wright, holding a biting baton in one hand and a bottle of chloroform in the other.

"I assume thou would desire the use of chloroform, Mr. Wright—or perhaps thou prefer to hardy the pain by *biting on the baton*?"

"Chloroform is preferable," Mr. Wright whispered through his pain.

"Dr. Wiltse will keep full track of your vitals throughout the process. An amputation at the wrist joint hath about a ten percent perpetual wink rate, Mr. Wright—thou shall survive the surgery in brave shape, I believe."

"How much shall thee take?"

"Not one smidgeon more than 'tis necessary, you can be sure of that. I shall use the flap method, which can only be done within forty-eight hours of the injury…it takes longer creating a flap of skin close to the raw stump, but shall allow for quicker healing."

Dr. Ward handed me the bottle and I commenced dripping the pungent liquid onto a cloth that I held beneath Mr. Wright's nose. Within the prescribed time, he succumbed to the chemical's vapors. I lifted his eyelids to confirm the drug had done its job, verified the patient's pulse, and indicated Dr. Ward could go forward with the surgery.

He then placed a board used for amputations upon Mr. Wright's chest and rested his mutilated hand upon it. With a circular amputation using a scalpel, he cut through the skin and with the Caitlin knife traversed the muscle, all the while keeping a close eye on Mr. Wright's respiration.

"How is our patient doing, Dr. Witlse?" he asked in his typical thunderbolt volume, knowing he could be heard by the family on the other side of the parlor wall, I believed.

"Mr. Wright's breathing and cardiac rate are normal and regular," I replied.

I thought I heard Mrs. Wright let out a sigh of worry.

Dr. Ward picked up the bone saw and cut through the bone until the hand was severed and placed it in a cloth bag. Next, he tied off the arteries with horsehair threads, and scraped the edges of the bone smooth. The flap of skin was pulled across and sewn close, leaving a drainage hole…after removal of the tourniquet some oozing was normal. Finally, the stump was covered with plaster, and bandaged.

"That's it—'tis finished," Dr. Ward said.

Mrs. Wright and the children appeared in the doorway.

Dr. Ward addressed Mrs. Wright: "Mr. Wright shall be miserable with pain for a week or more. I shall leave thee with sufficient quantity of morphine… We can talk about a prosthesis whenever he is ready. With all the returning invalids from war, 'tis quite a growing market of limbs available."

"We are grateful for thy help—Dr. Wiltse, too. I am unsure how we shall recompense thee, at least for now."

Dr. Ward continued: "With Mr. Wright laid up, I urge thee to submit a notice of your dire need for aid in the community," said Dr. Ward. "I am certain a good sum of money for your hardship shall be made available from the good people of Oxbow."

Mr. Wright awoke from the chloroform, and Dr. Ward and I helped him return to bed.

"Keep a watch over him…no food 'till mine return towards the morrow," Dr. Ward added.

Before leaving the home, Mrs. Wright presented Dr. Ward with a basket of fresh eggs, a fruit pie, and two caged chickens.

"My wife shall be grateful, thank you," he said.

Outside, we found a neighbor had led Dr. Ward's mare and carriage to the water trough by the stable. En route to the carriage, Dr. Ward informed me of his third and final sick call of the day.

"Do you remember the case of Mr. Thomas and the widow Mrs. Fay? There's been another love triangle—this time, *in Hazelton*—a dozen or so miles southeast of Oxbow, resulting in the murder of Juliette Thomas: *The State of Iowa vs. Daniel Thomas*… Surely, you've read of it in newspapers. Strychnine is believed used to dispatch the victim. Today we shall assist officials in the search for the poison on the Thomas' premises."

I nodded, having read of the case in newspapers.

Dr. Ward directed his mare southeasterly. A minute later the carriage hit a rough spot in the road that nearly hurled me from the carriage and into the weeds.

"Hold on, Wiltse… It'll be rough like this the whole way to Hazelton."

"It would help to slow down…" I said, but to no avail. The man was always in a hurry. In between the jostling, I attempted to strike up a conversation about testimony I had given at the Andrew Thompson trial in the murder of the Hagerty family of Clayton County some months ago.

"Thompson, a wealthy farmer, first became acquainted with Mrs. Hagerty at her husband's Bull's Head saloon in 1858; then, he employed her, when an intimacy began between them. In 1866, she gave birth to his son, the offspring of this intimacy— the child was murdered by the mother shortly thereafter, with the knowledge of Thompson and concealed by him. Thompson claims afterward he sought to get rid of the woman, but she persisted in remaining near him, and by threats obtained complete control of him… Are you getting' all of this, A. B.? It's a bit of a convoluted story."

"Go on, Wiltse, go on."

"His wife became alarmed, and Mrs. Hagerty then threatened her with violence. Mr. Thompson, so it was said, attempted to break free of the illicit relationship, but Mrs. Hagerty retained the power she held over him."

Once more I grabbed hold of the carriage frame as a wheel hit a large rock and for several seconds only three wheels of the buggy remained on the road.

Dr. Ward laughed and flicked the whip to hurry the horse along.

"Don't sell me a dog, Wiltse—what happened next."

"This is where things went really, really bad…" I said, continuing to hold on for dear life.

"On a December evening in 1868, Mr. Thompson took Mrs. Hagerty and her two boys and daughter into his sleigh for a ride, and at McGregor, Iowa they crossed into Wisconsin… And so, began the journey which ended in the murder of the mother and all her children.

"He killed 'em—*all of 'em?*"

"Thompson was Indicted in Clayton County and tried in the District Court of Fayette. The trial played out in the *Burlington Gazette*. He was convicted and sentenced to be hanged in early September. Then his trial was reviewed by the Supreme Court and the sentence changed to imprisonment for life."

Dr. Ward nodded. "I believe that I read you had been called when the trunk and other body pieces of the murdered were found by fishermen near Prairie du Chien, and you accompanied authorities in the aftermath on occasions to aid in searching the Thomson premises for the tool used in the murders—*an axe.*"

"Yes—and it does not please me to be a part of such an atrocity."

"I thought you rather enjoyed the excitement of murder."

"For a short while, murder investigation added a layer of excitement to my medical practice, which much of the time can be mundane, as you well know… Ever since the death of Dr. Stout it's been less so; I'm sure you understand."

We turned on to a less furrowed trail, and I relaxed my hand from the carriage frame, and turned my thoughts to our day's journey. Eventually, a burning question pushed to the forefront of my mind.

"As physicians, we see all manner of sickness and death… Perhaps this remark is insensitive, but this entire day you were hardly without a cough… How is this so?"

"I have consumption, Wiltse, as you hast surely diagnosed by now. Mine cough is a issue of the disease. O' recent, I have begun taking morphine… it seems to quiet my cough, of course—I put it off as long as possible, as there's an addictive quality to the drug. Sadly, I shall not live to see the end of the decade—and I am now only thirty-nine.

—

Sundown neared by the time we returned to Oxbow. Its golden glow aligned perfectly with the east-west Main Street and cast long shadows from the towering elm and maple trees planted fifteen years earlier. Most impressive was the reflection against the broad foliage that greatly enhanced the boulevard and gave the appearance of a town with *la perseverance*—staying power.

Dr. Ward halted his mare near the rebuilt mill, and from there he raised his tall, spindly frame in his covered black buggy to look easterly at the town.

"'Tis our returning men from the war that hast established so many new businesses: C. H. Procter, blacksmithing and wagon-making; A. R. Wolgomot, drug store; C. E. Redfield, hardware; J. C. Myers, hotel and general store—along with sundry shops: shoe, grocery, cooper, and harness, and an egg and butter packing house. W. H. Miller operates the mill previously owned by Minkler & Nichols. Many have constructed splendid homes in the township and developed prosperous farms in the area. 'Tis a town to be proud of."

Then, looking westward, he pointed to the roadway, barricaded, and vacant of a bridge across the river.

"The Buchanan County Board of Supervisors recently contracted with a company to build a wrought iron column and arch bridge, 145 long in a single span, with roadway of 16 feet in width, at a contract price of thirty dollars per lineal foot—it has been a hardship since the bridge washed out for those delivering their children to our fine two-story public place of learning that employs two full-time teachers. The Board recently declared that within five years every stream in the county shall be bridged at every road crossing."

"We are beginning a grand new age of innovation," I said agreeably.

"And didst I tell you, 'twas an Oxbow man who recently caught a pickerel with a hook and line, 34 inches long, 13 pounds—do ya fish, Wiltse?" he added.

"Only l'occasion, though I relish being on the water."

He sat back down on the bench seat beside me and signaled his black beauty to trot along South First Street.

As we clip-clopped along, once more I found myself enjoying the red plumb at the mare's headpiece top that bounced with its every step.

"Ere I deliver you to the inn, I shall take you past the Methodist Episcopal Temple nearing completion. The singers of the village are drilling for a concert in two or three weeks to raise money for an organ—and the church is steepless. I can get you a tour, if thou wish. I know you and Phebe are Methodists, and 'twill be the place of my final surrender in perpetual wink. Should thou wish to compose a contribution, 'twill be greatly appreciated."

A solemness overcame me, the kind one feels when the loss of something of weighty value is on the horizon.

"A visit to the church another time shall be welcomed when my Phebe can participate... And may I add, it has certainly been my pleasure to be in your presence for all these many years, A.B."

"Thank you, Wiltse, mine brave and loyal friend. 'Tis the same on my part."

CHAPTER NINETEEN

When Death Speaks Your Name

In Europe, the Franco-Prussian War of 1870 had commenced—which was of no importance to me, except from the conflict I learned of the tedious malady that would lead to my premature death. A part of me felt grateful I wouldn't die at the hands of a murderer, or by Indian massacre, or mob hanging, or prairie banditti, or on some battlefield far from home. Still, my end was clearly drawing near.

The familiarity of my diagnosis happened when reading an article written by French physician Apollinaire Bouchardat, wherein he noted his diabetic patients' symptoms had improved during the Franco-Prussian War, likely due to war-related food rationing. Sugar had all but disappeared in their urine. From this observation, he developed individualized regimes of diet and exercise as diabetes treatments. Forbidden foods included starches and sugars, including fruits and breads, while permitting meats, eggs, cheese, and wine. He taught patients how to perform an at-home glucose urine test as a way of monitoring their blood sugar levels.

I was aware during the previous year of my perverse thirst for water and polyuria—frequent urination. Performing Bouchardat's urine test, I knew, nearing my fiftieth birthday, I must begin to put my affaires in order.

Of utmost concern to me was Phebe. Now approaching our thirtieth year of marriage—and wishing to make our final years as meaningful as possible—I began writing and posting love notes for her to find...when she opened a cabinet in her kitchen...pinned to her lingerie...or attached to the garden hoe.

> *Beautiful is the morning of l'amour with its prophétique crimson, violet, purple and gold every day since first we met.*

It gave me great comfort knowing she would be well cared for into her old age. We had grown a considerable fortune of 340 acres—at $40 an acre; 70 acres of good timber, all adapted to stock raising; 6 milk Cows; 50 head of sheep; a span of good mares; Houdan chickens; 1 mower; 1 combined Reaper and Mower; 2 Cultivators; 1 Hay Rake; Plows, Drags, and other farm equipment; plus, a second house at the corner of 10th and Iowa Streets at The Point. Most recently, we purchased a lot in the cemetery for $3.00.

After my passing, Phebe would sell the farm and she and Sophia, age 10, would move into the house at The Point. We chose to designate a cow as Sophia's dowry. As for my other personal items, I left it up to Phebe's discretion what should become of my accordéon—none of the children had showed interest in learning to play the instrument that I so loved so dearly. Likely, Edwin would lay claim to my black bag, instruments, and a dozen medical books. Charles may wish to have my Parker shotgun. The conch shell should remain in the family, perhaps with one of the girls. Numerous other items would also need to be divided among our children—my mare, Boulon, the buggy I'd used to call on my patients, and Père Philip's gold watch. What should become of my portrait— perhaps it would be accepted into the library.

Vidella and Capt. Ennes had blessed us with Grandson Claude—though sadly, they resided in Ohio, and I had only seen him once since his birth. I would look forward to seeing him again, and any other grandchildren, in the afterlife.

I looked forward to seeing two of our children marry in the coming fall of 1872: Lucettie, age 16, and Francis Thompson, and Charles, age 22, and Anna Grannis. They planned their simple nuptials at the Methodist Episcopal Church to be officiated by Rev. James F. Heatwood.

Edwin was about to graduate Upper Iowa University and had begun working with me in my office at The Point. Together we healed sick persons everywhere—'twas a dream come true. He and Miss Lucy Dean planned to marry prior to his graduation from Bennett in 1873.

For as long as I was able, I would continue my medical practice, and it remained important to me to persevere in treating our Civil War soldiers.

Dewey Perry, even as he and his wife Matilda focused their energies raising their two children, reportedly awoke many nights from dreams of terrifying war battles. Starting over in the new state of Nebraska might reduce his trauma, they reasoned—plus, Dewey's mother, Mrs. Dewey, had died some time ago, so they had no reason to remain in the county. Her death had been from an accidental laudanum overdose. They stated their departure was imminent.

Cousin George and Emily had born their first child within the first year of their marriage, and they also talked of relocating, perhaps to Montezuma, Iowa—for reasons obscure to me, since both had family in the Clayton County.

Suicide had taken one soldier from The Point. After witnessing the worst atrocities of war, he, like so many other soldiers, was tasked with finding how to transition back into families, communities, and the world in general. His specific challenge was restoring his manhood after the loss of an appendage. I was certain some time ago the illusion had presented itself that the pain could all go away—insomnia…remorse…and fear of bankruptcy—with the gentle squeeze of the trigger of a Spencer repeating rifle brought home from the war. He left a note stating his wife was now free to marry another, knowing she only wanted him and none other.

I understood the man's struggle as much as one could without having gone to war, but I wished he had stayed. Such a mess he left for his family—mostly, his children. There was a time after Dr. Stout's murder that I, too, found myself in an unyielding struggle. Phebe, my faith, my family, and friends brought me through those dark days.

My good friend Dr. Boomer returned to his practice at Delhi and quickly resurrected the Delaware County Société Médicale—and not long after, he served as a member of the lower house of the state legislature; Most recently, he was making a bid for the Iowa Senate. He had continued to serve his countryman.

I was grateful that the event I had longed to bring to fruition, perhaps more than any other, happened in the spring of 1872. By then, The Point had grown to over six hundred people, and most were in attendance to witness the arrival of the Davenport & St. Paul Railroad. One newspaper exalted the long-awaited day:

> *At last farmers and villagers alike shall be able to look up from a field or step out onto the boardwalk and hear the neighing and puffing of the iron horse from his cast-iron lungs and brazen nostrils. The train signals prosperity. Jobs. And access to markets.*

I would never forget the expression of my anxiety when *la fumée* of the engine became visible in the distance, as had only been seen heretofore when a new and great actor was expected on the scene at the Opera House.

As the train neared—and the flags with which it was decorated could be seen waving in the breeze—shouts of "Welcome!" broke forth from the gazers.

The committee boarded the steam engine after coming to a halt.

I exclaimed to the conductor: *"Bienvenue to The Point!"*

We commemorated the extraordinary day and occasion with a photo of the colossal iron horse juxtaposed to committee members standing in front of the depot, and an ordinary sign STRAWBERRY POINT posted a few feet from the railroad tracks. I felt as giddy as a young boy with his own Christmas *Tourtière*—meat pie. I recorded the day with a little verse.

> *I couldn't recall when it happened*
> *that I became so fond of trains,*
> *their rhythm, their whistles,*
> *the dream*
> *of being transported to a place*
> *suspended between two unknowns;*
> *and, oh! the yearning it evoked,*
> *Vouloir, c'est pouvoir—to want is to be able to.*

In the afternoon, we rode the train to Oelwein, some twenty

miles west into Fayette County. My first train ride, with Phebe and our children, was all I imagined it to be. Though hardly did we expect such an accumulation of soot and fly ash on our clothing. Oelwein was to become a grand railroad hub with rails leading in every direction. I thought of Oxbow—ten miles beyond Oelwein; the village would have to wait a bit longer for the train's arrival, though already it was a beehive of activity.

No sooner was the D & St. P up and running at The Point when a young boy, while playing on flat cars in motion, fell between them and the cars ran over both legs, crushing them. The amputation surgery took several hours, even with the aid of another surgeon.

Additionally, over the next few months trains killed and maimed four of my calves. I filed a lawsuit against the railroad company and awaited my day in justice court.

—

Morose at it sounds, the thought of my impending death hounded me day and night. 'Twas Mark Twain who—writing on everything from slovenliness to governance, occupying more lines in newspapers than the doings of the Republican party—suggested the idea of including a little verse or two of comforting poetry with notice of obituaries. I placed one of his poems in the bureau where I kept a file, FUNERAL OF DR. ALEXANDER WILTSE for Phebe to find upon my death and read at the time of my burial.

> *That merry shout no more I hear,*
> *No laughing child I see,*
> *No little arms are around my neck,*
> *No feet upon my knee;*
> *No kisses drop upon my cheek,*
> *These lips are sealed to me.*
> *Dear Lord, how could I give* [this beloved man] *up*
> *To any but to Thee?*

The economy began a fluctuation in 1872, as it had in the

months preceding the Panic of 1857, which was worrisome to me, having lived through that difficult time. The price of wheat was down. Corn, flat. And oats, not lively. Some farmers happily bit upon a new business venture which commanded liberal prices—that of trapping prairie chickens for shipment east for about $4.90 in greenbacks per dozen. The venture went sour when the Iowa legislature brought forth a law making the enterprise illegal. A few other enterprising farmers traveled to California in hopes of luring Chinese immigrants for field laborers, but most found it impossible to get them at a profitable rate.

With considerable sadness, in August Phebe and attended a Clayton County sheriff sale respective to Uri's property for non-payment of a tax debt of $676.25. Uri, age 48, Libbie, with their two sons—Warner, age 10, and Albert, age 1—were unsure where they would relocate. Fortunately, the federal government had amended the homestead law to allow any soldier, without distinction on account of race or color, who'd served at least ninety days if discharged for wounds received or disability incurred in the line of duty, to acquire or up to 160 free acres on any public land in the United States. Uri and Libbie eyed Kansas, which had grown considerably in population since the Civil War's end. Of course, no one would miss Libbie more than my Phebe.

A horrific event followed that led me to question whether the Civil War had really ended, even though I knew Confederate Gen. Robert E. Lee had surrendered at Appomattox in 1865. The "Colfax Massacre" occurred on Easter Sunday, April 13, 1873 in Louisiana, the seat of the Grant Parish. A mob of former Confederate soldiers, now members of the Ku Klux Klan and the White League, killed over a hundred Negro militia men while in the process of surrendering.

The massacre would represent a crucial turning point in the downfall of American Reconstruction in the south—and adoption of Jim Crow laws. Once again, African Americans found themselves subjected to slavery, albeit a new form.

—

Preparations for Edwin, age 22, and Miss Lucy Dean's, age 19, wedding day induced a flurry of activity on our farm. Her guide had been William Andrus Alcott's book, *The Young Wife, or Duties of Woman in the Marriage Relation*. The bound book informed how to bring health, wealth, and success to the marital union. I observed she paid less attention to the chapter heading "Submission," where Alcott established the origins of woman as a *helpmeet* rather than an equal of man. Phebe reminded me that Lucy had been raised without strong governance of a male figure—and in that void, she had developed a strong female spirit.

Lucy ordered wedding bands of white gold from a catalogue; hers would be a halt loop style that had a half dozen diamonds in a crown setting. Her dress would come from Godey's ladies' book, a hoop-skirted and white, rather than the usual black. The guest list grew to well over one hundred. She and Edwin would honeymoon for a week at Niagara Falls before beginning his medical practice in Fayette—though only long enough to raise the funds necessary to construct a two-story hostelry in Oxbow, where he would relocate his office. I surmised the hotel was Lucy's attempt to reconnect with her mother. Phebe again defended Lucy: "Or, perhaps she has a strong inclination for business."

My cares were few, except for payment of the wedding as plans progressed. In the end, the event was a happy, memorable time for all. I recalled the words of the Rev. Theodore Parker, who had inspired many of President Lincoln's speeches:

> *Young people marry their opposites in temper and general character, and such a marriage is commonly a good match...a happy wedding is a long falling in love.*

The economic worries fully materialized in May 1873 with a global panic and great depression. Newspapers relegated the cause to repercussions from economic dislocation in Europe resulting from the Franco-Prussian War; major property losses in the Great Chicago Fire in 1871 and the Great Boston Fire in

1872, which together helped to place massive strain on bank reserves. Additionally, Jay Cooke & Company, a major component of the country's banking establishment, found itself unable to market several million dollars in Northern Pacific Railway bonds, and many railroads were destined for failure.

Then, in January 1874 came the winter of the Big Snow—Nebraska to Minnesota, northwestern Iowa, and southeastern South Dakota. *Harper's Weekly*, depicted it, thusly:

> *Many pioneers perished as they were unprepared for a tempest of such magnitude. Many became completely disoriented on the prairie in the white-out and collapsed, then became buried. Cattle were completely suffocated by the fifteen-feet deep drifts, which also stopped and buried trains for more than a week. At least seventy reportedly died with multiple corpses that would not be found until the snow melted away in the spring. One dangerous signal reported was the winds were so strong that homes lost roofs, causing some to be exposed to the elements and even succumb.*

Like other families, it was the gravest of times for us Wiltses. If grasshoppers or hailstorms ruined our crops in the spring—we might still need to consider removing ourselves back to Ontario.

CHAPTER TWENTY

An Ordinary Life

One's own death is perhaps the best teacher. The things I had clung to in life, death would take away the moment that I took my final breath. Death makes all men equal, regardless of race, creed, or color—Union or Confederate, Republican or Democrat. We will all die. The final lesson that death teaches: I am not my body—'tis only the body that dies, not the *esprit*.

The previous year, Dr. Ward had begun to call on me with regularity, though his consumption disease continued to progress. In the winter of 1875-1876, impassable roads prevented him from traveling to our farm until late April.

I heard Phebe greet him at the front door then his long strides as he moved across the plank floor to my desk. Seconds later, the tall, spindly, grey beard stood before me.

In the light of the vapor lamp, he appeared pale and a shell of his former self. The damnable consumption struck down young and old, rich and poor—physician or farmer—without discrimination.

"My apologies, Phebe," he began, "Maria has business with the Temperance Women today. She shall surely accompany me on my next visit."

"Give her my salutations… May I bring you a hot cup of coffee to warm you?"

Dr. Ward nodded.

"You're looking quite well, Wiltse."

"You and I both know neither of us are well men, but 'tis nice of you to say."

"Whatever you are doing is an improvement from last fall."

"I have strictly followed the diabetes *régime* put forth by Dr. Bouchardat," I added. "I eat anything, even abuse mealy, floury foods with wise moderation…three days a week, I eat absolutely nothing but meat. Previously, I consumed almost exclusively flour and sweet fruits, and abused sugar to the point of almost constantly having a piece of Gunther candy in my mouth. It's not an easy disease to manage, as you well know."

He motioned his wish to examine my legs and feet.

I slid off my socks and slippers and rolled up my pant legs.

Phebe arrived with his coffee and chose to remain for the examination.

Finally, Dr. Ward commented on his findings: "The harkening attack of gout hast nearly disappeared."

"I believe I shall live longer than first believed— *À votre santé*! for Dr. Bouchardat's observation from the war."

"It's essential a physician's mind is always curious—'tis true," he said.

Phebe smiled approvingly and turned to depart, explaining: "I must focus on the *crème anglaise* on the cook stove."

I replaced my socks and slippers while telling Dr. Ward of my premier surgery in March—not involving an amputation.

"Dr. Rawson and I assisted Dr. Myers—along with my Edwin, who observed—with removal from W. E. Little's adipose tumor that had grown to seven pounds over his vertebra. The liposuction method took three hours... Mr. Little has survived, though whether the cancer shall reappear remains unknown."

"Success, Wiltse! Congratulations."

"More importantly—this marked a dream come true: Edwin and me, working together in surgery—father and son. Dear God, merci! for this this unspeakable joy and blessing."

"A splendid memory that shall ne'r be diminished, for certain."

"And I had success with mine first appendectomy," Dr. Ward said. "It was revolutionary surgery and made quite a splash in Iowa newspapers. I also wrote about the procedure in a state medical journal so others may course mine success."

"Yes—read of it...and am extremely proud to call you *mon ami*... I imagine Griffy is impatient to follow in your footsteps."

"Griffy, at age 20, having graduated Cornell College in Mount Vernon, hath chosen to teach at a school near Oxbow for a few years."

"Teaching is an honorable path... He has time to attend medical school, as he wishes."

"I should'st care to take him into mine practice whenever he chooses," Dr. Ward added.

"Yours will be difficult shoes to fill."

I was reminded of a topic that medicine does not speak of at société médicale meetings, but in private, a conversation between two friends who had grown to know each other well, it was appropriate.

"I read of the arrest of the Ossian, Iowa doctor for performing not one, but two abortions, at the request of the women. One was married, the other unmarried; both lay near death. His bail is fixed at five hundred dollars."

"You ever been asked, Wiltse?"

"You are aware of my long-held fascination with murder investigation. Perhaps, 'tis the pleasure of playing a role in seeing the guilty brought to justice. But as you have witnessed, even the pleasure of hunting and killing animals for sport 'tis largely a mystery to me—even then, 'tis a tragedy.

"But to answer your question, I have been asked...and I understand the woman's plight in making the request, as who would volunteer to bear a dozen or more children in a lifetime if the mother's life has been in jeopardy from a previous childbirth? Or, who would choose to incur the social *la stigma* of a child born out of marriage? while the other party gets off scot free of any responsibility. Mental health is central to the question."

"Well said, Wiltse. While I never object to flushing the inside of the uterus with injected water, and other normal remedies...If there's quickening, that requires more thought.

"And Alexander—I care to add that you should'st not hast such a low opinion of yourself... Hunting wild game is not your craze, but I see you as a man who's sought the same adventurous spirit you knew as a young boy. You've certainly not lived an ordinary life and have acted responsibly for the choices thou made. Iowa hath greatly benefitted from your decision to become an honorable physician."

"'Tis kind of you to say."

Dr. Ward quite suddenly found himself struggling to breathe. I hurried to his side and loosened his coat and shirt. He coughed violently for some time, making several deposits of white mucus and blood into a handkerchief that he pulled from a pocket. No longer did he make any attempt to hide the severity of his illness.

The rest of our spring day we spoke of myriad topics. Gold had been truck at The Point a year earlier. A mining company was formed, dams built, and sluices under construction. One party dug up a piece of quartz as large as a chestnut containing $2.50 in gold. Again, hundreds of people flocked into the region. The Hon. Joel Bailey, now age 61, was among those along the Turkey River panning for gold.

A rap on the front door turned our attention to Phebe, who wiped her hands in her apron to attend to the caller.

"I have just been made aware of Dr. Wiltse's illness and wish to submit an invoice for the timberland purchased some years since—and half is owing."

"Certainly," Phebe said with a voice of uncertainty, grasping the invoice from the man's hands. "This is surely an oversight and shall be paid immediately."

She delivered the invoice into my hands with a quizzical look on her face.

"It is difficult to keep incoming funds aligned with the outgoing," said Dr. Ward. "My wife keeps abreast of our finances and informs me when I need to collect on what's owing—I imagine 'tis the same with you, Wiltse."

—

My case against the D & St. P Railroad Company was heard in the H. H. Court in February 1876 in Keokuk—a scandal in itself, as by then my health was very *mauvaise* and the trip nearly did me in. A judgment of some eighty dollars and costs was ultimately assessed upon *me*! In my protest, I was further arrested for contempt of court, though I returned to my home the following day.

News of my arrest quickly spread at The Point, and Dr. Boomer and his wife Charlotte called within the week—arriving with a half dozen prairie chicken. Phebe gratefully received them and prepared to remove herself to the exterior kitchen to perform the feather and gutting removal, with Charlotte on her heels.

"Stay for prairie poulet stew with yam biscuits?" she asked, before departing.

"We gratefully accept, but only if alexander agrees to entertain us *wi'* his accordion after phebe's *bonnie* meal," said Dr. Boomer.

I nodded, approving his proposal.

Dr. Boomer, at age 54, had also grown grey like an old dog, though he always carried himself with the dignity of a physician, a military man, and a legislator. The beloved man had tried to retire from public life but his old neighbors were reluctant to dispense with his services, particularly as family physician.

"'Tis good to see you, *mon cher ami* Scottish friend," I said.

Almost immediately, he inquired of the details of my arrest.

"The Tribunal refused to hold the railroad responsible, and instead, laid the blame *on me* for not fencing my animals that were killed by the train… My cows run free like most all others. I insisted the railroads should run barriers along the tracks, as is done in Germany," I explained.

"The trains that shall crisscross our nation require fresh light to our laws, ah imagine—ah kin look into it further, as ye require."

"No, it's *fini*—let it be," I said.

"There wull always be a fresh war oan th' horizon… That seems to be th' plight of mankind: to rammy ower another, rather than to use reason to solve problems. Mah years in th' General Assembly has alerted me to th' polarizing over th' temperance question—Prohibition will be the next muckle war Americans will face, mark mah wurds. Legislators wull have a go to pacify th' most rancorous, bit you must question whither legislation solves anythin', really.

"The 14th Amendment granted citizenship to Negroes born in th' United States, and in 1870 th' 15th Amendment was ratified, explicitly prohibiting racial discrimination in voting.…bit bloody conflicts in massacres over voting rights have continued to erupt o'er th' nation.

"We've bin good Methodists, Alexander, fur over thirty years, you and me—'n' know at th' heart of religion is th' ability to transform hearts and minds. When religion is reduced to window-dressing, it becomes the "Tale of the Ugly One With all the Jewels," and the *second sight* that comes through one's faith cannot occur. It's a story as old as time."

"'Tis true, particularly in the south—and the affect nearly cost us our democracy," I said. "I wonder whether our nation shall be able to keep it."

"When Phebe and I arrived in 1855, Iowans were just recovering from a financial depression, plus a hailstorm of such magnitude that many lost crops, animals, and farms. The financial Panic of 1857 followed. Nonetheless, the people quietly pursued the even tenor of their ways, doing whatever their hands found to do—working the mines, making farms, or cultivating those already made, erecting homes, founding cities and towns, building shops and manufactories. In short, the country was alive with industry and hope for the future.

"They paid but little attention to the rumored plots and plans of the slave states of the South, who lived and grew rich from the sweat and toil, blood and flesh of others—aye, even trafficked in the offspring of their own loins. Then came the struggle for American independence—when red-handed rebellion raised its hideous head and threatened the very life of our nation.

"Whoever dreamed there was even *one* so base as to dare attempt the destruction of the Union of their forefathers? Our nation was baptized with the best blood and all its attendant horrors the world ever knew."

We spoke, too, of the plight of the Indians. The Ho-Chunk's removal from Iowa began in the summer of 1848. After their arrival at Long Prairie, Minnesota, many Ho-Chunk missed their previous homes. They traveled south and east to find provisions and weapons at trading posts on the eastern banks of the Mississippi. Some never made the journey north from Iowa. For the remainder of their days, they were shifted around like a piece of unwanted baggage.

At one point in the afternoon, Dr. Boomer remarked of the unforgettable day at Stone's Grocery when our colleague Dr.

Stout lost his life.

"Whenever ah see yer face, ah think of him, though it's been twenty years ago."

"Do you question what we could have done differently to save his life?" I asked.

"For a long time, ah did—but nae fur a lang time. It's done 'n' over."

"I completely agree," I said. "Last I heard, Dr. C. C. Sharp had a medical practice in Columbus, Ohio—the place where he was raised. No word on the number of wives he's accumulated…he doesn't divorce one before taking another, or so it's said. The Ohio Sharps were big supporters of the Underground Railroad. It's my understanding the Ohio Sharp family was not on speaking terms with Dr. Sharp.

"His son, Alonzo, served on th' Union side—the Illinois Calvary, ah believe," Dr. Boomer added.

"Something else—I read Dr. Sharp has organized a *home for invalids*."

The news took me by surprise and elicited a long silence.

"Making up for wrongs of the past, perhaps?' Dr. Boomer suggested.

"I'm quite without words," I said.

The conversations this day had been stimulating, as they always were. Finally, afternoon shadows began to move across the floorboards, and Phebe and Charlotte reappeared before us.

"Our evening meal is on the table," Phebe said. "Charlotte is at last in possession of the recipe for my prairie *poulet* stew. Now she and Dr. Boomer may enjoy this special meal often— and think of our friendship."

Arm in arm we strolled to the table. Before eating, I played "Pass Me Not, O Gentle Saviour" on my accordéon while softly we sang the words in unison. 'Twas a double blessing for me, feeling the billows of the instrument gently open and close at my chest, and hearing the deep sonorous notes resonate from depressing ivory buttons and keys at my fingertips.

Never could I recall eating a more splendid meal. As I looked across the long table of prairie *poulets*, yam biscuits, and wine, I realized that those at my table were responsible for my melancholy mood. I could not take my eyes off my Phebe, especially. Her eyes sparkled of charity and kindness; her smile was warm and embracing. Her long hair, sparkled with gray, pulled back and piled high above the nape of her neck—now appeared as a crown upon her head. I beheld her every word as though a goddess speaking.

In the evening, I played more hymns, closing out our wonderful day's journey by reading a poem that I'd sketched on paper, as Dr. Boomer and I had conversed throughout the day.

> *Appreciate the splendid people and all things in your life.*
> *Pardon those who have injured you.*
> *Listen to your interior voice, follow, and obey.*
> *Be the bonnie person you are destined to become.*
> *'Tis a grand péché—sin—to live a life without passion or purpose.*
> *Choose your relationships with good judgement.*
> *Embrace change and enjoy your life as it unfolds.*
> *Everything about soi-même—the self—fades out to nothing.*
> *Life is a voyage courageous, or nothing at all.*

—

In early autumn of 1876, I acquired a harmless sniffle that progressed into my chest, but nothing to alert me of anything suspect to come of it. A week later, I finally took to bed to rid myself of it once for all. Phebe remained at my side caring for me day and night.

The same day Mr. Bomgartner stopped by to submit an invoice for miscellaneous items—rubber boots, collars, and miscellaneous things the family and I had picked up at the mercantile day to day as needed… The new owner requested the account be brought up to date as soon as possible, he said.

"I'll have Charles attend to it right away," I said, preferring not to discuss such matters in front of Phebe.

I stared at what had once been his roving, misaligned eye.

"Are you satisfied with the outcome of your eye surgery?"

"Ya—meine eyes work besser now," and for a few seconds he demonstrated moving his eyes in tandem left to right. "Less double vision… *Danken Sie*," he added.

I smiled agreeably. What a loyal friend Mr. Bomgartner had been these many years. I would remember on the morrow to inform Phebe to bequeath the beehives to him after my passing…and ask him to remember to cover the hive with a black cloth so they wouldn't fly away upon my demise.

Mr. Bomgartner had barely departed our home before Phebe demanded to know how much of the estate was in arrears, and to whom we were owing?

"You should prepare a list…you are not well, my dear, and I fear our predicament should your sniffle turn worse.

"Charles knows all my business," I said to soothe her qualms.

Over the coming days, Phebe and I spoke of many remembrances, of our marriage and years in Ontario—and of our impromptu voyage to Iowa, at a time when so many thought we would fail—or more precisely, that I would fail.

"How many states are there presently in the Union, my dear," I inquired at one point.

"Why, there are thirty-eight—with Colorado added just this past August."

"Quite right, we've been privileged to see seven states added since our arrival in our new homeland. And hasn't our adventure in America together turned out so very grand?"

She smiled. We embraced. Our aggregate tears fell like the water flowing over Niagara Falls. Never had I felt closer to my Phebe. We were as one.

"Did you know I held her in my arms for hours the day she was born before her passing?"

"What are you speaking of?" Phebe said, touching my forehead with her hand as though to check for fever.

"*Annetta*—I'm speaking of our Annetta."

I heard Phebe gasp and saw her raise a hand to her face. Fresh tears flooded her eyes and dribbled down her flushed cheeks.

"After Sophia was born earlier that morning… I listened for the second heartbeat that had grown increasingly faint. As you rested in your state of exhaustion, I felt for the *enfant* and withdrew her, feet first. Swaddling her blueish body, I carried her to the kitchen where I tried with all that I knew to save her. At dusk, while gently rocking her in my arms, I felt her *espirit* release and rise.

"For a long time, I regarded her long, dark eyelashes as they lay upon her soft, pallid cheeks; I caressed the folds of her wrists and fingers and toes. Twice I gently kissed her on her forehead— once for me and once for you, my love. Then, bathing her in perfumed water, I dressed her in the baptismal gown you made, and carried her to the corner of the Osage-orange hedge outside our bedroom window and buried her in a warmed blanket in the snow. A flat stone shaped like a half-moon marked her grave— you know, the place where the hedge bloomed so prolifically.

I paused to reach for Phebe's hand.

"Such a deed might have been wrong, my love, but I simply could not ask you to bear the loss."

She buried her head on my chest, weeping as though releasing years of repressed feelings.

"I knew there was another born all along, I was certain of it."

I stroked her shoulders and kissed her hair that smelled of sweet perfume and redemption.

"All is forgiven, my Love, all is forgiven," she said through her tears.

I felt my breathing become shallower.

The thing happened again, where it felt as though a hand brushed against strands of the hairs along my forehead.

Involuntarily, I lifted one hand to the place. Once again, I felt nothing, not even the slightest breeze blowing across the room through the open window.

When I arrived at heaven, I would ask God if that was His touch.

"Tell my children that I love them," I said. "I love them so very, very much."

Then, feeling very, very tired, I closed my eyes to sleep.

DIED.

Dr. Alexander A. Wiltse

***North Iowa Times*, October 7, 1876**
Dr. A. Wiltse, an old and respected citizen. He was 54
years of age and resided at the Point for many years;
was an active businessman and had accumulated a
line of property.

—

As had been Père Alexander's wishes, I, Charles, was charged with closing his estate, which went into probate upon his death. Together with Mère Phebe, I secured the aid of Attorney S. Chesley, to act as administrator. Atty. Chesley posted notices in newspapers requesting those with debts to come forth. The estimated value of the estate which included 416 acres was $10,000.

Creditors came forth, many submitting requests for $2.00—and up some with an invoice or signed contract; others stating a verbal agreement had been made, saying, "We shook hands on this, and Dr. Wiltse promised me he'd pay," according to Atty. Chesley.

I submitted expenses on behalf of Mère Phebe for wearing apparel of the deceased, and support for her and Sophia, a minor child, who was to be given a cow of three years, valued at twenty-five dollars.

Père Alexander also had stacks of unpaid invoices in his desk, in bureaus, and other places throughout the house of $3.50, $6.25, etc.

After nearly a year had passed, Atty. Chesley ascertained there weren't enough funds on hand to pay the estate's debts, and a sale of all assets and real estate was deemed necessary. I provided him with a list of assets, and he arranged the date and hour for an estate sale.

The probate continued…and after another year, I submitted the first petition asking for a full statement of all claims against the estate.

Ultimately, Mère Phebe, Vidella, Edwin, Lucetta, and I charged Atty. Chesley with wrongdoing and fraud for not recording exact payments of debtors, reduced, or nothing at all.

The probate was finally settled after five years. All that remained from the sale of estate assets after expenses was three hundred dollars to be divided among Mère Phebe, Vidella, Edwin, Lucetta, and me.

The last note I received from Atty. Chesley was his statement that the funds remained in his possession, and no one had come forward to claim them.

—

DIED
Dr. Alexander B. Ward
***Independence Conservative*, March 31, 1879**

The esteemed Dr. A. B. Ward came to Oxbow from Ohio almost 60 years ago and during his practice here from 1855 to 1879 made many calls with his carriage in both hot and cold weather for miles around. He departed this life March 31 at 8:35 AM. He was born in 1832 at New Lisbon, Columbus County, Ohio. At the age of 15 years, he moved to Akron, Summit County, Ohio. During his residence in Akron, while quite young, the Doctor commenced the study of medicine. He attended the medical department of the University of Michigan at Ann Arbor. He then returned to Ohio where he practiced until he moved to Center Point, Iowa, remaining at Center Point between one and two years. Diligent in business, warmhearted and generous, he soon gathered around him a host of sincere friends and an extensive practice. The funeral was largely attended, the stores were all closed. Consumption was the disease from which he suffered so long.

—

DIED
Phebe Wiltse
***Elkader Weekly Register*, Elkader, Iowa,**

Oct. 20, 1887

Mrs. Phebe Wiltse died Oct. 6, 1887, age 59 at the home of her son-in-law J. Malone, in this place, last Thursday at this place. The funeral took place from the house, Saturday afternoon, Rev. Norton coming from Clinton to officiate. Mrs. Wiltse leaves two sons and three daughters and a large circle of friends to mourn her death.

—

DIED

Dr John Acers

***State Democrat**, Norman, Oklahoma, Sept. 5, 1895*

The funeral rites of the late Dr. John Acers occurred at the residence of his son A. D. Acers last Saturday at 2 p.m. and were attended by quite a number of those who had known and respected him. President Boyd of the university conducted and spoke in an impressive manner of the excellent qualities of the deceased. The service was a striking tribute of respect to the dead and emphasized the esteem in which he had been held by those who had the pleasure of knowing him. Prof. DeBarr offered a very appropriate prayer, and Mesdames Boyd and Winans and Messrs. Tate and Brooks sung Cardinal Newman's "Lead, Kindly Light" in an impressive manner. The pallbearers were Messrs. Hullum, Ambrister, Kendall, T. E. Smith, Bessent, and Bixler. Mr. A. D. Acers accompanied the remains to Manchester, Iowa, where they will be interred beside his wife.

Dr. John Acers was born in St. Lawrence Co., New York, Dec. 13, 1810. He entered college and graduated at Brattleboro, Vermont, and began the practice of medicine and soon after attaining his majority. He moved to Jackson, Michigan in 1840 where he was married in 1844. He practiced his profession in Jackson until 1850. He made a trip west in 1848-1849, and moved from Jackson to what afterward became Manchester, Iowa, where he practiced until 1873, when he moved to Texas, where he has since made his home.

He acquired a competency early in life and always was a man of affairs and at times was interested in manufacturing and other business endeavors in which he accumulated a fortune of ample proportions. Dr. Acers was a man who would be classed as a leader among men, no matter where he was placed. He was broad, liberal, and tolerant in his views. His nature was such that it rebelled against anything that was cruel or tyrannical, no matter where such a force was found. He stood at the head of his profession and was a man who could note the progress in the sciences and kept up with the advancement of his profession. He was a hard worker and despised a lazy man. He always enjoyed good health and retained his mental faculties until the last. Surrounded by those he loved he died of old age, after having many years passed his allotted time of life.

—

DIED
Dr. Christopher C. Sharp
***New York Times*, November 5, 1898**

Dr. Christopher C. Sharp, an old physician of the Western States, died on Saturday at his residence, 412 Amsterdam Avenue. Dr. Sharp was seventy-seven years old, and was born in Albany. He studied medicine in Cincinnati and paid special attention to electric therapeutics. He lived several years in Lexington, KY., and was physician to the eldest son of Henry Clay, who presented him his father's portfolio. Dr. Sharp fitted up a home for invalids in Indianapolis and was a member of the Hendricks Club in that city. He also invented several electric appliances, some of which bear his name. Five years ago his health failed, and he came to live in New York, where his son lives. Death was caused by bronchial pneumonia. The funeral will take place at 2 o'clock this afternoon at the residence of his stepdaughter, Mrs. Fabius M. Clarke, 154 West Eighty-second Street.

—

DIED
Hon. A. Boomer
Manchester Democrat, April 19, 1899

The death of Dr. Albert Boomer at his home in Delhi last Saturday at the age of 72 years, takes from this county one of its leading citizens, a man who has been closely identified with the history of the county during his long residence here. He was by profession a physician and served during the Rebellion as assistant surgeon of the 27th Regiment of Iowa Infantry. At the close of the war, he resumed the practice of his profession at Delhi.

He represented this county in the senate of this state in the fourteenth and fifteenth sessions of the legislature.

Dr. Boomer was a consistent Christian and it is truly said of him, "Kindly in all his ways, upright in all his dealings, honest as the day itself, he was the type of the old-fashioned men who believed in the morally right and followed it without thought of compromise."

His wife died several years earlier. Two sons survive him: Merton A. of Pipestone, Minnesota, and Allen L. Boomer of Delhi .